"As of this moment, we're engaged.

"I move into Alyssa's cottage with you and keep an eye on you." His voice was a low, raw rumble in her ear.

"Engaged? Living together?" Brooke shook her head. Thoughts somersaulted as her jaw dropped open. *That*, she definitely couldn't handle. She could only take so much intensity at a time. And there was definitely too much raw power exuding from Jack Chessman. The force of his personality would hem her, control her. "Aren't you taking responsibility just a bit too far?"

His hands took hold of both her shoulders. The reach of his touch went much deeper than the skin. She wanted to back away from the unnerving sensation zigzagging through her. "I *will* keep you safe."

In his eyes, she saw his need ran as deep as her own, and relented.

Happy New Year, Harlequin Intrigue Reader!

Harlequin Intrigue's New Year's Resolution is to bring you another twelve months of thrilling romantic suspense. Check out this month's selections.

Debra Webb continues her ongoing COLBY AGENCY series with *The Bodyguard's Baby* (#597). Nick Foster finally finds missing Laura Proctor alive and well—and a mother! Now with her child in the hands of a kidnapper and the baby's paternity still in question, could Nick protect Laura and save the baby that might very well be his?

We're happy to have author Laura Gordon back in the saddle again with *Royal Protector* (#598). When incognito princess Lexie Dale comes to a small Colorado ranch, danger and international intrigue follow her. As sheriff, Lucas Garrett has a duty to protect the princess from all harm for her country. But as a man, he wants Lexie for himself....

Our new ON THE EDGE program explores situations where fear and passion collide. In *Woman Most Wanted* (#599) by Harper Allen, FBI Agent Matt D'Angelo has a hard time believing Jenna Moon's story. But under his twenty-four-hour-a-day protection, Matt can't deny the attraction between them—or the fact that she is truly in danger. But now that he knows the truth, would anyone believe *him?*

In order to find Brooke Snowden's identical twin's attacker, she would have to become her. Living with her false identity gave Brooke new insights into her estranged sister's life—and the man in it. Officer Jack Chessman vowed to protect Brooke while they sought a potential killer. But was Brooke merely playing a role with him, or was she falling in love with him—as he was with her? Don't miss *Alyssa Again* (#600) by Sylvie Kurtz.

Wishing you a prosperous 2001 from all of us at Harlequin Intrigue!

Sincerely,

Denise O'Sullivan
Associate Senior Editor
Harlequin Intrigue

ALYSSA AGAIN
SYLVIE KURTZ

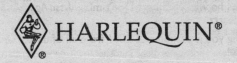

TORONTO • NEW YORK • LONDON
AMSTERDAM • PARIS • SYDNEY • HAMBURG
STOCKHOLM • ATHENS • TOKYO • MILAN • MADRID
PRAGUE • WARSAW • BUDAPEST • AUCKLAND

ISBN 0-373-22600-4

ALYSSA AGAIN

This edition published by arrangement with Harlequin Books S.A.

® and TM are trademarks of the publisher. Trademarks indicated with ® are registered in the United States Patent and Trademark Office, the Canadian Trade Marks Office and in other countries.

Visit us at www.eHarlequin.com

Printed in U.S.A.

ABOUT THE AUTHOR

Flying an eight-hour solo cross-country in a Piper Arrow with only the airplane's crackling radio and a large bag of M&M's for company, Sylvie Kurtz realized a pilot's life wasn't for her. The stories zooming in and out of her mind proved more entertaining than the flight itself. Not a quitter, she finished her pilot's course and earned her commercial license and instrument rating.

Since then, she has traded in her wings for a computer keyboard, where she lets her imagination soar to create fictional adventures that explore the power of love and the thrill of suspense. When not writing, she enjoys the outdoors with her husband and two children, quilt-making, photography and reading whatever catches her interest.

You can write to Sylvie at P.O. Box 702, Milford, NH 03055.

Books by Sylvie Kurtz

HARLEQUIN INTRIGUE
527—ONE TEXAS NIGHT
575—BLACKMAILED BRIDE
600—ALYSSA AGAIN

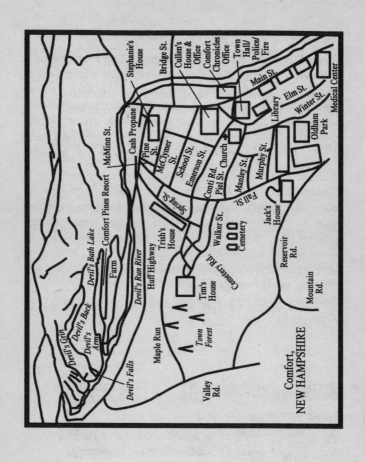

Comfort, NEW HAMPSHIRE

CAST OF CHARACTERS

Alyssa Snowden—Someone was willing to go to great lengths to see her dead.

Brooke Snowden—She assumed her comatose twin's identity to lure a would-be murderer into making a mistake.

Jack Chessman—He'd promised to protect Alyssa, but failed. Now he vowed to guard the beautiful Brooke…and prevent *her* from falling victim to her sister's fate.

Delia Snowden—Brooke and Alyssa's cold mother.

Walter Snowden—The father Brooke hadn't seen in twenty-four years.

Tim Hogarty—Alyssa's friend has a nose for scandal…and a secret of his own to hide.

Cullen Griswold—Alyssa had rebuffed his ladies' man charms. Had he crossed the line between love…and hate?

Trish Witchell—She and Alyssa were friendly adversaries, but had their rivalry turned deadly?

Stephanie Cash—She dreams of babies and white picket fences—but the man in the equation has a thing for Alyssa.…

Meg Kessler—Makeup artist extraordinaire. Her magic touch makes possible Alyssa's awakening.

Lauren Bell—The little girl and her dog Daisy warm Brooke's heart…and make her dream of a family of her own—with the off-limits Jack.

For sisters—

the blood kind: Madeleine, Joanne, Anick;
the writing kind: Yvonne, Tina, Stobie, Marci,
Lynn, Kelly, Kathy;
the soul kind: you know who you are.

A SPECIAL THANKS TO:

JoMarie Grinkiewicz, for her help
with my vacation resort.
Francis Langlois, for his mechanical assistance.
Fire Chief Robert A. Fabich, Sr. (retired), for his help
in creating a suitable explosion.

Any mistakes in procedure are the author's.

Prologue

Brooke watched her parents at the edge of the lake, glad the thick glass on the dirty attic window muffled their argument. Her father's arms flew fast and crazy like some cartoon character on TV. Her mother's face was hard like a statue. She didn't like it when Dad got mad, when Mom got quiet. Her stomach burbled. Tears smudged her view out the window.

"Don't cry, Brookie. This is a magic attic. No tears allowed."

Letting the tears fall anyway, Brooke turned to her sister. "I'm scared."

"I know. But I'll take care of you." Inching her bottom, feet and hands along the rough planks, Alyssa scooched closer to her twin. "Ouch!"

A splinter of wood lodged itself into Alyssa's thumb. Brooke felt the pulse of pain in her own finger. "Let me see."

Tears bright in her eyes, Alyssa held out her hand. With two fingers, Brooke slid the sliver of wood from Alyssa's thumb and kissed the boo-boo just as she'd seen her mother do. "There, all better." She smiled then. "I'll take care of you, too, Aly."

Arms linked, drawing comfort from each other, the

twins turned back to look through the window. It was pretty the way the yellow-orange light of the sun danced on the lake's black water. Brooke let her head fall against Alyssa's shoulder. "We'll take care of each other."

Chapter One

After twenty-four years, Brooke Snowden had found her sister only to lose her again.

This was not the meeting she'd envisioned. There would be no squeals of delight as they raced into each other's arms across the airport lounge, no squeezing hugs to breach the space of lost years, no heart-to-heart talks that would stretch deep into the night to fill the void of over two decades. There was only silence with its heavy, unnatural weight. And stillness.

"Alyssa."

Her twin lay in a hospital bed, a shell of herself. Her short blond hair was mostly hidden by a gruesome bandage. The outdoors tan was fading fast, giving Alyssa's skin a paperlike quality. The blue veins of one arm stood out, rivers of life pulsing on. The other arm was swaddled in a cast. Healing red-brown scrapes scuffed half of her face and one of her hands. Looking down at her sister and seeing a marred reflection of her own face was eerie.

Tentatively Brooke reached out for one of Alyssa's hands. But no remembered warmth seeped through her comatose sister's fingers, no communication of thought telegraphed itself through the *bump bump* of her pulse. Not even the vaguest sensation of pain transferred itself from sister to sister.

There was so much to say, to explain, to feel, yet this person who'd once been an extension of herself was now a complete stranger. One she desperately longed to rediscover.

"Do you remember…?" she started, then stopped herself, and put a hand over her heavy heart. She missed Alyssa, more now than when she'd thought her gone forever, missed what they might have shared now that they'd found each other again. In her mind the possibilities rolled one over the other, and always there was that wonderful feeling of comfort, of belonging, of acceptance.

"I didn't know." Brooke perched a hip on the bed, felt the mattress dip, then sprung up again for fear of disturbing one of the tubes tending to Alyssa's needs. "Mom told me you and Dad were dead. A car accident. Right after she…left."

Brooke broke the cool contact, turned away from the unmoving form that was her sister. Out the window, the early summer sun shone. Its heat beat against the glass, glazing the pane with its brilliance. Not that the view mattered. The only thing in Boston of interest to Brooke was Alyssa.

"I might never have known if Mom hadn't had a heart attack." Brooke felt foolish for talking out loud to someone who looked as if she were sleeping. Her voice seemed too loud, echoing off the stark walls and floor. Yet desperate to reestablish a connection, she couldn't stop speaking. She lowered her tone to a near whisper—the quiet voice she often charged her kindergarten students to use. "It scared her. I think she wanted to confess so she could die with a clear conscience."

Brooke closed her eyes against the memory of her mother's confession, of the twin threads of pity and bitterness that swelled within her even now. "She didn't. Die, that is. She's recovering at a nursing home in San Diego. She'll be just fine."

As Brooke paced the room, the rubber soles of her canvas shoes made little squeaks on the industrial tile. She stopped in her tracks, looked down in confusion at her feet, then sat in the chair with the beige vinyl cushion.

"I called as soon as I could. But...it was already too late." She stared at her sister, and twined her fingers in a fretful gnarl. "Someone named Franny Cotter told me about your accident. I had to come."

We'll take care of each other. The broken childhood promise warbled in Brooke's mind, fed by a stream of guilt for being unable to fix this injury. "I didn't know, Aly. I didn't know."

Driven by restlessness, by a need to outrun too-ready tears, Brooke shot up again. She needed to *do* something. She needed to *act*. Helplessness weighed her down. Yet there was nothing she could do for Alyssa.

Then the answer clicked, and hope along with it.

She could be there.

She didn't have to be back at school for another two months. She'd stay. She'd raid the hospital library, badger Alyssa's doctors, learn all there was to learn about coma. And simply be there for her sister.

This would be the first step toward healing for both of them.

Her decision made, energy filled her body, invigorated her muscles, provided a lift to her step. With purpose, she turned for the door and the public telephone down the hall.

There were so many things to do. As she walked, she fished into her purse for her notepad and pen, and organized a list. She had to arrange for a room close by, call her mother, then she had to talk to—

"Alyssa."

The harsh whisper stopped her midstep.

The man filling the doorway stared at her with an intensity that stole her breath. The dark eyes in a face seemingly chiseled from granite, the animal-like look of a predator, and the lean body tensed for action made Brooke take a step back. A shiver of apprehension snaked down her spine, raising goose bumps in its wake, speeding her heart.

Her pen and pad fell from her hands. Her purse slipped from her shoulder. Like enemy fire, they landed in sharp succession—ping, plop, plunk.

Instinct made her step back to shield her helpless sister against this unknown danger.

"ALYSSA."

The name was ripped from Jack Chessman's throat in a harsh whisper. Before him stood the miracle the doctors insisted couldn't happen. Alyssa was up and about—conscious again, ready to go home.

Backlit by the sunlight streaming through the window, she looked like an angel. Every detail of her was sharp, yet veiled in gauzy unreality. Her long, pale blond hair played across her shoulders, the soft look of its length intriguing in an odd sort of way. Her dress floated around her body in a wispy layer of pink and blue flowers, hugging curves he'd never noticed before. Her skin was golden and unscarred. As he reached to touch her, she took a step back.

A strange, cold feeling twisted through his gut. He wanted to touch her, hold her, drink in the subtle scent of summer flowers drifting toward him with a fierceness that frightened him.

It's Alyssa, for Pete's sake.

But something wasn't right.

He blinked, then frowned. Her light-green eyes were large and filled with fear. "Alyssa?"

"Who are you?"

The voice was all wrong, gentler than he remembered. Then he saw the finger with its polished pink nail poised over the nurse's Call button to raise an alarm.

And in the bed beyond, Alyssa's unmoving form.

As if he'd been punched in the stomach, air he hadn't realized he'd held gushed out.

Not Alyssa.

Someone else.

Someone who looked strangely like her—yet was very different. Sunshine seemed to gleam from this woman, whereas Alyssa always traveled with her own personal rain cloud. He found himself wary and implausibly... intrigued.

Who was she? Where had she come from? Why was she here?

"I'm a friend." Surprise had momentarily confounded him, but now he slid back into his professional state of mind to view the woman, the situation. As a police officer, he prided himself on observing from a distance, divorced from emotion. Instinctively turning his body into a ready stance, he held his left hand up in a gesture of cautious calm. He lowered the tone of his voice a notch to soothe her before she caused trouble, and gave the stranger in front of him all of his focused attention. "Jack Chessman. A friend of Alyssa's. You are?"

The woman's finger didn't leave the red button, but neither did she depress it. Her gaze pierced his with an equal wariness, her fear almost touching him with its sharpness. With concentration, he shoved away his irrational urge to comfort her.

"I'm her sister. Brooke. Brooke Snowden."

"Brooke Snowden." He moved closer, couldn't tear his gaze away from the face so similar, yet so unlike Alyssa's. The slant of eyes, the slope of nose, the angle of cheekbones, the fairy dust of freckles, even the eerie green of moss-colored eyes all appeared familiar, yet alien. He'd never wanted to explore Alyssa the way he wanted to study this woman. The tips of his fingers actually tingled from the force of his will stopping their movement.

Could this be true? Could Alyssa have a sister he knew nothing about?

No, that wasn't possible. Alyssa had shared every blow, every disappointment, every heartache with him. She wouldn't have kept something as important as a sister from him.

The woman shrank back, gripping the Call button mechanism tighter.

"I've known Alyssa since she was six." Jack took the Call box from Brooke's hand. "She doesn't have a sister."

The woman looked down at her empty fingers—long and slender like Alyssa's—then twirled away from him, and went to stand by the foot of the bed.

"I thought she died twenty-four years ago. My father must have told her Mom and I were dead—the same way Mom told me Alyssa and Dad were killed in a car accident."

She jerked a shoulder toward her tilted head—the way Alyssa did when she wasn't sure of something. Anger and an electric awareness of this woman waged a savage war inside him. He leashed them both, squelched the feelings running too hot, too fast, and scrambled to regain control of his mind, to analyze. "Why would they do such a cruel thing?"

"I don't know." Brooke's shoulders twitched up, her eyes became deep pools of bleak confusion. "Dad moved us to the lake house. They had a big fight. Then Mom took me and left. She never wanted to talk about Dad or Alyssa, about what had happened to them. I gave up trying to make her a long time ago."

Her eyes fascinated him. The green intensified with the

emotions playing over her face, drawing him into their warm depths. His heart thundered at the primitive hunger suddenly squeezing at him.

Angry with himself for letting emotions creep in, he lashed out, saying the first thing that came to mind. "There's no estate, you know." Instantly, he regretted the impulse. He was breaking his own rules and he didn't like it.

She gasped. Her face compressed into a mask of indignation. "You're out of line, Mr. Chessman—"

"Lieutenant Chessman of the Comfort Police."

"Lieutenant," she amended, a hard edge to her tone, her fingers tightening into fists. "I have no interest in Alyssa's estate nor lack thereof. After twenty-four years, I just wanted to get to know my sister." As she looked down at the unmoving body in the bed, her gaze softened. "I got here too late."

He studied Brooke intently, fighting the absurd flare of his response to this woman. Was he seeing enemies everywhere because he'd failed to protect Alyssa? She'd tried to tell him she was scared, but because she'd made light of her fears in the very next breath, he'd dismissed them.

Then he'd seen the shredded climbing rope on Devil's Grin. And known he'd failed her.

Now she was in a coma.

And because the Fish and Game officers who had investigated Alyssa's fall had ruled it an unfortunate accident, there was no one else who would look for her would-be killer, no one else to investigate which one of her friends could have wanted her dead. And it had to have been someone on the practice climb that day. As Alyssa was about to be airlifted to the hospital, he'd promised her that he would find who had tampered with the rope.

He always kept his promises. He couldn't let her down

a second time. Wouldn't let anyone hurt her again. She'd already suffered enough sorrow to last anyone a lifetime.

Anger scorched through him raw and red once more. He mentally grappled it and choked it down with a convulsive swallow, felt the burn of it in his stomach. He wasn't used to feeling such overpowering emotions, and he didn't like it one bit.

Thumbs hooked in the belt loops of his jeans, he kept scrutinizing Brooke, advancing on her. He used her fear to harness his control. "Just a case of bad timing?"

"Is that so hard to believe?"

They were dancing now. As he pressed forward, she retreated. Soon she'd be cornered. No way out. His irritation ebbed. Control was swinging back in his direction. "Alyssa's very special to me. Now that she can't fend for herself, I intend to do it for her."

"I see." She let out a long breath. Her shoulders relaxed as if she were shedding a burden.

Her reaction caught him off guard. He'd expected her defensiveness to increase. Instead she smiled a we're-on-the-same-side smile, and he felt as if he'd been sucker-punched. What was wrong with him?

"When you got here," she said, apparently oblivious to the turbulent air zapping around the room, "I was going to find out just exactly what her condition is. Do you know the prognosis?"

She glided past him, sat in the chair and leaned forward, looking at her sister with unmasked regret. Her hair fanned around her shoulder with the movement. At the silky sound, an erotic image flashed in his brain before he could stop it. Annoyed by his wavering concentration, he focused once more on Brooke. She and Alyssa looked so much alike. A twin? How could Alyssa have kept that secret from him?

And why did this woman fascinate him so when his feelings for Alyssa were solely of brotherly concern?

Because she's trouble. He could feel it all the way to his boots, see it in the sensuality that exuded with every little move she made.

Stranded on the opposite side of the hospital bed, he ignored Alyssa's chalk-white face, and concentrated on Brooke's sun-kissed skin. Professional curiosity, he told himself as he resumed his scrutiny—a curse of needing to tend to details, to solve enigmas.

"She suffered a trauma to the head," he said, uncomfortably aware of the hard check he had to keep on his body to show no reaction. "Her brain swelled. They had to drill a hole through her skull to drain off the pressure. Her right arm is broken. She's bruised on her right side. Otherwise she's fine." Regrettably he took no pleasure in Brooke's discomfiture. Instead the need to hold and comfort returned with an urgency that thrummed along his skin.

Brooke gently fingered the bandage on Alyssa's head. "Then how come she's…like this?"

"Her brain has to heal. This is the way it does it."

"So, she'll come out of her coma?"

Hope shone bright in her green eyes, causing a tension that had him scrambling to regain control once again. To understand her, to understand her preposterous hold on him, he needed her unbalanced. "Does that bother you?"

Focusing on Alyssa's still features, Brooke ignored his remark, though he hadn't missed the flash of temper streak through her eyes. "What is she like?"

"What brought you here, now?" he asked, determined to see beyond her distracting softness to the reason for her sudden presence.

Brooke sighed as if she were dealing with an exasperating child, and lifted her gaze to meet his squarely. "You're very protective of her."

"Yes."

"I'm not here to hurt her."

"Then why are you here?" he asked.

"My mother nearly died and wanted to clear her conscience before meeting her maker."

The tightness of her voice gave him the distinct impression she was leaving much unsaid. "A deathbed confession?"

"She didn't die, but it was too late to take back the confession."

Impassioned purpose vibrated from Brooke's body, in unmistakable contrast to the sterile starkness of the room. That was the attraction, he decided. And he resented his unwanted interest in this woman when he should be focused on Alyssa, on protecting her, on finding who had done this to her.

Wearily he scrubbed a hand over his face. He'd never been good with the gloom of hospitals. Hospitals meant death, defeat. He'd learned that at seventeen when, filled with depression, his mother had accidentally caused her own death.

"How did Alyssa get hurt?" Brooke asked, returning her attention to her sister. "The nurse wasn't quite sure."

"Climbing accident."

"Were you there?"

He stiffened at the question, then nodded once.

Brooke looked at him expectantly, waiting for details. What was he supposed to say? That he was responsible for her sister's coma? That Alyssa was in a hospital bed because he'd let her climb against his better judgment? That he'd let her sweet-talk him, as usual, because climbing was the rare joy in her life; because he couldn't stand to see the sadness in her eyes; because he figured he'd be there to guard against her distracted state?

Jack reached for Alyssa's hand, rubbed her cool fingers with his, willing the closed eyes to open, the still mouth to quirk in its usual self-deprecating way, for Alyssa to make a bad joke about her new shorn hairdo. For the feeling he'd failed her to disappear.

"She fell. Slammed against the side of a mountain."

He could still hear the sickening thud of her body crashing against the granite, then the windchimelike jingle of her gear as she dangled from her harness like a broken doll. And he wouldn't soon forget the horror of seeing the fraying rope, of reaching for her just as the last filament was giving way.

Someone had tampered with the rope—a rope he'd checked and rechecked. He wouldn't rest until he found out who. And he certainly wasn't about to let a magically appearing, long-lost sister he'd never heard of distract him from his intention.

He narrowed his gaze on her and said, "Someone tried to kill her."

Chapter Two

"No. You said it was an accident." Brooke shook her head in horror, her gaze not wavering from the flintlike hardness of Jack Chessman's eyes. How could Alyssa stand all this overwhelming intensity in a man? The boring gaze, the depth of his dislike for her made her feel raw, exposed. *What have I ever done to you?* "Who would want to kill her? Aly was the kindest, sweetest person."

"She hates being called Aly."

"I called her Aly. She called me Brookie. No one else was allowed to." Just as no one had shared their secret hug, their silent language, their bond of empathy. "What makes you think her fall wasn't an accident?"

"Just before she slipped into her coma, she told me."

Bile rose in her throat. Pain and panic mushroomed in her mind—Alyssa's pain, Alyssa's panic. Horror swelled to terror. A chill like she'd never known froze her to her very soul. She rubbed her arms to circulate some heat in her body. Was that why the first communication between them in twenty-four years had been so strong? Because the intention of murder was involved?

What would this hard man say if she told him the exact time Alyssa's head pounded against the rock? What would he say if she told him she'd felt the blow, that it had stopped her cold, made her drop a full glass of orange juice, knocked her to the tile floor in her kitchen, and left her feeling as if her head was going to explode, as if she were going to die?

"What happened?"

"The line stuck. She lost her balance trying to unjam it."

"And hit—" she flinched, reliving the sensation once again "—the rock."

"Yes."

Only after the pain had staggered her so badly had she thought of her dead twin, felt the urgency that drove her to challenge her mother for the truth one more time after years of playing the good daughter, of not questioning motives. She looked at him, seeking something in the stony set of his face. "Attempted murder?"

"The rope was tampered with."

She understood then his driving need to protect her sister. Anyone suspicious could be interpreted as the criminal who had sought to end Alyssa's life. And a sister he didn't know existed had shown up out of the blue.

Bending down, she reached for her leather purse by the bed, then drew out her wallet. She handed the stiff lieutenant her driver's license. "We were born right here in Boston. Dad moved us to New Hampshire just before we turned six. Alyssa is my twin."

He took the plastic-covered card. She didn't let go her end. She wanted him to understand the need to help stirring deep inside her, the connection she now understood had been severed only with Alyssa's recent accident, the cry for help she'd heard too late.

"My father had a handlebar mustache then. We used to sit one on each knee. Alyssa would ride hands above her head. I would hang on to each side of Dad's mustache as if they were reins. He'd bounce us until we were laughing so hard we'd roll off.

"Just before we moved, Alyssa fell off Dad's knee and bumped her head against the coffee table. My parents rushed her to the hospital to get stitches." She let go of the card, touched her jawbone. "Three right here."

She followed Jack's gaze to the thin scar nearly invisible on Alyssa's face, saw him frown.

"She was always the risk-taker," Brooke continued, remembering her awe at watching her sister throw herself headfirst down the slide, lift herself to the highest level on the monkey bars, climb the apple tree to touch the sky while she, Brooke, remained safe on the ground. "Dad was so upset she'd hurt herself, he got her a medal with a guardian angel to protect her."

As she rose from the chair, Brooke lifted the fine chain from the inside of her dress's neckline, drew out a piece of gold shaped like a crooked half-moon.

"She wanted me to be safe, too, so she cut the medal in half. Dad offered to get us each one, but we didn't want him to. We wanted this one. So he had the jagged edges polished, a hole drilled into each piece and bought an extra chain."

She held the half disc in her palm. He reached for the severed angel. She jerked her hand away. His fingers rubbed at the gold as if it were a magic lamp waiting to give him answers. Her pulse sped up.

"We took care of each other."

Suddenly he let the medal go. The half disc plopped against the material of her dress, unexpectedly burning her with the heat of his touch. She'd anticipated the metal to feel frost-nipped. He reached into his jeans pocket and slid out Alyssa's half of the angel. Carefully lifting Brooke's piece, he matched the edges. Complete once again. Tears momentarily blurred her vision.

Aly had kept her angel, too.

"She was the strong one," Brooke said.

He shook his head. "Then you don't know Alyssa."

His eyes were gray, Brooke noticed, not black. And definitely defensive. What had bred that defensiveness in him? Not that she wanted to know; she'd endured enough of her mother's frosty disposition to last her a lifetime. But every lean inch of his body was strung tight—hard to miss the telltale signs of tensed muscles when they were so visible through the age-softened jeans and navy T-shirt. Her body zinged with tension. He reminded her of a guard dog. All that was missing was the peeled-back lips to show off menacing canines and a deep-throated growl. Standing still and keeping her mind focused under the scrutiny of such a keen gaze was difficult.

"No, I don't know her. Not anymore. Not for a long time." That was the whole point of being here. "But I've missed her."

He cared for her sister, she reminded herself. He was worried about her. He wasn't going to allow anyone to take advantage of Alyssa. That had to count for something.

It counted for a lot.

So Brooke cut him some slack. She *had* appeared out of nowhere. She tore her gaze from the sharp planes of his too-handsome face, sat down once more and took in the slow rise and fall of Alyssa's chest. "Check me out, Lieutenant Chessman. You'll see I'm exactly who I say I am."

He was silent. She wished he would pace, move, do something rather than stand there like a statue, trying to X-ray her intentions. Though she wasn't watching him, she could feel the movement of his gaze by the heat its trail generated, by the unusual tension twining itself fiber by fiber all the way down to her toes.

"Why would someone want to kill her?" she asked, seeking to break the laser precision of his scrutiny.

"That's the burning question." He shifted then, leaning his rear against the windowsill. As he tucked her license into the breast pocket of his T-shirt, his gaze slid to Alyssa. Brooke expelled small bursts of pent-up breaths. "She's a very observant person. She can see things that most people don't. Unfortunately for her, she doesn't always keep her observations to herself. She can be gruff. And people tend to take her the wrong way."

"Someone tried to kill her for making an observation?"

He frowned. "Maybe. I know she was scared, but she wouldn't go into details. She…"

"She what?"

He looked at her again and the depth of his concern for Alyssa pushed her back against the chair. What would it be like to have someone care for *her* so deeply? Except that love required masks and she was tired of trying to fit herself to others' expectations. Her escape to Boston had been in part to free herself from that heavy mantle.

His jaw flinched. "She was troubled."

"In what way?"

He shrugged, examined the toes of his scuffed hiking boots. "It's almost as if she were looking for something, but couldn't quite find it."

Brooke sucked in a long breath. How many times had she felt that very way? Looking, always looking, but not knowing quite what for. Had she and Alyssa subconsciously been looking for a replacement for the missing part of themselves that was in the other?

Oh, Alyssa. I didn't know you were alive, or I would have looked for you a long time ago.

And now that she'd found her, she couldn't let go. Her sister represented the best memories of her life. She wanted the chance to build new ones, to find the free, happy girls they had been once.

Something took hold of her. Like a weed, the idea germinated and grew. She dismissed the thought. It returned. Larger. Thicker. Bolder. Brooke shot up from the chair and paced the room to untangle the urgency crowding her mind like a bramble of thorns.

Her world was an ordered one. Her mother had insisted on constancy and the military regimen had become habit. Everything had its place. Everything happened on schedule. Risks were kept to a minimum, and Brooke was almost never caught off guard.

But in the last month nothing had seemed real. She'd almost lost her mother. She'd found her sister, only to discover the essential part of her was unreachable. Her world was spinning out of orbit, tilting on its axis. Nothing was falling back into its rightful place.

Now that she'd found Alyssa, she *had* to get to know her. And if that meant finding out who tried to kill her first, then that was what she would do.

Brooke came to a standstill in the middle of the room, hands fisted by her sides. She faced the granite of Jack's eyes squarely. Her heart was beating fast. Her mind rushed like a waterfall. A bead of sweat trickled from her nape, snaked its way down her spine.

"You want to find who did this to Alyssa," she said.

Instant suspicion deepened his frown. "Yes."

"I can help you."

He straightened. His body shifted. His right hand crept to his hip. "You're in law enforcement?"

"I teach kindergarten."

"Kindergarten! How's that going to help me?"

She turned away from him, from the intensity chipping away at her self-confidence. Seeing her sister's still features, her resolve crystallized. This was the right thing to do. "You need a way to flush this person out."

Silence was his only response.

"I'll pretend to be Alyssa."

"No."

Brooke ignored the forceful blow of Jack's voice. Hands

knotted in front of her, she spun around to face him. "I'll pretend to be Alyssa. Then whoever tried to kill her will think he failed and—"

"Get another opportunity to get it right?" he scoffed.

"No." She paced the room, biting her left thumbnail as she concentrated on the plan firming itself in her mind. "Give you an opportunity to catch him."

"This isn't going to work."

"Of course, it will."

"You don't know anything about her life."

Pensively she reached up and touched her temple. "With the hit she took on the head, amnesia is believable. If I don't 'remember' things, nobody will be the wiser."

He stepped in front of her, an immovable obstacle. "No, I won't let you set yourself up as bait."

She held her ground, certainty giving her courage she didn't know she possessed. "How else are you going to catch him?"

"I've got suspects."

"If you're waiting for a confession, you'll be waiting a long time."

He crossed his arms. His eyes glittered with barely controlled rage. "And your vast knowledge of interrogative techniques comes from…?"

"You'd be surprised how tough five-year-olds can be. What I've learned is that the only way to solve a crime is to get the suspect to rat on himself or to get others to rat on him."

"I deal with the real world."

"Ten to one most of your calls are domestic disturbances." She paused, waiting for confirmation, and got none. "So are mine."

He just stared at her, all tough and hard-boiled, but in his silence, she sensed turmoil.

"And just what are you going to do with your sister?"

he asked finally. "It's easy enough for anyone to check the hospital to see she's still here."

She glanced at Alyssa over her shoulder. The need for physical closeness after their unnatural separation was feral. To let her go now would be another cut to the quick. Yet the most important thing was Alyssa's safety, and the only way to ensure that safety was to remove her from any chance of danger.

Her mother should have checked out of the nursing home days ago, but guilt was keeping her weak, unfocused. With her lost daughter to sit by and talk to, her mother could find a purpose again. "I'll send her home to San Diego. Mom can watch over Alyssa."

"What makes you think your mother will want to see her other daughter after all these years?"

"Because her message to Alyssa is one of regret." *Tell her I'm sorry. Beg her to give me another chance.* The tears in her mother's eyes had been the first real emotion Brooke had seen in years.

Jack forged on, forcing her to face him, making her feel like a swimmer caught in an undertow. "That'll be expensive. Can you afford it?"

"Mom can."

Jack started to reach for her, then scraped a hand through his dark-brown hair instead. "You don't know Alyssa."

"Amnesia—"

"Will only be believable so far."

She shrugged. "You can teach me how to be her."

He shook his head and she thought she spotted a shaft of fear in those flint eyes. It had to be a trick of the light. Jack Chessman didn't look as if he would let anyone or anything scare him.

"You don't look like her."

"We're identical." She fingered the ends of her hair. "I can have my hair styled like hers."

He eyed her up and down, measuring her. "You're shorter."

"By what? An inch? Will anyone really notice?"

His gaze latched onto hers, drilled, burrowed. "You're left-handed."

"I learned to use my right hand when I broke my left arm in high school."

He nodded toward Alyssa's cast. "The arm."

"There you go. It's the right one, so I'll have to use my left one anyway." She lifted her right arm. "Fake cast."

His gaze bored deeper. "What about the scrapes? It's not believable they vanished overnight."

"Makeup."

"You've been seen around the hospital."

"I just got here an hour ago."

"How did you know where to find Alyssa?"

"I called her home. A woman told me about her accident."

"You talked to Franny?"

"But didn't give my name."

"Your father'll know the difference."

"Not if you help me."

He let out a sharp breath that sounded like a muffled curse and shook his head. "I won't be a part of this ridiculous plan."

"I've got to do this."

"Why?" With a half step, he invaded her space, sending her senses reeling. She wanted more than anything to move away, to place a room, a building, a city between herself and this mountain of a man.

"Because..." She lifted her hands and arms in a helpless gesture. "Because I promised."

"Don't you realize how dangerous this could be?"

The dark, deep resonance of his voice lifted the fine hairs along her arms in a way no lover's touch ever had.

"You can't stop me."

"I'll blow your cover."

Heart hammering against her ribs, she was keenly aware of his mouth hovering too close to her face now, of the contradiction of softness and strength it presented. She swallowed hard, but held her ground. All her life she'd allowed others to bully her. Not this time.

"But you won't because you want to find who did this. It's eating at you. If it wasn't, you wouldn't have thought me a possible danger to her."

Giving in to impulse, she touched his cheek, laid her whole palm against the roughness, and played the one card she sensed would reach him. "It's Alyssa's only chance to get justice."

Swearing, he turned away from her, breaking their contact. As if she'd slapped him, he rubbed his cheek where her hand had been and stared at Alyssa. "This is crazy. You're putting yourself in danger. You have no idea who you're dealing with."

"But you do. You said you had suspects."

He shook his head, closed his eyes, hiding his brewing emotions from her. "I never thought one of her own friends would be able to kill." When he opened his eyes again, they reflected grim resolution. "Alyssa's attempted murder was officially ruled an accident."

"But you know it was intended to be murder."

"She told me."

"And you believe her."

"Yes." His expression dared her to contradict him.

"All the more reason for me to take her place."

He straightened, took a predatory stance. "All the more reason for you to stay out of it. This is no kindergarten field trip."

She paced again, trying to sway his steadfast gaze. "Will they try again?"

"The job is half-done."

Aware, always aware of that keen gaze following her every move, Brooke strove to keep going straight down the line of logic. "Then I have a better chance to survive a second attack than Alyssa does in her coma."

"She has nurses and doctors to protect her."

"Busy nurses. Busy doctors. I was here for a half hour before someone wondered who I was." She stopped and looked at him straight, too conscious again of the unsettling effect of his hard gaze. "If you don't prove this was an attempt on Alyssa's life, who will?"

"No one."

She lifted her arms in unabashed relief. "See, we agree."

"It's too dangerous."

"I'm going to do this, Jack. It may be the only chance I have to get to know my sister. A part of me has been missing for twenty-four years. I need to find it. I need to find her." *We'll take care of each other.* "I need to help her."

From his position by Alyssa's bed, his gaze speared her deeper, made her shiver. For the first time she saw something far-reaching in the intense gray of his eyes. Something softer, more personal. "She's here because of me. I can't take the chance something will happen to you, too."

A small catch skittered down her throat. So that was it. He felt responsible for Alyssa's accident, not just for finding who had caused his friend's—his lover's?—coma. Just how close were Jack and Alyssa? What kind of friendship did they share? That he loved her sister was clear enough by his words, by his actions—by the depth of his guilt.

"It's not your decision to make," she said softly, seeking to cushion her newfound determination, his guilt.

"You'll be in my town, on my watch. That makes your welfare my responsibility."

"When did New Hampshire become a communist state?"

He swore. More at himself, she surmised, than at her. "You're right. If you want to put yourself into danger, who am I to stop you?"

She smiled thinly. "I knew you'd see things my way."

"As the law in Comfort, it's still my responsibility to see to your welfare." She started to protest, but he held up one hand. "As I would do for any of the people who live and visit there. I let Alyssa down. I owe her your safety. Can you understand that?"

She nodded. Honor was a refreshing quality in a man. Alyssa was a lucky woman to have such a loyal friend as Jack Chessman.

Hands in his pockets, he turned to face the window. "Let me think."

"Take your time." She hardly dared to breathe as she watched him. His body was rock still, though she imagined his mind was a storm of lightning thoughts. She fought the urge to sit down in case any movement should cause a premature decision that would require a messy, unwanted confrontation.

Slowly he turned back to face her. His features were set, steely. He stalked toward her, stopped one step from her. She was sure his proximity was so she could see his intention.

In that instant an acute, primitive need stabbed her. Her body jerked from the blow as if it had been real instead of imagined. He was her sister's friend—lover?—not hers. This unnatural attraction was wrong. He was not the kind of man she wanted in her life. She wanted warmth. She wanted emotional honesty. She wanted a man who wouldn't constantly wear a mask of self-restraint. But her blood pulsed anyway, heated and charged.

"You want to play Alyssa," he said, his voice a low, raw rumble in her ear, "then I'll help you, and we'll do this my way. As of this moment, we're engaged. I'll move into Alyssa's cottage with you and keep an eye on you."

"Engaged? Living together?" She shook her head. Thoughts somersaulted as her jaw dropped open. *That,* she definitely couldn't handle. She could only take so much intensity at a time. And there was definitely too much power exuding from Jack Chessman. The force of his personality would hem her, control her, and the last thing she needed was to trade the prison of her mother's icy manipulation for his. "Aren't you taking responsibility just a bit too far?"

"Don't you understand that there's someone out there who claims to be Alyssa's friend who wants her dead?"

"Yes, you said so, but it's not necessary—"

His hands took hold of both her shoulders. The reach of his touch went much deeper than the skin. She wanted to back away from the unnerving sensations zigzagging through her. "I *will* keep you safe."

In his eyes, she saw that his need ran as deep as her own, and relented.

"We don't need to pretend we're engaged."

A crooked smile slashed his face. A rough laugh escaped his mouth. One hand slid from her shoulder to her left hand. He held her ring finger between two of his callused digits.

"You've just proved how inadequately prepared you are for the role you want to play. Her father's real big on family values. If Alyssa's living with someone at the Comfort Pines Resort, Walter's going to want to see a ring on her hand."

She looked down at his fingers on hers, felt the fire of

his touch forge a circle of heat more potent than hot metal. She was getting deep into a situation she didn't really understand, a situation she was beginning to sense could prove dangerous in more than one way.

But her discomfort would be nothing compared to Alyssa's. And to have the chance to know Alyssa again, to find herself, to find her freedom, she *had* to do something. She'd play this one last role.

Before she could change her mind, she drew in a long breath. "Okay, we'll do it your way. How do we start?"

TWO DAYS LATER, after a flurry of consultations and phone calls, they stood outside the office of the fixed base operator at a small regional airport on the fringes of Boston, watching a private jet taxi to the runway.

The stink of aviation gas filled his nostrils. The taste of hot tar scorched the back of his throat. The whine of jet engines attacked his eardrums. Heat rose from the asphalt, spiraled around Brooke so that she seemed to shimmer in the midday sun.

Complicated emotions stirred inside him as Jack studied the delicate curve of her spine—a caustic mix of anger, resentment, obligation and something warmer, needier. He didn't want to feel anything. Hadn't life shown him time and again that emotions only led to disaster? His mother had let her heart rule her life and ended up with a shattered spirit. His father had let greed dictate his actions and ended up in jail. Jack was determined to let facts and logic guide his behaviour. He was *not* going to end up like either of his parents.

His aim in life was simple: to observe dispassionately in order to protect the people of Comfort, and to climb every mountain in New Hampshire. Anything else skated too close to chaos, and chaos had to be contained.

But something about Brooke was drawing him from impersonal observer to a connection he didn't want to explore. He'd always seen Alyssa as a girl, a baby sister, but watching Brooke shimmering in the sun, he saw a woman—too soft, too fragile, too... complicated.

The image of an angel crept into Jack's mind, but he dismissed it with a shake. Brooke Snowden was no angel. She was nothing but trouble. Hadn't she already proved that with her stubborn determination to take Alyssa's place?

He shifted his weight restlessly from one foot to the other, suddenly needing movement to bring order to the storm of his mind, speed to tighten the loosening hold of his control.

"We should get going," he said. Brooke still stared at the sky, even though the jet taking her sister to San Diego had long since disappeared.

"Yes." She turned slowly, rubbing her arms despite the June heat, which had plastered the purple silk T-shirt to her skin.

He silently swore at the sheen of tears clinging to her golden lashes, and the more disturbing need to touch her, reassure her. His hands suddenly felt as fumbly as ten thumbs. He shoved them deep into the front pockets of his khaki cargo pants. "She's got a nurse and a paramedic with her. She'll be all right."

Twisting a finger around a lock of soft blond hair, Brooke attempted a smile but fell short. "I know. I just didn't think I'd have to say goodbye so soon."

"Your mother knows not to call the resort?" he asked as he led the way back to his car, keeping his hands, his control firmly in check.

For this to work, no one could know about Brooke. And a woman who had no qualms about letting her daughter risk her life would certainly think nothing of betraying her secret. Not that he was being a paragon of virtue in that department, either. Fresh anger assailed him. The fact remained, he was using Brooke, and didn't like it one bit.

Over the past two days, he'd given her plenty of chances to back out and each time she'd refused. The worst part was that there was a certain logic to switching places with her twin. In the throes of emotions, people tended to make mistakes, and if anything could throw the would-be murderer for a loop, it would be Alyssa's miraculous recovery. And he'd be right there waiting to apprehend the bastard.

Still, he didn't like the situation, didn't much like himself for taking advantage of Brooke's willingness to step into danger. But she'd handed him this opportunity to flush out a killer, to mete justice out, and he'd be a fool not to use it. It was the practical, logical, rational thing to do. If he didn't use Brooke, he'd have to examine the reasons, and he sensed that would get him into territory he'd rather not explore.

"I told my mother I'd call her." Brooke took one woeful last look over her shoulder before she jogged to catch up with him. "Mom thinks I'm a little old for a *Parent Trap* switch, but it was the only thing I could think to tell her."

"*Parent Trap?*"

"You know, the movie where Hayley Mills plays twins who meet at summer camp, then change places in order to get their parents together again."

"Your mother bought that?"

She looked westward to the sky. "Desperate people cling to desperate hope. Mom's arranged for Alyssa to share her room at the nursing home. She's so excited to have the chance to make amends for her past mistake." Brooke gave a halfhearted shrug. The wrinkling of her brow betrayed her inner turmoil. "It hasn't been easy on her."

Or on you, Jack guessed. He shook away the sentiment

and grunted as he unlocked the passenger door. "It was easy enough for her to separate sisters and make each believe the other was dead, then years later to interfere with their lives again."

Brooke stepped into the car and shot him a pleading look. "She knows she made mistakes. She's trying to make up for them."

"If you say so."

"We're both trying to understand. It's going to take time."

Once Brooke was seated, he closed the door with more force than he'd intended. She was swimming in a sea of emotions, and dragging him down to drown in them with her. When he'd settled himself in the driver's seat, a flick of the key brought the sports car's engine roaring to life. "It's not too late to change your mind."

She studied him frankly, the green of her eyes reminding him of woods, deep and wild, of his crazy hunger, sharp and strong. "I'm not going to change my mind."

Her rock solid determination was all he needed to retreat once more to his role of observer. The choice was hers. He didn't have to get involved; he just had to keep her safe. "We'll stop in Tilton, then."

"What's in Tilton?"

He shoved the car in reverse and gunned the engine. "A special effects wizard."

THE VISITOR spotted the empty hospital bed. An orderly was stripping sheets from the mattress.

"The woman who was here, what happened to her?"

The orderly dumped the sheets into a canvas laundry bag on wheels. "She leave."

Dead? The anticipation of victory pounded a fast rhythm in heart and pulse. "The morgue?"

The orderly shook his head. "She leave with her friend."

Jack? He hadn't said anything about Alyssa regaining consciousness. Was it possible? "When?"

The orderly glanced at his watch, shrugged. "One hour. Maybe two."

Fury blazed fast and furious. A hand tightened around the vial in the pocket, then loosened. *Stay focused.*

Two more nurses confirmed Alyssa's discharge, but neither were fountains of information. Efficient. Succinct. But facts were facts.

Alyssa was gone. Discharged.

Alive.

What would she remember?

In the glare of artificial light reflected on the window, everything was suddenly sharp and crisp.

It's just a minor setback. Alyssa won't get away with torturing people the way she does. It's gone on long enough. It will *stop.*

Chapter Three

"The movie studio's on the site of an old manufacturing plant just outside Tilton. It's still a dream in progress," Jack informed Brooke as he exited the interstate. He'd been acting like a robot tour guide since they left Boston and it was starting to get on her nerves.

"It's meant to draw Hollywood dollars to the Lakes Region rather than let them migrate north to Canada. The New Hampshire Film and Television Commission is trying to lure producers with the no sales tax, no state income tax and easy incorporation procedures angle."

"Jack," Brooke interrupted, digging the fingers of both hands into the soft leather of her purse. She'd never wanted to slap anyone before, but the urge now was nearly impossible to control.

"What?"

"That's all very interesting, but… Not right now."

There were more pressing things on her mind. Like the nervousness that knotted her insides. Like the doubt that was beating inside her head like a kindergartner with castanets. Like the anticipation that shouldn't be there, but managed to trip her heart into double time.

He glanced at her, nodded. Then he went silent, and that was nearly as unbearable. She couldn't think over the regular drone of the engine. She couldn't form words to carry on a conversation. All she could do was watch the scenery buzz by, the proliferation of trees thickening with every mile, her anxiety escalating with every roll of the tires.

Was she going to be able to pull this off? She'd never made the cut for any of the school plays for which she'd auditioned, never been good at controlling the emotions that flowed through her unfettered like water.

You're just like your father, hypersensitive and undisciplined, had been her mother's favorite admonishment.

For heaven's sake, Brooke, control yourself! Reproach had been obvious in the pinched tone of her voice, in the disappointment etched in her eyes. She'd tried and tried to be the daughter her mother wanted, but over the years she'd come to accept that nothing she did ever satisfied her mother.

Brooke had flown east to find herself, to be her own person, and now she had managed to put herself in the position of having to play a role again.

How could she even think of passing herself off as Alyssa? Assuming a person's identity took more than looks. Alyssa had been a risk-taker. While she had avoided risk whenever she could. She didn't smoke. She didn't drink. She hardly ever drove over the speed limit. And she never, ever would have even thought to climb a mountain. Her most dangerous pursuits were jogging along the beach every morning, feeding dead mice to the class snake she'd inherited and keeping twenty rambunctious five-year-olds safe while they were under her care during the school day. What had made her think she could pull this charade off?

And then there was Jack. He confounded her. She couldn't understand how he could fluster her with just a look, how her mind could become such a tangled mess when he was near. Over the past two days, he'd shown her he was an efficient, pragmatic man—exactly the kind of person she didn't want in her life. Still, no man had ever made her feel so unsettled.

She huffed a breath, shifted her weight from one hip to the other, centered her purse in her lap, and chewed pensively on a thumbnail.

Playing this was right. She'd be helping Alyssa. She'd get to know her sister. She'd see her father again. She'd help put a criminal behind bars. And when Alyssa was better—and she *would* get better—Brooke would have the reunion she'd dreamed of.

She was doing the right thing. She was.

As for Jack, well, she'd make herself view him as a necessary director in this play. She would learn from him, but she wouldn't be fool enough to fall for him just because he made her feel all jittery and hyperaware. This performance was for Alyssa.

Maybe if she told herself that long enough, she'd believe it.

Soon Jack turned onto a rutted road and stopped the car in front of a building that looked more like a warehouse than her idea of a movie studio.

A red barn, a traditional white farmhouse and a few other buildings dotted the background. An old apple orchard, various gardens, ponds, woods, even a riding ring offered a multitude of filming backdrops.

"Right now they're looking for funding to add a production facility with all the works—screening room, sound stages, production offices." He pointed toward the warehouse. "They've got everything crammed in here and they need more space."

He led her inside the warehouse through a maze of people, props and makeshift offices. Along the way several people called in greeting to Jack, arousing her curiosity. How did he know these people? He opened a door at the far end of the warehouse and the smell of paint, plastic and powder tickled her nose.

Hearing the door open, a woman looked up. A huge wine-red smile cracked her narrow pale face, giving her a Cheshire cat appearance. "Jack, how are you?"

Her long hair was burgundy and wound in a loose knot on top of her head. The knot was held in place with two black-lacquered chopsticks. A sleeveless black tank top and black capri pants shrink-wrapped her too-skinny body. Thick-soled black sneakers anchored her to the ground. She was busily applying color to a latex mask that looked like some sort of alien.

"Hi, Meg," Jack said, pulling Brooke inside. "Is this a good time?"

"Perfect." Meg plunked her paintbrush in a jar and wiped her hands on a towel, which had been white at one point, but was now a muddy green. "What is it exactly you want me to do? You were kind of vague on the phone."

He took two pictures from the breast pocket of his salmon-colored shirt. Both were of Alyssa. One was a snapshot taken two months before on a climbing expedition; the other was a Polaroid taken at the hospital just before Alyssa was prepped for her trip to San Diego. "Can you make my friend look like the girl in these pictures?"

Looking from Brooke to the pictures and back, Meg blew a bubble with her gum and popped it. A renewed slither of anxiety caused nausea to churn in Brooke's stomach. "Which version?"

"The scarred one," Jack said.

One artificially black brow shot up. "Are you working on a new project?"

"You could say that."

Meg rested her rear on the edge of a makeup table, adjusted the black-framed glasses on her nose and folded her arms beneath her nonexistent chest. "Details. I need details."

"I can't give you any."

Both of her eyebrows rose. "Which, of course, only makes me more curious. Jack, hon, you're going to have to give me something."

"Trust me, it's better if you don't know anything."

"You hand me this project and I'm not supposed to ask questions?" Shaking her head, Meg taped both pictures to the brightly lit mirror behind her.

"It's part of the challenge." Jack flashed Meg a smile. Brooke supposed it was meant to look disarming, but it looked desperate to her. Somehow seeing such a confident man uncertain was endearing. "You told me you like a challenge."

"Challenge is one thing. What I don't like is a possible misrepresentation of my talents." Brows drawn, she studied him for a minute, a veritable poster child for the temperamental artiste. "It's hard to get in the mood if I don't know what I'm supposed to be creating. I pride myself in getting the role right."

Jack scrubbed a hand through his hair, blew out a breath, then started to speak with stiff, exaggerated hand motions. "Think of it as a movie-of-the-week. *Terror in Tilton.* Melissa Gilbert and Bruce Greenwood star. It was a dark and stormy night. Melissa's car went over a cliff. She's got amnesia. She and Bruce have to find out who drove her off the road before the villain kills her for good this time."

"Mmm," Meg said, contemplating the pictures once more. "This movie of yours, how long does it last?"

"A week, maybe two."

"With makeup every day?"

"That's part of your challenge, Meg. I need something that'll last awhile."

"Mmm," she said again, blowing another bubble with

her gum. She got up, turned the barber chair in front of the large mirror around and motioned to Brooke to sit. She ran her fingers through Brooke's hair.

Brooke curled her hands around the chair arms. The metal was cold. So was her stomach. What was she doing? The shag cut she'd had in college had taken her years to grow out. She didn't like short hair. She didn't want short hair.

Meg squinted at the pictures and surveyed Brooke. ''Are the colors in the picture true?''

''As far as I know,'' Jack said.

''Then we'll need to lighten her hair a shade.'' She lifted a long lock from Brooke's shoulder and let it fall again in a soft cascade. Shaking her head, she *tsked*. ''Are you sure you want to cut this hair, hon? It's awfully nice.''

Jack slanted her a penetrating look, and Brooke realized he was giving her a chance to back out. She couldn't find her voice to assert her conviction.

''She's sure,'' Jack said and looked away.

''I wasn't talking to you.'' Meg turned her attention to Brooke once more. ''You got a name?''

''No names.''

''I'm starting to believe this girl doesn't own a tongue. Is he pressuring you into doing something you don't want to do? Cuz if he is, just say the word—''

''No. This was my idea.''

Meg cracked her gum, seemingly unconvinced.

''It's all right, Meg. I'm sure.'' Brooke's hard swallow stole a bit of certainty from her voice. She wasn't sure at all. What was she doing? This was crazy. She wasn't suited to subterfuge.

Meg shrugged and met Jack's gaze. ''Okay. You're sure you don't want to give me a hint what this is all about?''

''It's better if you don't know.''

''Secret police stuff?''

"Help-a-friend secret stuff."

"When it's over, you'll tell me then?"

"When it's over."

With that Meg gave her gum one last crack and got to work. She wrapped a styling cape around Brooke's neck. After shampooing Brooke's hair, Meg twirled fat locks and held them out of the way with butterfly clips.

"Got to see the final cut of *Mountain Rescue* a while back. Impressive." Meg grabbed scissors and a comb.

"What's *Mountain Rescue?*" Brooke asked.

"Jack's movie."

"You made a movie?" Brooke started to turn to look at Jack, but Meg firmly turned her head forward, then gave the air a few snips with the scissors to make her point.

"Didn't Jack tell you?"

"No."

Meg was only too glad to oblige with an explanation. "He consulted on a movie-of-the-week last winter. A search-and-rescue type thing. Filmed in his neck of the woods. He even has a small part in it." Meg smiled at Jack in the mirror. "And you thought it would end up on the cutting room floor! More like front and center. The camera loves you, Jack. It's all that fierce manliness in your face. Of course, I'll have to say that I did an excellent job with the blood. You sure looked like you'd been attacked by a bear."

As each hank of long hair fell to the floor, Brooke winced inwardly. Unable to look any longer, she closed her eyes. That was almost as bad. She could feel Jack's gaze on her. Laser keen. Burning. What was he thinking? What was he feeling behind that icy facade? Why did she care? Except that for some reason, she wanted his approval. She didn't want to let him down. And somehow she felt she was.

"There," Meg said, pleased, once she'd finished drying Brooke's hair.

Slowly Brooke opened her eyes.

Meg tousled what was left of Brooke's hair, leaving her with Alyssa's windblown look. The effect was unbelievable. For a second, Brooke didn't recognize herself. She thought she was looking at her sister. One of her hands crept to her chest and she was looking at it as if it belonged to someone else. She even felt different. How, she couldn't say, but different, as if a shift was taking place deep inside.

"What do you think?" Meg asked, obviously delighted by her effort.

"Great." Jack's voice was just a bit hoarse and hollow.

Brooke looked away from her reflection in the mirror and met Jack's gaze. It was narrowed, direct, filled with acute intensity that penetrated her.

She was Alyssa. Jack's expression confirmed it.

A thread of longing wrapped itself around her heart. She wanted someone to look at *her* the way Jack had just looked at her version of Alyssa before he restrained himself and shuttered his gaze once more. She swallowed hard. Why was she suddenly disappointed? She didn't even like him, didn't like his cold remoteness.

"Now according to this picture," Meg said as she ripped the Polaroid from the mirror's surface, "we'll need a scar on her temple. The look shouldn't change that much in a week or two. I've got stuff that'll hold for that long." Meg pressed a finger against Brooke's temple. "I'll need to shave a bit of your hair there to make it look like a hospital job."

Meg rolled a cart filled with prostheses next to the chair, tried a few scars on for size before she picked one she liked. Working with tiny paintbrushes, glue, makeup, something she called collodion and concentrated pops of her bubble gum, she applied a wound that looked so real Brooke reached up to touch it.

Meg *tsked*. "Let it dry, hon." Then she smiled. "Not bad, huh?"

"Jack called you a wizard. You really are."

Meg blushed. "Thanks."

"It won't come off in the shower?"

"I wouldn't scrub real hard or anything, but if you're gentle, yeah, it should be okay." Then she frowned. "About those scrapes. There's only one way to make them last long enough to be believed."

"How?"

Meg whirled the chair around and faced Brooke squarely. "Sandpaper."

"No!" Jack leaped from his stool. "You can't do that."

"I agree. It's drastic. I'm really going to hate messing up such great skin. But unless you want to come in every day to make it look as if they're healing…" Meg shrugged one shoulder.

"If that's what it takes, then that's what it takes." Brooke stiffened, already anticipating the sting of blood, of pain on her cheek.

"No." Jack's voice rang with authority. "I won't allow it."

Looking from one to the other, Meg said, "Okay. I believe that's my cue to exit. You two talk it over, and I'll be right back."

Meg left the room, snicking the door closed behind her.

"Are you crazy?" Jack's voice was rough and low as he grabbed both arms of the chair and leaned down.

There was nowhere for her to go, and if she let him see even a shred of fear, he would drag her right back to Boston. And she had to stay. She had to see this through. She straightened her posture, gathered up her courage.

"You heard what Meg said. It's the best way." Her

reflection in the mirror was too bizarre. It was like being out of her body, watching a wild-eyed puppet on invisible strings. Was the foreign appearance in the mirror the source of the strange disquiet gnawing at her?

"What if it scars permanently?" Jack's fingers hovered just above her cheek. Her breath caught in anticipation of his touch.

"Vitamin E oil will take care of that." Her heart was hammering against her ribs, making her wish he'd back off or come closer.

He shook his head. "Playacting is one thing. This...*mutilation* is quite another."

"We can't come here every day." She leaned forward, looking straight into the hardness of his eyes. As she licked her suddenly dry lips, she saw something hot flash in his eyes, then just as quickly be contained. "What if someone follows? It's too obvious, Jack. This way, it's real."

"I can't let—"

"It's my choice. I've got to do this. Don't make it harder for me." Freeing herself from her mother's hold had taken too long to just allow herself to slip right back into a demure role. Maybe it was because of the cross-country trip, maybe it was because of the shortened hair, maybe it was seeing Alyssa in such a precarious state; whatever the cause, Brooke needed to hold on to her burgeoning sense of freedom.

"Why?" The single word came out in a forceful explosion of breath and throttled emotion.

He was just like her mother. If that leash on his feelings was any tighter, he'd choke himself. She shook her head, calm radiating in her chest. "Because I'm here and Alyssa isn't. And if you could, you'd do it, too."

His slight backward jerk told her she'd hit the nail square on the head. Maybe there was something deeper to him than the emotionless front he presented to the world.

Before Jack could answer, Meg poked her burgundy head inside the door, cleaving the unbending tension of his gaze.

"So what'll it be?"

The silence in the room allowed the soft murmur of activity from the warehouse to float through the walls.

Breaking Jack's remaining hold on the chair, Brooke twirled to face the mirror once more. "Let's do it."

Jack swore, half turning away from her.

She reached for his hand, felt the callused fingertips, the hard tendons, the toughened skin. His gaze connected with hers. He silently spoke volumes with those flint eyes. But it was a foreign tongue, not as easily decipherable as the secret language she and Alyssa had once shared. She wasn't sure what she was reading, why she suddenly wanted to cry. But she knew without a doubt that acceptance was exacting a steep price. I understand, she wanted to say, but the words got stuck in her throat. Instead she gave his fingers a squeeze.

"Jack?"

He said nothing. She let her fingers slide back to her lap, twined them with her other hand to stay the sudden bereft sensation. What had she expected? Encouragement? Appreciation? Understanding?

Nothing. Don't expect anything and you won't be disappointed. Why did she keep forgetting that lesson? Because it was hard to remain calm and cool in the gush of conflicting emotions running hot in her blood.

The women looked at each other. Brooke frowned helplessly, unsure how to handle a man like Jack. Meg went to a locker at the back of the room, took out some change from her purse. She handed the coins to Jack. "Why don't you be a dear and get me a Diet Dr. Pepper?"

"I'm fine," Jack said and sat back on the stool.

"I'm really thirsty."

He glared at Meg. He was not a man used to being opposed. How had Alyssa handled his unyielding personality?

Meg shrugged. "Have it your way."

Sandpaper poised, Meg turned to her. "Ready?"

"As I'll ever be." Taking a deep breath, Brooke tightened her grip on the chair arms. Involuntarily her gaze sought Jack's.

In his eyes she saw that he would allow her to back out without rancor. He would spirit her to safety in a second without asking for an explanation. He would take her place in a flash if he could. Maybe there was hope for him yet. The softening depths of his gray eyes more than anything gave her the courage to go on, while filling her with impossible regret.

Meg held Brooke's jaw firmly in one hand, tilted her head slightly and applied the first scrape of sandpaper to skin. Brooke closed her eyes then. The fast pulsing of blood pounding in her ears masked the sound of her disfigurement.

Blood pearled on Brooke's newly abraded skin. Jack's stomach rebelled. With each tear of skin she accepted she was shredding his restraint. He wanted to rip the sandpaper from Meg's hand, drag Brooke to the nearest airport and send her back to San Diego. As it was, his fingers were making dents on the side of the stool. He couldn't watch. He couldn't tear his gaze away.

It's her choice, he reminded himself. He'd given her plenty of chances to back down. *All I have to do is keep her safe.*

Her fingertips were white against the chair's cold metal. Her lips were pressed tight. The gold chain at her neck jiggled erratically while Meg performed her transformation of Brooke from clear-skinned angel to scuffed imp.

Brooke was petrified, yet she wasn't allowing her apprehension to interfere with her decision. The girl had courage. No, not girl. Woman. Definitely woman.

He was suddenly very aware that if he let her cut any deeper through the skin of his detachment, he would lose his objectivity and place her in even greater danger.

Chapter Four

In the crowded space of the small car, Brooke shot Jack a sidelong glance. Since Meg had finished her transformation, he'd barely looked at her. Because she looked like Alyssa, but wasn't? Once again, she wondered at the intimacy of Jack and Alyssa's relationship.

He'd taken her to an out-of-the-way restaurant for dinner. Their conversation there had been stiff and stilted, the meal rushed. Now silence hung between them. She was uncomfortably aware of his body heat even over the blast of air-conditioning from the vents, of the clean outdoor scent of him over the rich smell of the leather seats. Shifting closer to the side window, she forced herself to study the landscape passing by.

With the summer solstice approaching, the days were long. The sun-drenched highway seemed to twist on forever. Once in a while, the relentless green of the trees opened up to give a breathtaking view of a deep gray lake or a faraway mountain a darker shade of blue than the sky.

Jack reached for the radio knob and turned it on. A shout or two from a rock and roll song belted out. He turned the knob off. His hands on the steering wheel and his bared forearms were a study of toned muscles and tendons under skin. There seemed not to be an ounce of fat on him, not an inch of give. Yet she couldn't help wondering how sensitive were fingers accustomed to feeling for the smallest of holds on a mountain side.

"What do you remember of the resort?" Jack asked, jarring her from her fanciful thoughts.

"Is that where we're heading?"

"No, we've got to give those scratches on your face a chance to heal. We'll make a quick stop at my house, then head to my grandfather's cabin in the woods for a few days."

"Oh." The passing scenery became a magnet, drawing her away from the discomfort gnawing at her. She was a little girl again, watching her parents fight against the sharp contrast of dancing water and dark woods. "The resort wasn't a resort the last time I was there. The house was kind of run-down. I remember the trees and the water." The musty smell of the closed-in house. The undercurrents of tidal emotions. The worms of fear. "Everything seemed so...dark."

He nodded pensively, keeping his watchful gaze glued to the highway. "They've got thirty cabins now. Most are on the water. Tennis courts. A picnic area where there's a barbecue every Thursday, daily activities for the renters and a family movie once a week. There's a boathouse for canoes and kayaks, which they rent out. Alyssa lives in the original cabin. Your father lives in the great hall. The business office is there, too. I'll show you around when we get there."

Brooke would be stepping into a whole new world about which she knew nothing. Alyssa's world. Anticipation and fear overwhelmed her, and tears of frustration started to burn her eyes.

Oh, for heaven's sake, Brooke, get a hold of yourself! In her mind, she could see her mother's pinched features, hear her harsh whisper. *You're making a public spectacle of yourself.* She blinked rapidly, and focused once more on the landscape.

Four lanes of highway narrowed to two. The trees on both sides formed a canopy over the road, allowing the shade of maples, birches, beeches and pines to encroach on the asphalt. The lengthening shadows darkened her mood. Could she handle herself well enough, long enough to do this for Alyssa?

Needing to keep busy, she foraged through her purse, not quite sure for what. Unaccustomed to the cast on her right arm, she fumbled awkwardly. Suddenly she stopped, folded the flap and positioned the mound of leather at her feet. One step at a time. She could do this. *Take it one step at a time.*

Brooke rearranged the shoulder harness so she could lean the back of her head against the window's glass, and tried to ignore the roll of the tires against the road as they rumbled dire warnings all the way to the marrow of her bones.

Jack stared straight ahead, his granite profile a wonder of nature. What had Alyssa seen in him? What was hiding beneath the rough exterior?

Then slowly, in the glacial cut of his features, there materialized traces of warmth—the dip of a dimple in one cheek; small fans of lines betraying laughter near his eyes…an earlobe, rounded, smooth, practically begging to be kissed.

"Tell me about her friends," Brooke said. She didn't want to delve into Jack Chessman's softer side. "Since you seem to think one of them tried to kill her."

"What do you want to know?"

"Enough to recognize them without introduction."

"Why? Amnesia—"

"Like you said, it's not enough."

Nodding once, Jack kept his gaze concentrated on the

road. "There's Tim Hogarty. He's the editor of the local weekly paper. Six feet. Short blond hair. Blue eyes. Glasses."

"That could be anybody. What's he *like?*" Distraction. That was better. She didn't want to think of Jack. *Keep things in perspective. Concentrate on the situation, on Alyssa.* Anything to avoid analyzing the strange stirrings in her gut.

He glanced at her, frowning. "What do you mean?"

"If I asked you to describe his car, you could probably give me half a dozen analogies and detail the thing down to the wheel nut."

The hint of a smile creased his cheek, deepening his dimple. "He's like one of those guys you'd see in a Calvin Klein ad. Polished, studious, silent."

"There you go." An answering smile curled her lips, lightening her mood. "Was that so hard?"

He made a noncommittal grunt.

"Why would Tim want Alyssa dead?"

Jack shrugged. "She calls him Mr. Squeaky Clean."

"Is he?"

"Alyssa calls him that because she thinks he looks like a choirboy. Maybe she found some dirt. If she did, I haven't found it yet. I'm digging deeper, but it'll take time."

"Could he—?"

"Have killed her?"

She nodded.

"Given the right circumstances, anyone can."

"But—"

"Is there a precedent?"

She nodded again, not quite sure she liked the ease with which he anticipated her questions. Was she that transparent?

"Not really. But I did have to jail him once for disorderly conduct."

"What did he do?"

"Punched out a senatorial candidate whose views he disagreed with."

"Doesn't make for impartial reporting."

"Is there such a thing?"

Brooke chewed on a thumbnail. "Still, there's no motive there for murder."

"That I know of yet."

"Okay, let's leave Tim for now. Next?"

"Stephanie Cash is Alyssa's best friend. Five-seven. Brown hair. Hazel eyes. She helps out at the office of her family's propane business. She hates it, but can't see a way out of it. She wants to be a mother so bad, you can almost hear her biological clock ticking when you're near her."

"No male prospects?"

"None who want to stay in Comfort, and Steph is basically a hometown girl. Earthy. She loves to hike and climb, but she wants to come home to that white picket fence."

"You're getting good at this."

He gave a small chuckle, and she found herself smiling in return. His face was a vision of charm when he smiled. Like a child with chocolate, she wanted another taste of this warmer side.

"Any bad blood in their past?" Brooke asked.

"No. They're very much alike, except for their expectations of life. Alyssa sees Comfort as a cage. Steph sees it as a nest."

"No fights, no hair pulling, no contests over men?"

"None."

"No skeletons in the closet?"

"With Steph what you see is what you get. Before the accident, I'd have said lying was impossible for her."

"Now?"

Jack shrugged. "Everybody's a suspect until proven otherwise."

"You didn't learn that philosophy at the police academy."

He shot her a pointed glance. "There are a lot of things they can't teach you."

Like loyalty. Like love. The thought sprang into her mind unbidden. She swallowed hard. "Next."

"Cullen Griswold runs a small real estate office right in town. Five-ten. Brown hair. Brown eyes. He's like…" Jack raised a hand and dropped it back to the steering wheel. "He's like a bear cub. He looks harmless until you wrong him, then the claws and teeth come out and there's always blood. Literally. He's also familiar with the insides of our lockup."

"A teddy bear with bite. Does he have any reason to kill Alyssa?"

"He uses people."

"And?"

"And nothing. Alyssa probably found out something he'd rather not get out. What it is, I haven't a clue yet. His finances look clean. No contract disputes. No lawsuits pending. There's probably a woman involved somewhere. And he and Alyssa have a history of flaunting their affairs in each other's faces."

"They were lovers?" Brooke leaned forward like a columnist toward gossip, disgusted by her eagerness.

"Could have been if they weren't so bent on hurting each other."

Would you have minded? "And you say he's a friend?"

"It's hard to explain. We've all known each other forever. In a small town, social options are limited. He likes to climb. She likes to climb. It's safer to climb as a group than alone."

"Oh." She chewed on her thumbnail, considering the complicated web of their relationships. "So Cullen's a ladies' man?"

"More like a horny devil with more appetite than discretion."

Now there was a picture ripe for blackmail. "But being a glutton for sex isn't a reason to murder, especially if it's common knowledge."

"Depends who you're sleeping with."

She leaned back against the door once more. "There is that. Who has he been sleeping with?"

"Only Steph as far as I know. If there's anyone else, for once, he's being discreet. Nothing's flying in the rumor mill. I've tailed him on and off when I've had the extra time, but so far nothing."

"He doesn't sound like the marrying kind. What's Stephanie doing with him if she's so desperate for marriage?"

"She's settling. She seems to think, if nothing else, Cullen also wants to stay in Comfort. So I think she decided to give him a shot."

"Oh," she said. "Next?"

"Trish Witchell runs the Web design business she and her brother started three years ago. Five-five. Her hair isn't blond, but it isn't brown, either, somewhere in between. Blue-gray eyes."

Jack glanced at her. A sparkle lit his eyes. "She's like the little engine that could. Her brother was our age. She's a year younger, but was in our class because she skipped a grade. When we were kids, she'd always tag along, no matter how hard we tried to ditch her. After a couple of years, we gave up and she joined the group."

"Is the tagalong still feeling left out?"

He shook his head. "Not that I know of. She pulls her weight—just like everybody else. Her brother had a crush on Alyssa. But that doesn't matter now. Rick's out of the picture.''

"Why is Rick out of the picture?"

"He died last year."

"How?"

He glanced at her. "He didn't take the right safety precautions during a rappel and fell to his death."

"Oh." No real motive for murder there, either. "Has Trish visited your jail, too?"

That brought a small smile. "No, but she was cited for demonstrating against the ban of Judy Blume books in grade school."

Ah, a woman who believed in free expression of thought. Brooke would have fought for the ability to read what she wanted, too. "No blood involved?"

"Not then, but she and Alyssa got in regular cat fights."

Brooke's eyebrows shot up. "Cat fights?"

"Over boys. Over awards. Over everything. Both of them were very familiar with the inside of the principal's office." He gave a half grin as he shook his head. "Trish chopped Alyssa's ponytail off in eighth grade."

Brooke's left hand strayed toward her own newly shorn locks.

"Right in the middle of lunch." He chuckled at the memory, the sharp lines of his face softening with breathtaking results. Was that what Alyssa saw when she looked at Jack? "You should have seen the food fight that erupted. The whole eighth grade got detention."

"Over a boy?"

"Ryan Alden."

"School jock?"

"President of the Nintendo club."

Now she was laughing, too, trying to imagine the picture of Alyssa and Trish fighting over this Ryan Alden and ending up with cafeteria mystery meat and mashed potatoes all over them. "So she and Trish are rivals then?"

"Friendly rivals. I think they like the competition more than the goal. Poor Ryan didn't get a glance from either of them when they both made the track and field team a week later."

Brooke tried to fathom the appeal of such an adversarial friendship. The thought provoked a memory of her and Alyssa's little contests involving everything from eating cereal to getting dressed to the mad dash to the mailbox to retrieve the day's mail. She remembered the thrills, the fits of giggles, the melting of one into the other in a heap like puppies tired from a hard round of play. She sighed. The contests hadn't mattered; the closeness had. Is that what Alyssa had sought in Trish?

"I assume you did a check on Trish, too," Brooke finally said, erasing the memories with a shake of her head.

"Other than a few complaints against her company with the Better Business Bureau, she's clean."

This exercise didn't seem to be shedding any light on the situation. "How many more on your list of suspects?"

"That's it."

"That's it? I don't see a motive for murder in any of that."

Jack signaled to turn. The road became narrower, the canopy of trees tighter. The shade from the woods all but choked the sunlight, leaving Brooke feeling a bit like Gretel lost in the forest without any crumbs in her pocket to mark her way—especially since she hadn't been paying attention to the outside scenery for a while.

"That's it," Jack repeated. "Unless you count the fact that no one else had the opportunity to tamper with the equipment. No one else was at the scene of the crime. For all her brashness, most people liked Alyssa."

"No enemies?"

"None that I've found so far."

Frustration hummed throughout her. "But there has to be *something*."

They passed a park where soccer games were still going on despite the fading sunlight, then turned onto a twisty road sprinkled with a variety of house styles—everything from traditional gambrels to a modern log cabin complete with sun panels. Jack reached a hand to his visor and pressed a button. The garage door of the small, light-blue Cape Cod at the end of the road opened in response.

He drove into the garage. Hands still gripping the steering wheel, he let the engine rumble. "The one thing that ties us all together is the Adventure Club."

"The Adventure Club?"

"A business we started together five years ago. We take clients out on weekends to climb or kayak or hike or cross-country ski."

"And?" she pressed.

"And lately, we've had a few differences."

"Like?" Was she going to have to pull every bit of information out of him?

"Like safety versus risk. Like growing too fast. Like money."

Again he stopped, and Brooke wanted to reach over and shake him. "And?"

His jaw tightened. "At our last few meetings, things got out of control. We even talked about dissolving the business. We were going to take care of the commitments we already had and weren't going to take on new clients until after we'd reached a final decision."

Brooke sensed there was more. "But?"

He turned to look at her. "Alyssa booked a group of businessmen who wanted to do a team-building climbing exercise. Cullen was for it. Tim was against it. Steph was upset Alyssa broke an understanding. Trish didn't care either way."

"And you?"

He looked away. "I wanted to strangle her."

"Three against two, with Trish being the swing vote. What happened?"

Again his jaw flinched with tension. "The deposit money disappeared, so we were obliged to provide the adventure."

With a jerk of the keys, he cut the engines—and the conversation. "I won't be long."

Business, even among friends, could create a motive for murder—especially if said business was going sour and money was involved.

Five minutes later, he returned with a small duffel bag, a cooler and a key on a chain shaped like a trout. He shoved them all into the miniature back seat.

Without a word, he set off again, retracing his path through the neighborhood. What little sunlight was left didn't reach the back road on which Jack traveled. He kept glancing at his rearview mirror, and seemed to grow more preoccupied by the second.

"Is something wrong?" she asked.

"We're being followed."

THE BLACK PICKUP HAD TURNED onto Reservoir Road after him. Not unusual. The soccer games were just about over and it wasn't out of the realm of possibility that someone would take Reservoir to Valley and on to a neighboring town. But something about the truck had instantly alerted his senses to danger.

The curse of small towns was that everybody tended to know everybody else's business. That was reason number one he'd chosen to take Reservoir Road rather than wind his way through downtown. The old biddies rocking on their porches were bound to notice his red car, notice the woman beside him, and he didn't want anyone asking questions about "Alyssa" quite yet.

The other reason was efficiency. The shortest point between here and his grandfather's cabin was through Reservoir.

But with the truck he couldn't quite make out in the deepening darkness tailing him, he regretted his choice. Reservoir wasn't paved, making all that power under his hood almost useless unless he wanted to strew parts behind him. On a straight, paved road, he could easily have outrun the truck. If anything, the truck held the advantage.

And he didn't know anyone who owned a turbocharged black pickup. Was he overreacting? Was he hyperalert because Brooke was in his care?

He spared her a glance. Her hands were knotted on the edge of the seat and she was looking at him with that wide expectant look again.

"Everything's going to be fine."

Why had he agreed to this idiotic plan? For Alyssa. Because he'd made her a promise. Except that by trying to help Alyssa, he could very well be endangering Brooke. *Not your brightest move, Chessman.* But now was not the time for second thoughts. He'd also made Brooke a promise. He would keep her safe.

The truck was keeping its distance, leaving plenty of room, but Jack couldn't shake the feeling that they were being followed. There were no side roads to make an escape. He was stuck on this long, lonely road with no lights, no people and no way to maneuver except straight ahead.

He slowed, giving the truck driver ample opportunity to pass.

Forty-five, forty, thirty-five.

Still the truck stayed back—just far enough so the license plate couldn't be read, the driver's shape safely obscured.

The truck's engine whined. The brights went on, blinding him for an instant. Before Jack could stomp on the accelerator, the truck rammed into his bumper. He heard Brooke gasp at the resulting jar. Wrestling with the steering wheel, he kept the rebelling car under control.

"Hold on tight," he said.

He put his foot on the gas, accelerating sharply. The truck sped up, too, advancing on the sports car's tail. There was no place to turn, no way of going back. There wasn't a turnoff for another two miles when Reservoir forked onto Mountain.

The truck outweighed the sports car. One good shove at this speed and the car would be knocked off the road to crash into the trees.

Did the driver have an accomplice with a gun? In the darkness, Jack couldn't tell how many people were inside the truck's cab.

Steering with one hand, he used his other to push Brooke's head down toward her knees. "Stay down."

"I'll get car sick."

"Better than dead."

The truck's engine revved again. The pickup drove parallel to the sports car. The driver intended to sideswipe him. Jack played the game, alternating braking and accelerating to prevent the attacker from either cutting in front to block him or ramming the rear end to force a change of direction.

"Can you reach the car phone without getting up?" he asked.

"Yes."

"Turn it on."

"It's on."

"Call office," he ordered.

At his voice command, the phone dialed the prepro-grammed number. Dispatch answered on the second ring. "Serena, it's Jack Chessman," he shouted into the hands-free phone. "I'm heading west on Reservoir and I've got some joker in a black pickup trying to run me off the road. Any chance of getting some help out here?"

"Stand by." There was a pause as Serena contacted officers on duty. "Jack, I've got two units on their way."

"Copy. Show me a mile from Mountain Road."

Serena signed off.

"Is there any way to stop him?" Brooke asked.

"Not if he's determined to stop us."

The truck veered right. Jack fought the impulse to steer away from the truck and turned into it instead to lessen the impact.

Metal screeched against metal. Jack struggled to keep the car on the road.

"Brooke, reach into the glove compartment and get my gun."

The little door squealed as she opened it. She fumbled inside and retrieved his holster.

"Got it."

He got the car under control again and drove his elbow into the electric switch to open the driver's side window. The truck slammed into them once again. The crunch of the collision sent the car skidding dangerously close to the trees. Jack wrestled with the car. Gravel flew. Sweat poured.

"Have you ever fired a gun?" he asked.

"No."

He swore, knowing that taking one hand off the steering wheel long enough to shoot would give the truck the chance it needed to run them off the road.

"What's in the cooler?" she asked.

He failed to see the relevance of the cooler's contents to their current situation. "Food."

"Any cans?"

"Coke."

"That'll work." She twisted around and reached into the cooler in the back seat.

"What good is that going to do?"

The truck hammered them a third time. The car swerved wildly. Brooke held on to a can with her left hand. She tried to hold onto the dash with her casted hand. Her grip slipped. Her forehead smacked against the dashboard.

"Brooke?" Blood trickled from her cut. He swore. With the truck ready for a final swipe, he couldn't take his hands off the steering wheel to help her.

"I'm okay." She sat up, seemed wobbly. As the truck came parallel to the car she said, "Heads up!"

He leaned back into the seat. She launched the soda can. It hit the glass of the passenger's side window of the truck and exploded on impact. Sticky brown syrup rained on him.

Startled by the unexpected missile, the driver of the truck overcorrected. Too light in the rear, it fishtailed onto Mountain Road, its rear fender grazing a tree trunk. Jack kept going on Reservoir.

Sirens blared in the background.

Brooke twisted in her seat and looked back. "He's backing up! He's coming after us again!"

"Backup is right behind us. You'll be safe." Jack hesitated, then pressed on the accelerator.

As much as he wanted to stay and give this jerk a piece of his mind—and more—with Brooke hurt and not knowing if the truck's driver was armed or not, he had to keep going. Brooke's welfare was his number one responsibility. Had to be. Backup was closing in and would handle the driver. He had to trust them to do their job.

And if he was lucky, the ensuing arrest would solve his case. The driver of that truck had waited for him, known the miraculously resurrected Alyssa was out of the hospital, known he would lead the would-be killer to her. This open attack left him no doubt. Someone wanted Alyssa dead. Someone wanted to finish the job.

"That wasn't just a bad case of road rage, was it?" Brooke's voice was taut, brittle. She wiped the blood from her forehead with a tissue from her purse. He cursed himself for allowing her to put herself in the way of danger.

"No."

"It didn't take very long to get a rise out of somebody."

His jaw tightened. "Someone must have gone to visit Alyssa at the hospital and found her gone."

"Then that's where we need to start. Find out who went to visit her today."

He couldn't believe she still wanted to continue the charade. "It can wait. Right now we need to get you somewhere safe and see to your head. How are you feeling? Any dizziness?"

"No, I'm fine. You let him get away." Her voice was spiked with accusation.

"My number one concern is your safety."

She nodded and looked away. "Thanks."

"I think you should go home." The sudden roll in his stomach was a delayed reaction to the adrenaline rush of the chase. Nothing else.

"I'm staying."

This chase should have scared the living daylights out of her, yet it seemed to have cemented her determination. Reluctant admiration made him back off—for now.

"I'll get him." He tightened his grip on the steering wheel. He had two reasons now to want this suspect behind bars.

"I know."

Confidence rang strong in those two simple words. The feelings that trust aroused were disturbing and unacceptable. He shoved them away. Right now he needed to take Brooke some place safe while he reevaluated his plan.

Not his grandfather's cabin, though. That would be what was expected. He couldn't take the chance of being predictable even though he suspected the suspect was being apprehended at that very moment. He'd take her to his captain's hunting lodge. He'd been on many fishing vacations there with Bert. He knew the combination and his captain wouldn't mind.

Then he'd let her close call with danger sink in, and in no time at all, she'd be ready to go home. Safer for her. Better for him.

"Good thinking with that can," he said to Brooke, not liking the leaden quality of her silence. She could think on her feet, and went beyond the obvious to the creative. Unexpected. Admirable.

"Thanks. Your driving wasn't half-bad, either. We make a good team." Brooke beamed him a megawatt smile that unleashed a string of fantasies better left unexplored.

No, not a team. I work alone, always have, always will. But for some strange reason, the independence that usually brought him comfort left him…strangely disturbed.

Chapter Five

Brooke waited in the car while Jack punched in the code to his captain's hunting cabin and entered. The building was dark. The thick woods around it were darker. The sky, cloaked with clouds and night, was darker still. She'd never been good with darkness. Even now as an adult, a light still burned in the kitchen when she went to bed—a tiny ray of reassurance should she wake in the middle of the night. Unlike Alyssa, who even as a child had found a certain comfort under the quilt of blackness.

A light turned on inside, spilling welcome illumination onto the porch from the open door and the two small windows on each side. Jack strode out of the cabin and opened her car door. Unlike the jarring crunch made by his door, hers swung smoothly.

''Everything's clear.''

Still reeling inside from their encounter with the truck, she didn't know how to respond, so she simply nodded and followed him. She'd known she was heading into danger when she decided to take Alyssa's place, but accepting that fact and living it were two different things.

Until that truck had rammed into them, she'd presumed the challenge to be one of finding justice rather than an actual physical threat. Though she wouldn't admit it to Jack, she was glad he'd taken her out of danger's way for the night. By morning, she'd have a chance to rebuild her flagging courage.

There wasn't much to the cabin, she noticed upon entering. Two sets of bunk beds were shoved against the back wall, one tiny window between them. A farmer's table was flanked by two benches. To the left, an overstuffed chair and a sofa—both had seen better days—lounged by the rock fireplace. To the right, a stainless steel sink, cupboards, a white enameled pantry, a small refrigerator and a stove made up the kitchen area.

"Make yourself at home." He flicked on a flashlight. "I'm going to go check outside, then call the station."

"You think we were followed?" A shaft of panic went through her.

"No, but it doesn't hurt to make sure the driver of the truck's been arrested." He pointed to a portable phone on the scrap of counter beside the sink. "I thought you might want to call your mother."

"Thanks."

Had it been only this morning that they'd seen Alyssa off on the airplane? It seemed much longer. Keeping the front door in her sight, she took the cordless phone, and headed toward the living area, then sank into the overstuffed chair.

A talk with her mother didn't help soothe her uneasiness. Delia Snowden's voice bubbled with uncharacteristic happiness and filled Brooke with a touch of resentment. The reaction was natural, she told herself, not a reflection of her mother's feelings, or lack thereof, for her. After all, Delia hadn't seen Alyssa in nearly twenty-four years.

Still, it was hard to squelch the little voice telling her she wasn't good enough, that if she'd been a better daughter, her mother wouldn't have been so sad, wouldn't be so glad to see her other daughter. She'd disciplined her thinking on the subject of her mother's cold distance a long time ago, but now, in a skin not quite her own, she was feeling just a touch vulnerable.

And her mother's explanation of the events of long ago only served to heighten her sense of hurt tonight.

Delia hadn't been able to forgive her husband for following his dream against her wishes, she'd told Brooke. Nor had she been able to forgive him for transplanting their family to a run-down cottage in the middle of nowhere. She'd sought to wipe him from her memory by moving across the country. She couldn't handle both girls on her own, but couldn't bear to leave them both behind, either. Though it broke her heart, she'd made the difficult choice to keep one daughter, while leaving the other behind. Then she'd told an unforgivable lie.

Brooke shivered.

"Are you cold?"

Jack's voice caught her unaware. He dropped an armload of firewood next to the fireplace. The logs clunked against the floor. Her shoulders slumped in relief. He was back. She was safe.

"A bit. Who'd have thought it could get so cool in June?"

"In the mountains, the nights are always cool. Here." He handed her a navy sweatshirt from his duffel bag. His outdoor scent clung to the material and she hunched her shoulders in order to bring the delightful aroma closer to her nose.

"How's your head?" he asked as he crouched closer by the stone hearth.

She reached up to the small cut. "It's fine."

She watched as he started a fire. His movements were sure and productive. Soon a blaze radiated from the hearth. She was glad for the warmth and light it provided. He'd think her childish if she'd had to ask for a night-light. This way she wouldn't have to.

"He got away," Jack said, his attention concentrated on stoking the fire.

"Those cops you assured me would get him didn't?"

Jack's shoulders rose and stiffened. "He disappeared in the maze of back roads off Mountain. All they found was a handful of glass from a broken taillight. They're running a computer check on the make and model, and tomorrow, they'll start calling on body and repair shops. We'll get him."

He didn't sound so sure anymore.

"Who's familiar with those back roads?" Brooke asked, seeking to narrow down the list of suspects instead of letting her imagination paint a picture of a predator truck on the prowl, searching for them through the dark woods.

"We all are." Jack threw another log onto the fire. Flames leaped to devour the dry wood, flickering golden light and stark shadows on his face.

"Any chance he knows about this place?" Not that it would make a difference. Brooke doubted she could sleep tonight even if Alyssa's stalker was securely behind bars.

Jack shook his head. "Friends and work are separate."

In the set of his face, Brooke saw that he would keep everything neat and tidy. No messy emotions need apply. How far did his desire for order go? *None of your business, Brooke.*

"What if he isn't one of her friends as you suspect? What if...what if it's one of your fellow officers?" She knew her question was far-fetched, but was too scared and tired to care. She drew up her knees and hugged them close. The hard cast on her arm offered no comfort.

"None of them are climbers."

But from the steeling of his spine, Brooke sensed he *had* taken that possibility into consideration. For him, *everyone* had become a suspect.

She was cold again, but it had nothing to do with the

room's temperature. The thought of murder could chill anyone's marrow. She wanted to sit right by the flames, to feel their heat against her icy skin. But that would mean getting close to Jack and right now she was feeling a little too vulnerable for that. After their close call with the truck, after the call to her mother, she wanted, needed, human comfort. But Jack's arms were the wrong place to find it. She still had enough sense to realize that much.

"There are clean sheets in the drawers under the lower bunk," he said, adjusting the burning logs with a poker. "I'll let you use the facilities first."

It was as good an escape cue as any. A warm bed wasn't the same as warm arms, but it would have to do. She'd gotten herself into this situation. Remaining in control was up to her. She made quick work of sheeting the bed and her nighttime routine.

In the small bathroom, the scrapes on her face, reflected on the blackening mirror, wavered like a carnival illusion. The purpling bruise on her forehead couldn't be mistaken for makeup. She wasn't herself anymore. She wasn't Brooke. She wasn't Alyssa.

"Who are you?" she asked the face in the mirror and was taken aback by the haunted quality of her own voice.

"Brooke? Are you all right?"

She gathered her clothes and toiletry bag and opened the door. "I'm fine."

His body blocked her escape. She was struck again by the masculine force of his bearing, by the forbidding starkness of his expression, by her unruly response to a man to whom she ordinarily wouldn't even give a second glance.

"Brooke," he said and frowned. His mouth opened as if he wanted to say something more, but no words came out.

The tip of his fingers brushed along her cheek, skimming along her scrapes. She shivered, a dull, needy ache rippling all through her body. The look in his eyes darkened. The frown on his forehead deepened. His head bent forward, hesitated.

Her heart gave a sudden leap. Her breath was hot and fast in her throat. *Not real. Not real,* her head said. But her body didn't care. Anticipation roller-coastered through her.

His head bent once more. Then a touch of lips. Nothing more. Skin on skin. It shouldn't have been earth-shattering. Yet it was. The earth moved under her feet, her universe shifted, tilted crazily. Her clothes, her bag fell from her hands. Distantly she heard them bang against the floor. She reached for his chest to balance herself. It was leftover adrenaline from the truck chase, she tried to rationalize. Anyone would be affected. She just needed a bit of warmth. That was all. She rose on her toes to taste more of him.

And heat smoldered. Her hands slid upward to his neck. She loved the texture of him, soft and hard. The raspy feel of his beard on her cheek. The surprising silk of his hair beneath her fingers. The sweet and salty fire of his tongue on hers.

His hands grasped her waist as if he wanted to push her away. Then, as if he sensed how much she needed to be held, his arms reached around her, cradling her nape and the small of her back strongly, securely. She sighed her pleasure and melted against him, finding a strange satisfaction in every hard muscle of his lean body.

With a husky groan, he deepened the kiss.

She wobbled against him, felt him tighten his hold. Mixed with the outdoor wild scent of him, the sensation was heady. She burned with heat. The power of the feeling shook her to her very foundation. More, she wanted more.

"Hold me closer," she begged softly, desperate now for the blazing heat of reassurance he offered. The breathiness of her voice sounded alien to her ears and seemed to shatter the torrid current between them.

When he lifted his head to end the kiss, she involuntarily gave a whimper of protest and followed the upward movement to lengthen the dizzying sensation.

Then his glorious heat was replaced with space, too much space. "Jack?"

"I'm sorry," he said, pushing her away. His breaths were short and heated against her lips. "This won't happen again."

"No," she said as she bent down to pick up her clothes, her toiletry bag, and tried to make sense of what had happened. She clutched her belongings to her chest and fumbled for a way around him to the cold safety of the bunk bed.

"Brooke." His voice rumbled through her like aftershocks. He touched her chin with a finger. The gray of his eyes was nothing but a small ring of smoke around the large, black pupil. She swallowed hard, wanting, needing, but not trusting herself to talk. "I will keep you safe."

She nodded mutely.

He touched her cheek once more before he moved aside. "I think you should go to bed now."

She walked stiffly to the farthest bunk, putting space between them. But even as she hurried, she couldn't outrun her thoughts, or help wondering where her greatest danger lay—in Alyssa's faceless would-be murderer, or in Jack Chessman's arms.

KISSING BROOKE LAST NIGHT had been like being caught outside in the middle of a summer storm. Invisible energy had electrified his nerve endings. Not even a night's sleep could erase the vestiges of his lingering craving for this woman.

She'd melted against him, responded to him freely, passionately. And he'd let himself get caught in the storm of sensation she'd drawn from him. He'd wanted her, God, he'd wanted her so fiercely that just thinking about her body soft and pliant against his was making him hard all over again.

All he'd meant to do was reassure her.

"Time to get up," Jack said tersely as he cracked another egg into a bowl. Already this wasn't shaping up to be a great day. He'd awakened with a headache and a needier ache that was better ignored. He'd made no headway when he called the hospital. No one seemed to remember anyone calling on Alyssa. "We've got a lot of ground to cover today."

"Ground?"

Her voice sounded sleepy, but he didn't turn around to look at her. Her eyes sparkling with intelligence, her expressive face vivid with life were etched on his brain, troubling him, fascinating him. He'd vowed long ago that he'd never get involved with the type of woman who wore her heart on her sleeve. He wasn't about to change his mind this late into the game. "Transforming you into Alyssa."

"Oh."

Using a fork, he scrambled the eggs and poured them into a hot pan. His relationship with Alyssa had never been this complicated. Difficult, uneven, yes, but not complicated. She got into trouble; he got her out of it. Alyssa had needed his ability to ground her, but she'd made no emotional demands on him.

With a spatula, he slapped the cooked eggs onto two plates, not understanding where the anger growling inside him was coming from. Since he couldn't seem to chase it away, he decided to simply ignore it. Working with brisk efficiency, he put the eggs and toast on the table and hunted for jam.

Dressed in her usual uniform of silk T-shirt and skirt—

both in shades of green that annoyingly managed to make her eyes seem bigger and brighter—Brooke joined him at the table. The clothes were too soft, too sensual for Alyssa; they would have to go. How was he going to imbue Brooke with her sister's hard edge?

"What next?" Brooke cut off a section of toast. She delayed swallowing it by repeatedly spreading a dab of strawberry jam.

Pouring coffee into mugs, Jack forced himself to speak in a remote, neutral tone. "Next we shoot for the impossible."

"Which would translate to what in English?"

"You and Alyssa are worlds apart in behavior."

She watched him as emotionlessly as he watched her. Trying like him to pretend last night's kiss had never happened? Was it as difficult for her as it was for him?

"Well that's not surprising since we were raised three thousand miles apart."

"This is no joking matter. For this to work, the suspects have to believe you are Alyssa. Amnesia will only cover so much."

"Who's joking?"

"The doctor said she would probably remember her skills and habits, if not the recent events of her life." He shoved a mug of coffee toward her. "She takes hers black."

Brooke made a face. "I don't drink coffee."

"You do now. One cup in the morning before you attack the changeover paperwork."

"Changeover?"

"Getting the bills ready for the guests that are leaving. Making sure everything is ready for the guests who are arriving."

She looked at the black liquid as if he were asking her

to drink straight mud. "Couldn't I have tea instead? Who's going to notice what I drink in my own house?"

"You're going to drink coffee because Alyssa drinks coffee. She drinks it at the office because she has to."

"What do you mean has to? No one *has* to drink coffee."

The subject had to come up. There was no way around it. Yet he found himself reluctant to expose Alyssa's carefully guarded flaw. Even to her twin. He toyed with his eggs, scooped a forkful and chewed on them as he tried to order his thoughts. "Your sister is…unconventional."

"Unconventional?"

There was that damned curiosity lighting her eyes again. That would have to go, too. "She's never colored within the lines."

Brooke carefully put her knife down, rested her elbows on the table and her chin on top of her folded hands. "You don't strike me as the kind of guy who beats around the bush. Spit it out."

He put down his fork, wrapped his hand around the mug of coffee. "Alyssa has a creative personality."

"I'm not sure I understand."

"Think absentminded professor." Over the years Jack had had to learn more than he wanted about the workings of a creative mind in order to help Alyssa function in a world that seemed to do its best to beat her down.

"How does drinking a cup of coffee fit in?" Brooke asked.

He drank deeply from his mug. "It helps her focus without taking away the only thing she likes about herself."

"Her eye?"

"Yes." He was surprised at Brooke's insight. "Alyssa sees the world in a whole different way and it comes through in her photographs. She can sit for hours waiting for just the right lighting, for just the right move of a butterfly wing, for just the right perspective. Caffeine helps to keep her on task.'' Uncomfortable trapped in the curious beam of Brooke's gaze, he changed the topic of conversation. ''You're sitting all wrong.''

She looked down at her feet on the ground. Her spine was tall and straight even without the benefit of a chair back. ''What's wrong with the way I'm sitting?''

''You look like you just graduated from a Swiss finishing school.'' There was that anger again, churning inside him like a bad case of food poisoning. What was it about Brooke that made him want to kiss her silly one minute and send her packing the next?

''So?''

''So Alyssa sprawls. Kick off your shoes—she has a hard time keeping shoes on her feet.''

Reluctantly, Brooke did as he asked. The white canvas shoes she wore had not one speck of dirt on them. Alyssa's shoes looked ready for the Dumpster after a week of wear.

''Now scrunch down.''

She contorted and twisted and shrank, looking at him with those green eyes, trying so hard to please. And what did he do? He barked at her.

''No, more like a stoop. No, no.''

Exasperation built with the disturbing sensuality of her every move. If he didn't know better, he'd think he was going through his teenage years all over again. Though come to think of it, they hadn't been much fun the first time around. He'd had too many responsibilities even then. And he had too much now to give in to adolescent cravings.

She pitched a napkin at him. ''Well, jeez, Jack. Demonstrate then.''

His jaw twitched, then he nodded. He let his body sag, his shoulders droop, as if his spine was soft instead of rigid. Mistake. Another part of his anatomy took his relaxation as a go ahead to react. He was thankful for the table's cover.

"That looks awfully uncomfortable." She tried the twisted pose.

"Stop complaining." His voice was gruff as he straightened, but he didn't care. She didn't have to like him. In fact, it was better if she didn't. "This was your idea, remember? And stop looking at me like that."

"Like what?"

"I don't know. Wide-eyed." *Too damned desirable.* Had Alyssa's eyes been that green? Had they pinwheeled with each of her thoughts? Had they revealed her soul for the world to see? No, she'd always been lost in her own little world, a world he'd never understood.

"I can't help the way my eyes look."

"You're going to have to," he grumbled. "Narrow your gaze. No, don't frown. Try suspicious."

"Suspicious?"

"No, that's not right, either. How about wary?"

She gave it a shot, exaggerating the look.

"You're not taking this seriously."

"I'm doing my best." She tried again.

She still didn't look like Alyssa. And Jack was starting to understand that, to him, she never would. He could never mistake the frank heat in her eyes for Alyssa's distracted gaze. He could never confuse the soft, sensual moves of her limbs for Alyssa's purposeful motions. And he could never pretend brotherly concern, not when his body was so ready to betray him.

"It'll do for now." His gaze dropped to her plate. "You're eating too slow."

"Kind of tough to eat when I'm under the microscope." She picked up her fork and dutifully put her attention to the task of consuming the eggs he'd prepared.

He sensed her withdrawal under his criticism, yet he

couldn't seem to stop. He needed to toughen her up, he rationalized, ignoring the little voice calling him a liar. "Use your right hand. Alyssa's right-handed."

She lifted the casted arm. "Cast."

"She'd use it anyway. Because of her distractibility, she's become a creature of habit. She's very spontaneous when it comes to her photography, but not about her daily habits. Change is tough for her."

That more than anything was now niggling at his conscience, he realized. Looking back, he saw all the signs of Alyssa's escalating fear: her father's growing displeasure at her work; her preoccupation; her unusual silence and disappearances. Why hadn't he seen them sooner? Why hadn't he pushed for an answer instead of accepting her assurances that nothing was wrong? Because change was tough for him, too, and Alyssa had been changing for a while.

"Tell me more about Alyssa," Brooke said, pushing her empty plate away from her.

He suddenly didn't want to talk about Alyssa anymore. Didn't want to spotlight his failure. Didn't want to dissect how this whole situation could have been avoided if only he'd taken charge of it sooner. "She's impatient, reactive, restless—which reminds me. If you're sitting there doing nothing, you need to be jiggling your left foot."

"Jiggling?"

"Lift your heel off the floor and let it drop." *Tap, tap, tap* drummed his foot in a quick tattoo. She joined the concert. The disjointed noise got on his nerves—always had. "That's it."

"What else?"

"She's also fun-loving, tireless, independent, artistic. She's got a quirky sense of humor." He shrugged. "There's only one Alyssa...."

Brooke looked away, but not before he saw the touch

of hurt in her eyes. "And somehow I've got to become her."

"Yes."

"Go on with your lesson then."

Dangerous emotions reemerged deep inside him at Brooke's perseverance at what seemed like a losing proposition. Those emotions made him feel alive in a way that was disturbing. But he'd learned his lesson long ago. He wouldn't repeat his parents' mistakes. He would not let base feelings dictate his actions. He was doing this for friendship, for justice, and for no other reason. Certainly not to bask in the sunshine of Brooke Snowden's smile.

THREE DAYS LATER, as Brooke was bracing herself for another day of impossible lessons, Jack announced they would leave for Comfort after breakfast.

"Before we get there," he said once they were packed and in the car, "there are a few things we need to talk about." His voice took on the bite of authority, instantly sparking resistance in Brooke.

In the last few days, Jack had done his best to make her believe she was falling short of impersonating Alyssa, and she hated being judged lacking by someone who knew nothing about her, by someone whose emotional temperature seemed barely to rise above that of granite in winter—when he wasn't burning her into a pile of ashes with a blistering kiss, that is. Her cheeks warmed at the memory of that kiss, of her easy response, of his hard and ready body. She shook her head, returning her thoughts to the present.

He slowed the car to turn onto a dirt road. The ruts bounced her in her seat. Brooke hung on to the car door with one hand and the seat's edge with the other.

"You're to go nowhere without me."

Rocks pinged against the undercarriage. "Don't you have to go back to work?"

"I've taken two weeks of vacation."

And burned several days of it already—because of her. Tree branches scratched at the side window. "What if we don't find who we're looking for by then?"

He downshifted. The engine raced. "You go back home."

"No."

He speared her with his flintlike gaze. "That's the way it's going to be, Brooke. No ifs, ands or buts. When I can't watch over you 24-7 anymore, you go home."

"Don't I get a vote?"

He slowed for a curve. "No, I've already let you have too much slack as it is."

"She's my sister. I have a right to find out what happened to her."

"Not if it interferes with my job."

"Jack—"

The car shot into sunlight. "We do it my way, or you go back home now."

"But—"

He halted the car and jerked the parking brake on. "I need to be able to trust you."

And she gleaned from the sad set of his eyes that trust didn't come easy. He was used to being in the driver's seat and now he was going to have to share that control. They were after the same goal. Like it or not, they were partners in this charade. She'd agree—for now. "Okay."

With a sharp nod, he looked away.

"Here we are." Both hands gripping the steering wheel, he stared out at the white cottage in front of them. The house faced the water and stood on a hillock. Trimmed rose bushes shrouded the sloping foundation. "Home."

Brooke's gaze slowly panned her surroundings. Nothing

was as she'd remembered. Bathers and boaters frolicked in the sun-freckled water. Their gleeful chatter floated across the coarse sand on pats of wind. Bright beach towels flapped in the breeze against whitewashed cottages. The scent of water was sharp and clean with overtones of pine and earth and hot dogs on coals. The whole presented a picture of a vacation paradise.

But the dark and gloomy woods surrounding the resort hadn't changed. They made her think of a setting for a gothic novel. All that was missing was a lantern glowing eerily in the dark, and the moan of ghosts on a damp gust. A chill made her shiver. She shifted her attention back to Alyssa's cottage.

Home.

For better or for worse, this was her home for the next week and a half. Once she was out of the car, she found herself lingering. She shouldn't have been so rash. She should turn around and go home. She wasn't Alyssa, could never be Alyssa. Jack had made sure she understood that fact loud and clear. Could she really deceive the friends who knew Alyssa so well?

She shook the thought away. She would have to.

A wreath of white roses and dried herbs hung on the red door of Alyssa's home, bidding a cheerful welcome. The sentiment was echoed in the painted piece of slate hung on a nail just above an old-fashioned triangle, in the pots of purple and white pansies spilling onto the three stairs in an ever narrowing path.

If she stepped through that door, Brooke sensed she wouldn't be able to turn back. It would be like opening Pandora's box and allowing disaster to escape.

Then she remembered what had remained trapped in the box—hope.

Hope had saved the world, allowed it to survive. The promise of hope surged through her now.

WITH A HARD TWIST OF HIS HAND, Jack switched off the
engine, and stepped out of the car. He looked at Brooke
as she stood before Alyssa's home, the yellow of her silk
T-shirt a beam of sunshine against the dull white of the
cottage. Her shortened hair gave him an unhampered view
of her nape. In his imagination, he could see himself rubbing the tender spot, kissing it, could feel her shiver of
delight.

He brushed past her, catching a whiff of her summer
sweetness. His step slowed. He started to lean closer until
he remembered he needed to keep distance between them.

He wrenched the front door open, frowned at the fact
that it had opened freely, then held it wide. How often had
he reminded Alyssa to lock her door? "Watch out for the
second stair. There's a spot of rot."

Brooke's steps were slow, but not afraid as she followed
him inside. She stood in the middle of the living room,
absorbing it with all her senses.

And he saw the place again through her eyes.

Alyssa was alive in all the small details: the stone fireplace, its age-grayed wooden mantel and its collection of
well-used scented candles; the Flying Geese quilt tossed
haphazardly on the rocker, which faced the window, not
the room; the pieces of pottery chosen for their eye appeal
rather than their function; the photographs plastering the
wall, displaying her gift for unique observation.

And when he could stand the reminders of Alyssa's sadness no longer, he shattered the spell. "There's one other
thing."

"What?"

Brooke glanced at him over her shoulder. A strange light
filled her eyes and ignited a slow burn in his solar plexus.

"The ring."

He toyed with the velvet box in his palm, then reluctantly lifted the cover. The diamond winked at him as if it were in on the joke.

This pressurized piece of carbon was the only thing of value his father had ever given his mother. Not that it had gifted her with any happiness. Long before the time it took for a baby to grow inside a womb, his father had left Comfort for livelier pastures.

He'd never known his father. They had met only once when Jack had braved a visit to the Concord prison to tell his father that his mother had died. His father's concern had not been for his dead wife or his orphaned son, but for himself.

Jack reached for Brooke's hand. The skin beneath his fingertips was smooth, without the calluses Alyssa had earned climbing. He poised the ring over her finger, and missed the pink polish that had adorned Brooke's nails earlier, missed its cheer. It was a little thing, a detail. And everything had to be right. A swipe of acetone had taken care of the oddity, but not the remembered effect of tender warmth, of vulnerability.

As he slipped the ring onto her finger, a thread of something close to terror vibrated through him. The simple act of pushing the gold band over Brooke's knuckle felt much too legitimate.

This isn't for real.

Neither had his parents' marriage been genuine, he reminded himself. Just one big production with more bang than lasting power. This was going to end the same way, too.

No, not the same way.

He wasn't going to lie to Brooke to get what he wanted, then leave her, as his father had done his mother. He wasn't going to promise to love her forever, then break her heart. He was going to stay. He was going to see this through all the way.

As he slipped the ring in its place, he renewed his promise.

I will *keep you safe.*

"Get changed," he said as he dropped Brooke's hand and turned abruptly toward the kitchen before he did something he'd regret—like kiss her again. "Then we'll get this show on the road."

She swallowed hard. "How?"

"We're going to go say hello to your father."

Chapter Six

That was a close call. There had barely been enough time to slip out of the cottage before getting caught. Good thing Jack's car had such a distinctive signature roar. Had Jack recognized the truck? Probably not. No cops had come sniffing around the house asking questions. The truck was hidden once again, back in its dusty home. Out of sight, out of mind.

Even knowing Alyssa was alive didn't take away the shock from actually seeing her in living color. She'd always been too pretty for her own good. The scars didn't take anything away from her, and that broken arm probably wouldn't slow her down. She'd be back to her old thoughtless tricks in no time.

Yet…there was something different about her, something uncertain. Had her close call with death kindled a little fear inside her? And Jack, what was wrong with him? He looked positively green with worry. He was clinging to her as if she were some helpless creature.

Was Alyssa not as well as Jack had professed she was? Just where had they been for the past few days? Not at Jack's fishing cabin. Not at Alyssa's secret camping spot.

No matter. Time for a new strategy. Time to let Alyssa know the past wasn't forgotten. It was only right she should feel some of the pain she was inflicting on others before she died.

"Welcome home, princess."

"ALYSSA! ALYSSA!"

As Brooke exited the cottage, a streak of girl and beagle speeded toward her. Anticipating the collision, Brooke lifted her casted forearm out of the way and used her free arm to cushion the small body's blow against hers.

Two sets of big brown eyes sparkled up at her. The girl, who looked to be about six, hugged Brooke's thigh, and the puppy danced up on its back legs and batted at Brooke's bare calves with its front paws.

"You're back," the girl said, beaming. "I missed you."

"I missed you, too," Brooke said and patted the little girl's shoulders.

Her mind reeled, trying to place what couldn't be placed. Who was this girl so full of eagerness for Alyssa? Jack hadn't mentioned her, and Brooke still hadn't recovered from entering Alyssa's world and trying to fit in as if it were her own. That would take time and Jack hadn't given her any. Her sister's khaki shorts and tight red cotton top clung to her with the stiffness of a new Halloween costume. The borrowed boat shoes on her feet, though they fit, made her feel like a little girl playing dress-up. The fake cast surely branded her an impostor—at least to herself.

The little girl frowned and pouted. "You don't remember me."

How can I? I've never seen you. But that wasn't going to cut it. She glanced toward the cottage door, but Jack was still inside, looking for Alyssa's master key to lock up. Brooke had to make this charade work. She crouched down to the girl's eye level. With one hand she brushed the wild tangle of brown hair stuck with sweat to the girl's cheek. With the other she tried to avoid a tongue bath from the beagle. She turned her head so the scar on her temple was visible. "I hit my head really hard on a rock and some things got knocked out of me—like names."

"Oh. I'm Lauren." Lauren wiggled her fingers in front of her. "Finger painting. Remember?"

"I'm sorry, I don't."

With a serious look scrunching her forehead, Lauren reached a chubby finger toward Brooke's scar. "Does it hurt?"

"Just a little." Brooke flinched inwardly. She hadn't expected the lies to be so burning and scalpel sharp.

"We had fun." Lauren leaned forward, half-sitting on Brooke's lap and whispered, "Holly doesn't do crafts as good as you."

"Tell you what," Brooke whispered back, glad to find she had the love of children in common with her twin. "Tomorrow, you come by and we'll plan a really fun craft to do. You choose and we'll put it on the weekly schedule."

Lauren smiled, pleased. "Just you and me?"

"Just you and me."

"I choose?"

"You choose."

Lauren disentangled herself from Brooke's lap. "I'll come after your kayak ride."

Kayak ride? This was not good. She and water had never gotten along. Another little detail Jack had forgotten to mention. Brooke looked up to find Jack smiling at her. He was enjoying her discomfort much too much. He was testing her, but for what, she wasn't quite sure. Something told her it was more than for the role she had to play. She swallowed hard. "After my kayak ride."

"Can I be the muffin girl tomorrow? Jessica did it two days in a row."

Again Brooke, feeling a bit like Alice lost in Wonderland, glanced at Jack for direction. He nodded and said, "Sure."

Lauren yipped with delight. The puppy barked and danced around them until they were all knotted.

"Why don't you go tell Miss Franny so she knows," Jack said, unraveling the squirming puppy from leash and legs.

"Oh, right. Before Jessica." Lauren scuttled away, tugging on the beagle's neon-yellow leash. "Come on, Daisy. See ya tomorrow," the little girl tossed over her shoulder with a wave.

Brooke waved back. "One of the renters?"

"Regulars," Jack confirmed. He led her down the path to the road. Their feet crunched on the coarse pebbles. The breeze stirred the heat around them, making Brooke uncomfortably aware of the foreign T-shirt clinging to her skin, of Jack's nearness.

"Lauren's family rents a cabin for the summer," Jack continued. "She's got an older brother, Robby—a regular terror. The father commutes from Nashua every weekend."

Brooke reached for a nonexistent length of hair to twirl, covered the reflex habit with a sharp movement of hand through her shortened hairdo. "Oh. So Alyssa would know her."

"Yes, but you handled it well."

"Awkwardly."

He stopped in the middle of the road and grabbed her forearms, forcing her to a standstill, too. "You can't expect to jump into this situation and not make mistakes. It took Alyssa a lifetime to build these memories. I've given you some coaching, but you've been here only an hour. Alyssa's trauma lets you get away with not being perfect."

She looked down, away from his piercing gaze. But it

was too late. In the gray mirror of his irises she'd seen a reflection of her imperfection. The weight of it descended on her shoulders and bowed them. "But you want me to be perfect. Wasn't that the point of the past few days?"

With his index finger he lifted her chin. A tiny electrical charge skittered down her spine. "You don't have to be perfect all the time."

She nodded. Perfection. There was the rub—at least according to her friend, Crystal, who was a counselor at the school where Brooke taught. Perfection was an itch she couldn't help scratching. Her mother kept telling her not to take life so seriously, but how could she believe that when Delia's sadness was an example of how imperfect life could be? Brooke heaved her shoulders, stifled a sigh and moved on.

"Brooke—" He swore and raked a hand through his hair. "I can't call you Brooke, but I can't call you Alyssa, either."

"Why not?"

"Because."

"That's not an answer. Don't I look enough like her?"

"That's not the problem."

Did he communicate any better with Alyssa? Their conversations were like trying to start a fire with two water-soaked stones. "Then what?"

His jaw tightened. "You don't feel like her."

"Oh." How could she not have thought of that before? Every time Jack looked at her, it was a cruel reminder that the woman he loved was lost to him to coma. This charade couldn't be easy for him, either. Not when he probably longed to be with Alyssa and felt he had to stay here to protect her.

"There's always, 'hey you.'" Brooke slanted him a small smile. He answered with one of his own. Something in her stomach fluttered.

"That's not going to work, either."

"We'll think of something."

"Yeah." Hands stuck in his cargo pants, he resumed walking.

"What's this muffin girl business?" She'd seen a copy of a weekly schedule hanging on Alyssa's fridge, but nothing about muffins.

"Franny bakes muffins for the kids to take around and sell in the morning. It's kind of a tradition. The kids learn about it fast and there's always a rush to see who gets to carry the basket."

She shook her head. "There's so much to know."

"Don't worry about it. You did fine."

For now. Would fooling her father and Alyssa's friends be so easy? "Alyssa kayaks?"

"Every morning at least once around the lake."

Brooke gulped. "I don't do water."

"You live by the ocean." Disbelief tinged his voice.

"I don't go *in* the water. I just look at it. At least with this cast, I'll have an excuse to skip that ritual of hers."

He chuckled. "You don't know Alyssa."

A sigh reverberated through her. "I wish you wouldn't keep saying that. It's not helping my confidence level any."

"You're the one who wanted to play this game," he reminded her.

And put you on the spot, she finished silently. They'd already had one brush with the evil stalking her sister. Now the faster the game got in motion, the faster they would catch Alyssa's would-be murderer, the faster they could both return to their respective lives.

"I'm sorry," Brooke said.

"For what?"

"For not being her. For making things so difficult for you."

Jack slanted her an odd look, then stopped. "We're here. Ready?"

"As I'll ever be."

BROOKE AND JACK STOOD BEFORE a large building painted brown. Behind them the sounds of summer fun echoed in the air. A car slowly crunched along the gravel road, giggling children hanging out the back windows. The scent of bug spray and lunchtime burgers wafted. Life was continuing in its usual way.

Even though ivy climbed over one wall and a basket of artificial flowers hung on the door, the lodge made Brooke think more of a camp dormitory than a home. With the toe of her shoe, she drew an arc on the soft earth before the ramp leading up to the door. "What's he like?"

"Dour."

A row of carpenter ants marched along the edge of the sparse grass. She followed their trail until they disappeared beneath the ramp. "Did they get along, Dad and Alyssa?"

"As well as they could, considering."

She glanced up at Jack, could read nothing in the stern set of his face. "Considering what?"

"You'll see."

"Shouldn't you tell me?"

"It's not something you can explain."

The door at the opposite end of the building banged open and Lauren, puppy in her arms, shouted to a nearby friend, "Jessica! Jessica! I'm the muffin girl! I'm the muffin girl!"

An older woman came out to rescue the door and spotted them. Her ample curves gave her a motherly roundness. Streaks of gray painted her short, no-nonsense auburn hair. Her open smile of delight crinkled all the way to her eyes and won Brooke over in a heartbeat. The woman tottered over, both hands covering her mouth.

"My Lord, Alyssa, why didn't you tell us you were coming home?"

"She wanted to surprise you and Walter, Franny," Jack answered for her, clueing Brooke to the woman's identity.

"And what a surprise it is! Come here, girl."

Franny enveloped her in her capable arms and hugged her tightly. "I knew you'd come out of it. I never believed those doctors. You're too ornery to let one little rock knock you out of circulation. It's so good to have you back."

"It's good to be back." Brooke stiffened in the woman's dizzying embrace, wanting to take in the warmth, yet needing to draw back because the feeling of being a charlatan was growing bigger by the minute.

Franny's hazel eyes searched her face, narrowed at the sight of the scar. "How are you feeling?"

"A little disoriented," Brooke answered truthfully. She stepped out of Franny's grasp.

"Her memory's a bit scrambled." Jack draped a hand around her back, and rubbed the tips of his fingers on the bare point of her shoulder, silently telegraphing his intention to establish himself in his role of fiancé. He might be acting, but the frisson of heat racing down her spine was far too real.

Franny frowned, then brushed her worry away with a sweep of one hand. "Oh, well, that's normal, what with you just getting out of a coma. It'll take a bit to get back to your old self."

More than you know. Knowing that Alyssa still lay in a coma, a shaft of guilt skewered Brooke. This woman was so nice, so concerned.

Franny turned to Jack who was silently taking in the scene. "She is fine, isn't she?"

"She's as good as can be expected." So much, so little lay buried in those words, in the gentle smile that didn't quite reach his eyes.

"Well, come on then, let's go say hello to that father of yours." Folding Brooke's hand within her large one, Franny led her up the ramp. The wood thundered beneath their feet.

"How is he doing?" Brooke asked, trying to delay the meeting.

"Worse than usual. He's missed having you around. He was worried you'd…" Franny shrugged.

"I'd what?"

"Not come back."

Inside, the room was dark, resentment palpable in the stale air. A ceiling fan paddled lazy circles, but didn't seem to stir the air. The only light came from the window by which someone was sitting, staring out to the water. Her father? Of course. Who else? Anxiety coursed through her. This crumpled man was not the father she remembered.

The being in the wheelchair was a husk of the man who'd lived in her memory. He seemed shrunken, sucked of all life. Loose folds of skin lay over brittle bones. His spine was bent as if burdened by a heavy load. His mustache was gone. His hair was thin, white. His hands lay knotted on his lap as if each needed the other for support.

Franny snapped on the light and strode over to the wheelchair. With gentle fingers against his cheek, she drew his attention to her.

"Walter, look who's here." With an overly bright smile Franny turned the wheelchair around and was rewarded with a surly grunt and a cutting glare. "Alyssa. Your daughter's home, Walter. Say hello."

Smiling, Brooke went to him and crouched by his chair. With one hand she reached for his. There was no strength in his fingers. They lay lifeless in her palm, then retreated in a shunning curl.

"Daddy? It's me. I'm back." She held her breath in

anticipation of his answering smile, of his laughter, of his big bear hug.

His gaze, cold with disinterest, cranked back to the window. She reached forward, tried to wrap her arms around his neck, to draw him into a hug, to inhale his smoky wood scent. "Daddy?"

But he shrugged away her hold.

Brooke stumbled back, holding empty space. Her smile melted. *Daddy, aren't you glad to see me?* Her insides squeezed, convulsed. She tried to hold back tears, and the bitter taste of abandonment.

"What...time...is it?" Walter asked, his words slow, slurred, and painful.

Trying to shove his rejection in the closet of painful things deep inside her, Brooke glanced at her—Alyssa's—watch. "N-nearly one."

Did he not care for Alyssa? Did he not love his daughter? Didn't he want to know how she was doing after her accident?

Don't think. Don't ask. Shut it off. Close it out. It's better that way. The less you see of him, the less chance there is he'll see the differences.

Walter turned his flat blue gaze to her. "Then what...are you...doing here...wasting time? Don't you have... business to...tend to?"

Franny gasped. "Walter, that's no way to speak to your daughter. She's had an accident. Don't you remember? She's been in the hospital, for heaven's sake. She needs to rest, not to be bullied by you."

"She's a...quitter. Just like...her mother." Walter shoved Franny's hold away and wheeled his chair back to face the window.

Franny shook her head in a slow, sad arc. "I'm sorry, Alyssa. He's in one of his moods."

"That's okay."

But it wasn't okay. It was a nightmare. Never could she have imagined her father so stark and cold. What kind of life had Alyssa led? Had he been like this since her mother had left, or had the change come with the stroke?

"She was never a quitter, Walter," Jack spoke up. The controlled emotion ringing in his voice seemed to catch everyone off guard. "You're the one who gave up on her. I'm going to be taking care of her from now on."

Walter turned his upper body and speared Jack with a withering look. "What?"

"We're engaged. I'll be living at the cottage with her, helping her with her recovery."

"No living…together. Not while…I'm alive."

"You've got no say."

Walter punched an ineffective fist on his wheelchair's arm. His reddened jowls quivered with his anger. "This is a…family resort. I've got…principles to live up to."

"And look where all those principles have landed you!"

Brooke reached for Jack. Why was he coming on so strong? "Jack—"

"No, sunshine, he's got to understand that you're not your mother."

For a minute Brooke thought Jack meant it, thought he was fighting for her, then she remembered he was only trying to establish his position in Alyssa's house the only way he could—by force of personality. And what did her mother have to do with this?

"Get…off…my land. Now."

Jack bent to look Walter in the eye. "No, it's more than past time someone woke you up. I should have done it long ago. Alyssa will be resuming her duties on a very limited basis. I'll be taking care of her, in her house. Find a way to deal with it."

A shift of power was taking place. Two strong males were drawing a line in the sand. But her shrunken father was no match for Jack. Walter knew it and withdrew. What had happened to destroy so much of her father's spirit?

Franny tried to wedge her way between Jack and Walter.

"Give him time, Jack." The sadness in Franny's eyes made it obvious she was devoted to Walter. Just as obvious was her father's oblivion to Franny's feelings. Was he no longer able to care at all?

"He's already had too much time," Jack said, straightening.

"He's hurting...."

"So is Alyssa. Put yourself in her shoes for just a minute. She's been through hell and he doesn't have the decency to ask how she's doing. Things can't go back to normal."

Franny lowered her gaze and nodded. "I know. I—"

"It's not your fault. You do your best." Jack took Brooke's hand. "Come on."

The steely grip of his fingers on hers made her realize he was her only anchor in this unfamiliar world, her only champion. Her first instinct was to withdraw before pain struck again. She didn't like the idea of being dependent on anybody—on him—to navigate Alyssa's world. But she didn't want to create a scene and raise questions that couldn't be answered right now, so she closed her hand around his and accepted the silent support he offered.

Play the role.

"Let's go back home." His voice gentled, allowing the tears she'd held back to rise up and constrict her throat. Swallowing hard, she nodded and turned away from the heartbreaking mound that was her father.

"Don't you worry about a thing, Alyssa," Franny said, patting Brooke's shoulder. "Don't listen to your father. Everything's under control with the resort. You go home and rest. I'll take care of everything. And congratulations on your engagement."

"Thank you."

Tightening her grip on Jack's hand, Brooke glanced over her shoulder.

If she told her father she was Brooke, would it make a difference? Would he be as happy to see her as her mother had been to see Alyssa?

But she'd already agreed to keep their charade from Walter in order to keep things as normal as they could so they would have a better chance at catching whoever wanted Alyssa dead.

First things first.

Before she turned away, something caught her eye. Her father's shoulders were shaking. A run of tears shone in his reflection in the window.

"Daddy?"

"Give him time," Franny's soft voice cautioned. "He just needs time."

How much time had Franny already given Walter? How much time was Franny willing to give? How much was too much?

If love was involved, was a lifetime worth waiting? Maybe one day soon her father would look into Franny's eyes and what he saw in them would spark his soul back to life. Maybe then he'd be able to let go of his resentment still so strong for Delia.

Brooke nodded and followed Jack back into the deceptive sunshine showering the resort.

She would give her father time.

And when Alyssa's would-be murderer was caught, she would give him back what Delia had stolen from him.

I'M SORRY, SUNSHINE. As Jack led Brooke back to Alyssa's cottage, he let her hand go. Her palm felt just a little too good nestled against his. Stripped of purpose, his fist clamored for something to do. He stuffed it into his pocket, the feeling of Alyssa's master key a comfort. Earlier it had taken tense moments to find it.

Brooke shouldn't have had to endure this rejection from her father. No one should. As much as he wanted to protect her, there were certain things about Alyssa's life that couldn't be sugarcoated. Her father's coldness was one of them. Her friends' brutal honesty would be another.

Watching the brightness dim on Brooke's face under Walter's abuse had been hard. Alyssa was used to it, but he'd wager what memories Brooke had of her father were little girl soft.

Never had Jack wanted to strangle someone as he'd wanted to strangle Walter at that moment. His new understanding of Walter's complicity in allowing the girls to believe each other dead had shone a whole new light on Alyssa's situation. And seeing him shun Brooke because of his own internal pain had snapped something inside Jack. He'd returned Walter's verbal slap with one of his own. Worse, he'd liked it, wished he'd done it sooner, and freed Alyssa from this grip of indecent dependency.

"Two down. Four more to go," Jack said, still trying to understand the surge of protectiveness that had made him act out when he'd vowed to remain a simple observer.

Brooke's released hand fluttered like a leaf for a moment, then she shoved it into her short pocket, an unconscious imitation of his own stance. "What do you mean?"

"I've invited our suspects to dinner."

She frowned. "I don't think I'm ready yet."

"No sense putting off the inevitable."

The waiting, that was the hardest part. He wanted this charade over and done. It wasn't that he wasn't a patient man. Ordinarily he was. Dissecting took time. But he was used to setting the pace, to calling the shots. He worked alone; always had. He didn't like being dependent on someone else for results. It bent the odds. It took control away. It left too much up to chance. One miscommunicated intention. One small step taken out of turn. One unanticipated twist. That was all that was needed to rip apart this fragile lie.

Then what? He might never identify the guilty person. And his world would change because now the trust he'd extended to his friends would be permanently broken.

He'd made Alyssa a promise and he intended to keep it. He would find who had harmed her. And he would keep Brooke safe, too.

He glanced at Brooke once more. The painful frown creasing her forehead tugged at him. He'd seen her face crumple, felt her heart wrench, sensed her unshed tears rasp her throat when her father had twisted away from her hug. Just like Alyssa, her brittle spirit would need bolstering against the blows to come. He wasn't sure he could go through this heartache one more time. Not when she could reach through his barriers and touch him so easily.

But for a chance at justice, he had to play out the lie.

"You should know I don't cook." The teasing note in Brooke's voice caught him unaware. Twice in the space of an hour she'd used humor to skate through a patch of discomfort.

"That's okay, neither does Alyssa. The Comfort House of Pizza delivers."

Brooke smiled up at him, chuckled, and his breath hitched. "Apparently often."

As he climbed the cottage steps, Jack chortled. "She doesn't even have to give her name. As soon as they get an order for a pizza with jalapeños, they know where to deliver."

"Jalapeño pizza?" Brooke burst out laughing. The sound rippled warmly in his chest. "Don't tell me she has pineapple on the side to cool things down, too."

Too? "Cucumber spears. You like jalapeño pizza?"

He dug Alyssa's master key from his pocket.

Brooke lifted her foot to the edge of the second step. "Let's just say that's one thing that won't be a stretch."

She stepped on the stair he'd avoided out of habit. A piece of board gave way under her foot. She lost her balance, clutched at the railing. The railing cracked, broke beneath her weight.

He dropped the key, stretched out a hand.

She was falling. Just out of his reach.

Just like Alyssa.

Chapter Seven

Jack grabbed for Brooke. He caught the waistband of her shorts, felt gravity pull both of their bodies down. Holding on to her waistband, he sought to grip a stronger hold, snagged a fistful of T-shirt.

She clutched at his arms. The look on her face was the mirror image of Alyssa's when she'd realized the dire extent of her situation on Devil's Grin. Horror and guilt pummeled him. He should have foreseen this. He couldn't let her fall.

Brooke's T-shirt ripped in his fist. He swore. She slid toward the thorny arms of the roses below. He shifted his stance, braced his legs and slid one arm beneath her shoulders. Her fingers dug into his collarbone. Carefully he climbed over the splintered wood and stepped down on the slanted ground. Balancing her weight in his arms, he put himself between her and the rocks beneath his feet.

"I've got you."

She nodded, the green of her eyes still wild with apprehension. "I'm okay."

If she'd fallen, the rosebushes wouldn't have stayed her. They would have shredded her skin, then plunged her down against the sloping embankment of rocks serving as a retaining wall. No two ways around it, she'd have been hurt.

On his watch.

While in his care.

Jack glanced at the piece of wood railing staring up at him. Nothing out of the ordinary. Just the splinters of neglect.

Accident or planned incident? Not enough to kill her, but enough to terrorize her all over again. Just like him, Alyssa would have avoided the step out of habit. He'd told her time and again to get that step fixed, but she'd never gotten around to it. He should have done it himself. Accident or planned incident?

Everything was suspicious to him now—even something as innocent as wood rot.

What had Alyssa done? Who had she hurt enough with her meddling to warrant vengeance? In these past few months, why had she kept so much from him?

Swallowing back his anger at himself, at Alyssa, he carefully freed Brooke from the clutches of the rosebushes.

One thing was certain, to keep Brooke safe, he'd have to heighten his vigilance.

JACK'S TOUCH WAS IMMENSELY tender as he sought to disengage her from the thorny limbs holding her prisoner. Brooke clung to his shoulders while he disentangled the branches sticking to the back of her ripped T-shirt. But the tenderness of his fingers soon seemed more menacing than the thorns because it made her forget the sting and focus on impossibilities.

"Sorry about your shirt," he said once she was free again, concern evident in the wrinkling around his eyes.

The fall hadn't caused any real damage. A few cuts smarted the backs of Brooke's legs, but otherwise she'd escaped her misadventure unharmed.

"I'm fine. No damage done. Really."

He let her go just when she was wishing he'd take her

deeper in the cradle of his arms. She brushed imaginary thorns from her legs, taming the shivers still racking her body, hoping at the same time to dismiss her inappropriate desire to lean her head against his chest and hear the strong drum of his heart.

Jack examined the broken step, frittering the decaying splinters of wood between his fingers. "I told Alyssa to get that fixed months ago. I'll get Tony to do the job."

Once again she wondered at the degree of intimacy between Jack and Alyssa. Close enough to know the idiosyncrasies of her home. "Tony?"

"The handyman who takes care of maintenance for the resort."

As soon as she'd cleaned her cuts and changed her shirt Jack ushered her right back out, determined to keep them in motion.

Infinitely worse than her illogical wish for Jack's touch, she discovered as the day progressed, was the thrill and horror that the longing and regret weren't waning. She was drawn to him as surely as thunder to lightning.

Yet Jack seemed unaffected by her, going about business as if his hands weren't magic.

As he should.

After all, she wasn't truly Alyssa. She was just a stand-in—a twin of convenience to reach his goal of justice. So why did frustration hum along her skin?

Jack spent the afternoon going over resort procedures and showing her the lay of the land. He introduced her to Tony, the handyman, and asked him to repair the broken stair and railing at Alyssa's cottage. From a distance he introduced her to Holly, the activities director, April, the bookkeeper and Bryce, the boathouse/beachfront manager. Jack informed her that a couple of college girls helped out during the summer season with cleaning and readying the cabins between changeovers and with clerical work in the office.

They skirted the edges of activities, allowing Brooke to absorb the constant hubbub of resort life without participating. By the time they returned to Alyssa's cabin, Brooke's brain was on overload and she didn't know how she was going to manage to keep everything straight.

With his usual brisk efficiency, Jack called in the pizza order and helped her put together a salad as she awkwardly learned her way around what was supposed to be her own kitchen.

Their guests arrived en masse at the same time as the pizzas. Jack's descriptions proved accurate, and Brooke had no difficulty recognizing Alyssa's friends.

Sniffing appreciatively, Cullen scooped the two large pies from the delivery boy while Jack paid for the food.

"I like the way you've redecorated your front entryway. What happened?" Stephanie scowled at the scratches on Brooke's face, clucked at the cast.

"Procrastination," Brooke said, trying to inject levity in her voice.

"Gets you every time."

"You know that from experience?"

"Oh, she's in rare form tonight!" Stephanie made Brooke sit down, plumping the flowered decorative pillows around her as if she were about to keel over. "Welcome back, sweetie."

"Better get Tony to fix that step before someone falls and sues you," Tim said as he and Trish made themselves at home in the living room.

The evening was awkward at first. Plates, napkins, forks, the pizza and salad were laid out on the coffee table in the center of the living room. The conversation started slow, and it seemed as if everyone was trying hard to avoid the obvious subject of Alyssa and her miraculous recovery.

Tim sat in the corner straight chair, simply observing her with a narrowed gaze. What was he seeing? Was he comparing features and discovering anomalies? Would he expose her secret through his newspaper for all the world to see rather than keeping it in the small circle of their friends?

From his perch in the recliner, Cullen commandeered the conversation and filled it with boisterous stories about the charm he'd oozed on clients to whom he'd shown houses today, and about the sale he'd closed on an overpriced lakefront chalet. Had he noticed Alyssa's return—or that she'd even left? Was his indifference on purpose, or was this part of his character? His cover?

"Speaking of sale, when are you going to get around to updating my home page, Trish?" Cullen asked, picking out the jalapeños from a slice of pizza. "I gave you the information weeks ago."

"I'm getting there," Trish answered curtly. "There's only one of me."

Trish flitted from place to place as if she were trying to see Brooke from every angle. Did something about "Alyssa" seem out of place? Brooke resisted the urge to fiddle with her shortened hair.

"If you're that busy, maybe you should hire some help," Cullen said.

"Maybe you should mind your own business. From what I hear, if you did more minding and less meddling, you'd have more success."

"Children, children," Stephanie tsked as she returned from the kitchen with a glass of iced tea. "This is supposed to be a celebration of Alyssa's return. Do we really need to hear this bickering?"

There was a mumble of agreement.

"Speaking of celebrations," Trish said. "I hear congratulations are in order, Tim."

He blushed and dabbed a napkin at his mouth. "Yeah, I guess they are. One of my reporters is up for 'Writer of the Year' in the New Hampshire Press Association's Better Newspaper Contest."

Congratulations abounded.

"Oh, come on, Tim," Trish pressed. "Don't be shy. Tell them about your nomination for 'Best Editorial.'"

Everyone fussed over Tim's nomination, then the conversation changed to Adventure Club business.

None of them was acting the least bit guilty. Maybe Jack was wrong and Alyssa's accident was just an accident.

Juvenile, she told herself, was the way they were acting. It was as if none of them had graduated from high school. They still teased and pestered each other like... like siblings. A touch of envy ate at Brooke as she watched them interact.

Alyssa might not have had her father's undivided attention, but she'd had family. A cloak of loneliness draped itself over Brooke's shoulders.

Jack's piercing gaze caught her attention. He glanced at her hands and gave an almost imperceptible shake of his head. She looked down at her plate. She was cutting her slice of pizza with a knife and fork, and Jack was letting her know Alyssa wouldn't do that. She should have remembered from the constant grilling at the hunting cabin that Alyssa's table manners left much to be desired. Putting down her utensils, Brooke pretended absorption in the conversation and took hold of the slice with her left hand, remembered Alyssa was right-handed and shifted it to the right, despite the cast, then awkwardly took a bite.

One slight, sharp nod from Jack told her she'd gotten the right message. His approval shouldn't have sent a small wave of pleasure through her, but it did. He was playing her like a puppet, she reminded herself—the way her mother had. A lump formed in her stomach. She put the slice down on the plate and pushed it away.

She didn't belong in San Diego where the crush of people and traffic made her long for wide-open spaces. She didn't fit in here, either. The shadows of the dark woods were too claustrophobic, too reminiscent of a fairy tale gone wrong. Jack's constant monitoring of her every move made her too conscious of her failings. And sitting on the outside looking in, the feeling of being alien increased.

Instead of dwelling on the growing dark cloud in her mind, she decided to focus on the assembled group once more.

Could one of these gregarious people really want her sister dead?

Periodically Stephanie filled plates and poured drinks and otherwise made herself the unofficial hostess. She was stuffing a moundful of salad into her mouth when the ring on Brooke's hand caught her attention.

"Oh. My. God. She's wearing a ring!" Pounding her plate on the lamp table, Stephanie tumbled out of the rocker and lunged to Brooke's side. "Would you look at that rock! When did this happen?"

The whole room exploded with a buzz of disbelief. She sought out Jack and relief sighed through her when she found his reassuring gaze.

"Engaged? To whom?" Tim straightened and leaned forward, adjusting his glasses to peer at the ring.

"To me."

Cullen nearly choked on a piece of pizza. "To Jack?"

"You two are engaged?" Trish looked from one to the other with a stunned expression on her face.

"I can't believe this," Stephanie said, still examining the ring on Brooke's finger. "Who'd have thought!"

In the sudden crush of their disbelief, a shaft of panic

went through Brooke. Had she done something wrong? Had she said something that had given her away?

"These things happen." Jack stepped to Brooke's side and put a hand on her shoulder. Standing by. Standing guard. She wasn't alone in this.

"Not to you, Jack. Not with Alyssa." Cullen guffawed. "She's not your type."

"What's my type?"

"He's blushing. Stop it, Cullen, you're making Jack blush." Stephanie rose and batted Cullen on the arm. "And Alyssa, too. Look, she's beet-red."

"Well, don't keep us in suspense, man. Give us the details." Sensing time-sensitive news, Tim probably wanted to break the story of their engagement in tomorrow's paper before anyone had time to spread the rumor through town and beat him to the scoop. "When's the big day?"

The next time a blue moon falls on a Thursday, Brooke wanted to say.

"We haven't set a date yet." Jack stood solidly by her, a mountain of confidence.

"We're taking our time." *Until one of you makes a fatal error,* she couldn't help thinking.

"So what brought this on?" Trish discarded her half-eaten plate of food on the coffee table and studied Brooke with renewed fervor. Brooke found she didn't like the ardor in the woman's gaze. Did Trish expect the rivalry between Alyssa and her to bloom in this aspect, too? Should she encourage the competition in order to draw out the possible murderer?

Jack sat next to Brooke on the love seat and reached for her hand, lacing his fingers through hers the way a lover would. Maybe she should have eaten more than half a slice of pizza. The shakiness had to be from hunger, not just his touch.

Magic hands, she thought again, then dismissed the notion. No magic. The practical hands of a practical man on a mission.

He shrugged. The becoming pink blush of embarrassment still colored his cheeks. He looked at her a bit googly-eyed. His smile bordered on the daffy. Meg was right, Brooke thought with a start, the man could be a consummate actor when he set his mind to it. "Seeing Alyssa so close to death made me realize I had...feelings for her."

"Feelings? That's rich!" Cullen teased. He stuffed most of a slice of pizza into his mouth.

"Why can't he have feelings?" Stephanie challenged, brows furrowed. "I think it's wonderful. Finding love on the edge of death is so romantic." She turned toward the happy couple once more, favoring them with a smile. "Congratulations!"

The longing in Stephanie's expression suggested both happiness for her friend and a touch of jealousy. She reached for a piece of pizza, dripping with cheese, and sat back down in the rocker, but her gaze kept drifting to the ring on Brooke's finger.

Jack draped an arm around Brooke's shoulder—a protective umbrella in the rain of disbelief showering all around them. She snuggled into him. A soft sigh escaped.

"I'll be moving in to help her with her recovery," Jack announced, brushing her cheek with a gentle swipe of thumb. "I don't want her doing too much, too soon."

His voice was friendly, his smile warm, yet his words sounded like a warning. Why would he want the would-be murderer to know she wouldn't be easily accessible? Wasn't it part of the plan to make it seem as if she were an easy target? They should have talked more about this before setting the play in motion. She'd never been good at improvisation.

"Aw, that's so sweet of you, Jack," Stephanie said, smiling dreamily. "She does tend to get carried away."

Trish flopped back in her chair and hitched an ankle over a knee. "Well, I still can't believe it."

Their juvenile banter was starting to get on her nerves. Why couldn't they be happy for Alyssa? "What's so hard to believe about Jack wanting to marry me?"

Throwing his legs over the recliner's side, Cullen snorted. "You're kidding, right?"

"No. Tell me." Brooke folded her arms beneath her chest, crossed her legs, and her dangling foot jiggled with irritation.

"Well, number one is that you don't exactly have a good track record where men are concerned. That would be, what, engagement number six? I've been toying with the idea of calling the *Guinness Book of Records* people to see if they have a category for 'Most Runaway Bride.'"

"People change." Alyssa had been engaged six times? Her surprise must have shown in her face. Tim, Trish and Stephanie all seemed to notice it. What about Cullen? She caught the flash of worry in Jack's eyes and decided to ignore it.

"Number two," Trish added, counting off on her fingers, "you and Jack get along more like cats and dogs than lovebirds."

Cats and dogs? Just what kind of relationship did Jack and Alyssa share? Trish seemed to relish the notion of acrimony between Jack and Alyssa a bit too much. Should she encourage Trish's competitive streak?

"What's wrong with a little spice in a relationship?" Brooke cocked her head, giving Jack a coy smile. She savored the rush of pleasure at his discomfort, at her new-found spine. "Right, honey?"

"I've always liked spice."

"In your food," Cullen teased. "Not in your women."

"Cullen," Stephanie warned.

Cullen raised both hands. "What did I say?"

"Spice is one thing," Tim said from his corner. "Marriage is quite another."

Stephanie leaned toward Jack. "Is she all right? You did mention a problem with her…memory."

"Why don't you ask her?"

Stephanie's face turned red. Lowering her gaze, she tucked a strand of hair behind her ear. "You are all right?"

"I'm perfectly fine." Brooke shrugged. "Just a little…"

"What?"

"Disoriented. Because of the head trauma," Jack said and waited for a reaction. Brooke followed his gaze. Stephanie seemed properly horrified. Tim waited expectantly for more detail. Trish appeared unconvinced. And Cullen looked as if he wanted to change the topic of conversation. So what did it all mean? They all looked slightly uncomfortable. That didn't necessarily make any of them guilty.

"It's normal," Jack continued, not missing a twitch of muscle, a slide of eye, a shift of body. "The doctor said she'll probably regain most of her memories, eventually, but may never remember the accident itself."

The bait was planted. Who would bite?

"You don't remember the accident?" Stephanie gasped.

Brooke lifted a shoulder. "No."

"Not at all?" Trish said with a pensive frown.

"You don't remember paddling up Devil's Run, the picnic, the climb?" Stephanie added, twisting her hands in her lap.

Brooke shook her head. "Sorry."

"Well, imagine that! Alyssa without a memory," Tim said, leaning back in his chair. "Are you still going to be able to take the occasional picture for me?"

"I don't see why not," she said, glancing at Jack for confirmation and seeing nothing in his eyes but a wall as impenetrable as granite. She had a feeling she'd get an earful of his disappointment in her behavior later.

"You still remember how to use your camera?"

"Of course," she said, hoping he wouldn't actually ask since she barely knew the difference between focus and f-stop.

Tim leaned forward again, bracing elbows on knees. "Even with the amnesia?"

"Memory of processes is unaffected," Jack said, zeroing in on Tim's interest. "Events, emotions are what the trauma affected. That's why she didn't have to relearn to walk or talk."

"So she can still climb and run the resort and drive everybody nuts," Cullen said with a teasing smile.

"That about sums it up."

"Then nothing's changed at all. She's the most forgetful woman I know."

"So, what's the last thing you remember?" Tim threw the question with nonchalant care, but Brooke sensed a deeper interest. As a murderer fearing discovery, or as a newspaperman itching for a story?

"Bits and pieces," Brooke said, parroting the doctor's opinion of Alyssa's possible path of recovery. "Nothing really clearly until the first day I saw this house."

A shot of alarm streaked through Jack's face. He straightened and his grip on her hand tightened. She dug her nails into his flesh.

"But that was twenty-four years ago!" Stephanie said, reaching for Brooke's knee.

Trish shook her head. "Unbelievable!"

"So, you don't even remember us?" Stephanie's expression reminded Brooke of a hurt puppy's.

"Of course I do." Brooke reached for Stephanie's hand and squeezed it. "I just don't remember details. I couldn't completely forget my best friend now, could I?"

Stephanie gave a small smile. "I guess not. But if your memory's not all there, why would you want to rush into marriage then?"

Tim laughed. "Now that's a strange question from someone who'd be willing to pay a guy to walk her down the aisle."

"Shut up."

"Because..." Brooke looked up at Jack and contorted her features in what she hoped looked like dripping adoration. "Because feelings can't be helped and what I thought was just friendship seems a whole lot more potent now."

Jack rubbed his thumb on the back of her hand. She couldn't decide if it was nerves or a warning. All she knew was that his touch caused small heated waves to lap up her arm down to her stomach.

"Well at least you're giving yourself time to get your senses back and aren't rushing into matrimony," Trish said.

"Exactly." Brooke snuggled closer to Jack. Her head fit perfectly in the crook of his shoulder. Her hand strayed to his thigh. "We're taking it nice and slow."

Jack nearly crushed her hand and she realized her fingers on his thigh were causing a stir of reaction. Heat colored her cheeks. Change the subject. Now.

"We had a bit of excitement a couple of days ago," Brooke announced. Might as well get straight to the heart of things. "On the way home from the hospital someone tried to run us off the road."

Jack choked on his iced tea. Brooke pounded on his back.

"I caught the call on my scanner," Tim said, interest gleaming in his eyes. "Since I was headed home, I decided to swing by and cover the story myself. When I got to Reservoir, I saw nothing."

"That was us." Still rubbing Jack's back, she turned to her attentive audience. "It was quite exciting, really. Jack's maneuvering had me on the edge of my seat."

"You would think a brush with death was thrilling!" Trish said, shaking her head. "What happened?"

Brooke leaned forward, gestured grandly and injected a shot of enthusiasm into her voice—just as she thought her thrill-seeking sister might. "A truck rammed us from behind, then tried to sideswipe us."

"That's horrible!" Stephanie exclaimed.

Cullen took a swig from a beer bottle. "How much is that little thrill ride going to set you back, Jack?"

"Let's just say I'm glad my insurance is all paid up."

"What about the truck?" Tim asked. The fingers of his right hand twitched as if he were itching to write. "Who was driving it?"

"He got away," Jack said. The muscle in his jaw tightened.

Tim leaned back in his chair, his nose wrinkling with disgust. At the thought of a missed scoop, or at something else?

Brooke snuggled back into Jack once more, playing her role of adoring fiancée to the hilt. "We were never in any real danger. Jack's such a great driver. I figure it must be someone who'd had too many beers at one of the soccer games. Right, honey?"

Jack shot her a warning glance. She was pushing her luck. To her surprise, she found she liked being on the edge like this—like Alyssa.

"Or maybe lost a game." Cullen chuckled and snagged Stephanie into his lap as she went by with an empty glass. "I've seen how rough those games can get. And road rage is a problem these days."

"You're no stranger to road rage, are you?" Tim asked.

"I do believe you're one ticket short of having your license suspended."

Cullen shrugged indifferently, but his gaze narrowed. "There are a lot of people out there who shouldn't be allowed to drive. I can't stand Sunday drivers putzing around at thirty-five in a fifty-five zone."

"We're safe and that's all that really matters," Jack said, clearly trying to regain control of the situation. But the caress of his thumb along the side of her hand was causing a small riot inside her. "I think we should call it an evening, sunshine."

"Sunshine? What's that all about?" Cullen groused.

"It's a pet name, you idiot," Stephanie said, staring at Cullen reproachfully. "People in love do that. Not that *you'd* know anything about it."

Not a pet name, Brooke thought, just part of the act. But she liked it anyway, liked the way Jack's voice softened when he said sunshine.

"Jack's right." Trish rose and put her plate on the coffee table. "Alyssa's still healing, we need to let her rest."

Stephanie scrambled out of Cullen's lap and reached for her plate on the lamp table. "Want me to put this stuff away for you?"

Brooke shook her head, got to her feet and took the plate from Stephanie. "I'll take care of it."

She was aware of Jack's gaze following her progress, but rather than feeling unsettled, a warm sensation trickled through her like honey on hot toast.

"At least let me help you take everything into the kitchen." Stephanie grabbed the two pizza boxes and followed Brooke into the kitchen.

A new sense of confidence seeped through Brooke's bones, giving a lightness to her step. Wearing Alyssa's skin was starting to feel pretty good.

JACK'S HAND FELT EMPTY, where once he'd held Brooke. After she left the room, he rubbed his palm on the leg on his pants. Her hand fit so well, so naturally inside his that it had felt like a part of him. And her touch had had him fighting for control of his thoughts more than once. The sudden urge to go hiking struck him full force. He had to get rid of these people, get out and hit the trails in the woods around the resort.

Trish located her purse and extracted a lipstick. Cullen headed for the bathroom down the hall. Tim collected empty beer bottles and set them on the coffee table.

Had any of them noticed his uncharacteristic show of emotions? Jack wasn't sure what he wanted the answer to be. If his friends believed he was in love with Alyssa, this charade could work. If they didn't, it could very well heighten the would-be murderer's suspicions and put him—or her—on guard, making this an exercise in futility.

He wasn't comfortable with the lie, but the idea of someone getting away with the near murder of his friend, in his town, was even less palatable.

But emotions were dangerous. His parents' example had shown him that. Especially this kind. Especially now. They distracted. They left a person weak and vulnerable.

His father had exploited his mother's unfettered emotions and broken her heart, and her sprit. Alyssa's father had suffered a similar fate with his wife's leaving.

He should be continuing to examine his suspects, searching for telltale signs of discomfort and lies instead of dwelling on the fire Brooke stoked in his blood with just a touch.

Her amateurish venture into investigation had muddled the situation. Brooke's face was too easy to read. Her attempt at looking indifferent only made her appear too eager. Restlessness had him on edge.

Just as he rose, someone pounded on the front door. Glad for the distraction, Jack answered the summons.

"You the manager?" A huge, bald muscle man stood on the other side of the door. He sported no shirt under his black leather vest, exposing a large tattoo of an eagle with spread wings on his chest. He wore chaps over his jeans, thick-soled biker boots with fringe and an expression of acute irritation.

Jack barred the biker's entry with his body. "No. The manager's not available right now."

The biker took a handful of Jack's T-shirt. "I said I need to speak to the manager. *Now.*"

Grabbing the biker's wrist, Jack pressed until the man released his hold. "What do you need? I'll take care of it."

"Is there a problem?" Tim flanked him.

"No, this gentleman was just about to tell me how I can help him."

"Someone broke into my cabin," the biker barked.

"Which cabin, Mr....?" Jack asked, keeping his voice low and calm.

"Herbie Johnson. Cabin 16."

"Anything missing?"

Red-faced, the biker scowled. His movements were choppy. "Yeah, something's missing all right, and I swear if anything's happened to Cuddles, I'll sue the hell out of this resort."

"Calm down, Mr. Johnson."

"*Dr.* Johnson."

"You're in luck, Dr. Johnson," Tim announced, slapping Jack's shoulder. "This just happens to be the finest police officer in this lovely little town. He's a master at search and rescue."

The biker ignored Tim and kept his frozen expression on Jack. "My pet's cage was open. Deliberately. And I know I locked the cabin door. I can't find Cuddles any-where."

"We'll help you look for her." Jack pegged the good doctor for a dog man—a boxer, maybe a pit bull. The sun would give at least half an hour more of light. Time enough to find the mutt before coyotes or a fisher gobbled it as an appetizer.

A shriek came from the kitchen. A chair crashed against the linoleum. Then there was a mad scramble.

"God, oh God." Stephanie exploded out of the kitchen, shoved Jack and Dr. Johnson aside and ran out the front door.

Jack swiveled to run to Brooke's aid.

"Dr. Johnson?" Brooke's voice floated from the kitchen.

"Yeah?"

"What kind of pet is your Cuddles?"

"She's a six foot boa constrictor. Just a baby."

Before Jack could reach the kitchen, Brooke rounded the corner. A brown snake with irregular dark blotches draped around her shoulders, making her look for all the world like a pagan goddess. In the wonder of the picture Brooke painted, he almost forgot Alyssa had feared snakes since her near encounter with a timber rattler on a Con-necticut hike.

"I think we've found her," Brooke said.

Yelping, Trish jumped on the love seat and used Tim as a shield. Tim didn't look too happy with the snake's presence, either. Neither seemed to have noticed the anom-aly of Alyssa carrying a dreaded snake.

The transformation in Dr. Johnson, on the other hand, was worthy of a Meg Kessler job. His whole demeanor softened, turning this angry biker into a molasses-eyed Saint Bernard. "Cuddles, my sweet, come to Daddy."

Gently Dr. Johnson relieved Brooke of her scaly burden

and wound Cuddles around his own shoulders, kissing the reptile's face. "How did she get in here?"

"I have no idea," Brooke said. "She was in the cupboard beneath the sink. We'll have the lock on your cabin changed in the morning and won't charge you for today. I promise you this won't happen again."

"Thanks."

The key. Someone had duplicated Alyssa's master key. That was why he hadn't found her key chain on its proper hook by the door, but in the kitchen, half-hidden between the coffeemaker and the food processor on the counter. The unlocked door had *not* been due to Alyssa's forgetfulness.

Dr. Johnson left, cooing at Cuddles. As Jack closed the door, the snake's elliptical pupils stared coldly at him. The reptile's long, curved fangs and forked tongue added to the impression of something sinister.

Danger. He could feel it closing around him, tightening like a boa's coils around a kill.

His hike would have to wait. He couldn't leave Brooke. Not now. Not with the scent of death strong on her doorstep.

Chapter Eight

Very deliberately, Jack closed the door behind their last guest. Brooke gathered the last of the napkins and utensils, trying to ignore the stiff anger vibrating in every one of his muscles.

"Alyssa is afraid of snakes." Jack's expression was forbidding under his scowl.

Brooke bristled. "How was I supposed to know?"

"You jump at every shadow. How could you pick up that snake and wrap it around your neck?"

She dumped the napkins and utensils into the empty salad bowl. What was the matter with him? Where was all of this righteous anger coming from? Certainly not just because of a snake. "I inherited a boa when I took over my classroom. The kids love it, and I had to learn not to show fear. The worst part is feeding the thing. I've got to get mice from the pet shop and stir them around with a stick so Phoebe thinks they're still alive." She shuddered as she did every time she had to feed Phoebe.

"In the future, leave the investigating to me."

She whirled around to face him. "I'm part of this, whether you like it or not."

"You're not a trained detective."

"How many murder investigations have you solved?" she tossed back at him without missing a beat. *Let me handle this, Brooke. It'll go faster.* How many times had her mother said that to her while she was growing up? Jack's uncompromising attitude struck a nerve that was much too raw.

"None, but I'm a tracker and I've never failed to find my quarry."

"You hunt?"

Of course he did—man, beast, clues, it didn't matter. The signs were there in every taut muscle of his body, in the piercing keenness of his gaze. He was a hunter by nature. He could no more tame that aspect of his personality than she could still her too-liquid emotions. For him, the act of hunting was separate from its quarry—no emotions need be involved. But not for her. Everything was tied together. The basic difference between them lay raw and exposed like a fresh kill's underbelly.

"For lost souls. Search and rescue." He gave an exasperated sigh. Irritation chafed her. "Checking details is a tedious, but necessary part of any investigation. You can't go off half cocked just because you're impatient. If you go too fast, you can miss a clue and it can cost a lost hiker his life."

"I'm as patient as the next person, but we can't just sit here and wait for things to happen. Isn't that the whole point of me coming here in the first place?" For an intelligent man, he was being quite dense. She banged the salad bowl on the coffee table and stooped to pick up an empty glass.

"If we go too fast, too soon, we could blow the whole thing. Just do as I ask, Brooke. I know what's best for you."

"No, you don't. You can't possibly know what's best for me. You don't know me. Not at all." Her grip tightened around the glass and slowly, deliberately, she straightened. "Alyssa wouldn't let you get away with that caveman attitude."

"You're not Alyssa."

His words struck like a land mine, hitting dead center. *I don't want to talk about this, Brooke. You never do, Mom.* And Delia would walk out, leaving Brooke standing there with her heart in her hands. "No, I'm not. But I'm not a puppet, either. You can't pull my strings when you want, then just toss me in a corner. I'm *not* going to let you walk all over me."

"Brooke—"

Head high, shoulders squared, she shoved the dirty glass at him, leaving him no option but to take it. "Good night, Jack. I've had enough manipulation for one day."

With that, she headed down the hall, leaving him staring after her. Alyssa or not, she was through living up to any expectations but her own.

Moments later, in the privacy of the shower, she let the cold spray needle her skin. Her tears mingled with the streams of water pouring from the shower head. Eyes closed, mind concentrated on forgetting everything but the feel of water sluicing over skin, she didn't notice her hand creep up to press against the tender bruise of regret aching in her heart.

NOW, NOW. WASN'T THAT an interesting evening? Amnesia. Beautiful amnesia. How permanent would it prove to be? Apparently Alyssa had forgotten her Connecticut misadventure and that she was deathly afraid of snakes.

Kind of took the edge off the welcome home surprise.

From the darkness of the boathouse, the view of the cottage was unimpeded.

For a couple who professed to be so in love, what was up with separate bedrooms? Had Alyssa forgotten how to tease a man to the edge of madness, how to play with him until he saw nothing but her siren's smile, how to reveal just enough of her black soul to lead him into hell?

I don't buy it. Not for a minute. No one could change that much. Not that fast, not that completely. She was up to something.

My memory's fine, princess. I won't forget so easily.

In the cottage, one light winked out, then the other.

With Jack at her side, so damnably protective of someone so undeserving, it would be harder to make Alyssa learn her lesson of compassion. Maybe it was time to teach Jack a little lesson of his own.

THE DAY HAD BEEN LONG and exhausting. Brooke had expected to fall asleep as soon as her head touched the pillow, but her surroundings were too unfamiliar, and her thoughts spun on a never-ending merry-go-round—most of them having Jack at their center.

Moonbeams pierced through the sheer curtains hanging from the open window. Soft light silvered the contents of the room and blurred the sharp edges of shadows. She'd never thought moonlight could be so bright. She could actually read the cover of the photography magazine lying on the floor next to the dresser.

She was used to the city sounds of cars and airplanes lulling her to sleep. Here, the grating of crickets in need of a good oiling clashed with the off-key warble of tree frogs and the eerie ululation of a distant coyote. Tree branches shook in the breeze, and the rub of their leaves conjured up the image of dry-boned skeletons walking. Even the lap of the water on the rough sand sounded evil. This strange lambent darkness with its ghoulish concert made sleep impossible.

"How can you sleep with all this noise?" Brooke asked her absent sister.

The clock on the nightstand read three past midnight.

With a sigh, Brooke heaved the sheet covering her and got up. If she wasn't going to sleep, she might as well use the time constructively and examine Alyssa's things. She wasn't about to quit trying to find who had tried to kill her sister just because it gained her Jack's wrath.

Without turning on lights, she headed for the living room. Bright moonlight allowed her to peruse the room almost as easily as if it were day. She spotted the love seat she'd shared with Jack, placed her hand against her cheek at the memory of his gentle touch. Jack had made it plain he was playing a role, that he was disappointed in her performance. Shaking her head, she focused on the past.

She and Alyssa had cozied on this sofa in their house in Boston, watching *Sesame Street*, *Reading Rainbow* and countless repeats of Disney movies from its sagging cushions. The peach flowers and moss-colored foliage clustered on the cream fabric had faded with time. The arms now displayed threadbare patches.

She ran a hand along the back of the tan recliner, stooped to sniff it. If she closed her eyes, she could almost smell her father's smoky scent, hear his laughter roar. *Which one of you girls wants to go riding?*

Me, Daddy, me!

No, me first!

You're in luck, girls. I've got two horses with me today.

She and Alyssa would squeal and clamber up each on a knee.

I wish you wouldn't do that, Walter. One of these days, someone'll get hurt.

Brooke turned at the sound of her mother's ghostly voice, could see her rocking in her rocker, flipping through the pages of a decorating magazine. Tension floated even through the folds of time. Had she and Alyssa felt it then, the building stress between their parents? Was that why she'd been such a nervous child?

Hugging herself, Brooke moved to the window. Under the caress of the moon, the lake water shone.

What is this place, Walter?

It's our new home.

Are you crazy? It's a dump.

Delia, you've got the eye, can't you see it? Can't you see the potential?

The eye. Alyssa had it, too. The framed photographs tacked to the white walls displayed her talent. A ladybug reflected in a dewdrop hanging from a flower leaf. A squirrel gripping a branch with hind legs and tail, greedily robbing a suet cake. A Monarch butterfly against the yellow petals of a sunflower. A cardinal feeding its young. An iridescent hummingbird sucking nectar from a vine. A spiderweb in the rain. Forest magic. Mountainscapes. She had captured color-rich, emotion-filled vignettes of her world.

"When you're well…" Brooke started, then shook her head. What? A showing of some sort? "The world needs to see this beauty."

The wind outside brushed against the house, causing the woodwork to creak and crack. The noisy settling reminded her of her first and only night in this house. Unlike tonight, there had been no radiant moon. Their bedroom had been so dark she hadn't been able to see her own hand in front of her face. The wind had howled and sounded like soughs from the dead. She remembered slipping into Alyssa's bed.

"Chicken," Alyssa had said, giggling, but her twin had turned around and hugged her, and they'd fallen asleep in each other's arms.

The wind gusted again, jarring a screak from the ceiling. Brooke's gaze strayed to the dark beams supporting the ceiling.

Another memory floated up. She and Alyssa were crouched in a dark and musty attic, looking through a dirty window at their parents arguing by the lake's edge. The contrast of sunshine reflecting off the lake and the dark shadows from the nearby woods had added to her anxiety, and when she'd started crying, Alyssa had patted her back and told her the attic was magic and no one was allowed to cry there.

Guided by impressions, Brooke headed toward the kitchen. Alyssa had scaled the empty pantry shelves to reach the panel in the ceiling. Brooke looked up and spotted a rope dangling from the panel. She pulled on it. Attic stairs creeped down, stopped at her knees. Looking around the kitchen, Brooke found a flashlight, then started up the stairs.

She'd anticipated spiderwebs and dust and forgotten boxes. Instead Brooke found a cozy nook. A red fleece throw blanketed an olive-green corduroy-upholstered chair. A braided oval rug covered the rough wooden planks. Two stacked milk crates served as an end table and supported a bean-pot lamp. Brooke clicked it on. Soft, yellow light spilled into the space. She turned off the flashlight. Tucking one leg beneath her, she sat, felt the chair's high wings wrap around her like a mother's arms.

"Nice place you've got, sis."

Waist-high bookshelves lined one wall. More books lay in piles. Here Alyssa had fed her secret hunger for knowledge. Brooke recoiled at the thought. Had Alyssa had to hide her love of reading? Kneeling in front of the shelves, Brooke explored the titles. She found everything from bestselling thrillers to photography books, from mythology tomes to field guides.

Brooke pulled a photo album from the shelf. Sitting cross-legged on the floor, she turned the pages, laughing and crying at the memories they evoked. The past and the present blended in a sweet-and-sour cocktail of pictures and emotions.

Then she came across a ragged pile of what appeared

to be journals. There were twelve of them—oversize, canvas-covered books. She slipped the top one onto her lap, then hesitated. Would the answers she sought be inside? What had Alyssa confided to these pages? Daily routines? Photographic details? Parts of her soul?

"Hey." Jack's unexpected husky voice should have made her jump, but it didn't. She looked up from the journal's cover and spotted his head poking through the attic opening. "What are you doing here?"

"Exploring."

He climbed up. Because of the slanting ceiling, he had to stoop. He was wearing nothing but jeans, showing off hard pecs and a washboard stomach. Her fingers itched to play along the ridges and sample the firm flesh. His hair was sleep mussed. She wanted to sweep away the stray lock dangling in front of his eye. A heavy shadow of beard darkened his jaw. She yearned to rub her cheek against it and feel the prickly softness. But she did none of those things. She would not let him know he could wipe away her anger at him with just a crooked smile.

He sprawled beside her, wiping a hand over his eyes as if to whisk away sleep. Her body instantly tensed with a double-barreled dose of desire and anxiety. She hugged the journal close to her chest.

"You should be in bed," she said, still debating whether or not to pry into Alyssa's private musings.

"So should you."

"I couldn't sleep."

"I thought I was hearing mice." His gaze swept the small space. "How did you find this place? I didn't know it existed."

"I remembered it from the day I was here with Alyssa, all those years ago."

He bent his knees and leaned back against the bookshelves. The tent formed by his legs now housed her left knee. Their shoulders were separated by no more than a thought. She had to fight the urge to slant her head to his shoulder, to tip her chin up and kiss the steady pulse at his neck.

"I'm sorry," he said.

She didn't want his apology. She wanted to hang on to her anger. Irritation would make dealing with Jack's over-whelming masculinity easier to handle. How could she want to kiss someone when she was mad at him? Then he had to apologize and melt away the remainder of her anger.

"About what?"

"Being overbearing. It's a bad habit."

"Yeah, well, you need to work on it."

"What did you find?" he asked, pointing at the journal in her lap.

"Maybe the answer to our questions." She glanced at him. "I'm not going to stop looking, you know."

"I figured as much."

After a moment more of hesitation, Brooke turned the cover. Unlined pages stocked the inside. Alyssa had filled them with words and drawings. She'd started the book with a title page bearing the year in an ornately colored fashion. The second page held, along with sketches of bal-loons, champagne flutes and confetti, a list of eight New Year's resolutions: "convince Cullen to walk the straight and narrow; destroy the negatives of Tim; talk to Gary about Trish; find Stephanie a decent guy; set Jack free; find a manager for the resort; move to Boston; establish a studio."

"Set you free from what?" Brooke asked, curious about the exact nature of Alyssa and Jack's relationship. Had she mistaken the essence of their friendship? Not if she lived by Alyssa's friends' reactions to her engagement to Jack. Yet jack's care for her twin seemed to go deeper than friendship. *Don't go there, Brooke. He's not for you, no matter what the circumstances are.*

"Alyssa broods. One minute she depends on me. The next she's telling me she's a burden and trying to send me away."

Self-sacrificing for the man she loved? Or something deeper? "Depression?"

"Probably, but she wouldn't see anybody about it."

Do you love her, Jack? Does she love you? Were you lovers? Brooke shook her head and concentrated on the written words. "It sounds like she was trying to tie up loose ends before moving on. Did you know about this studio idea?"

"She mentioned it, but with her, it's hard to tell when she's serious and when she's just talking."

Was Alyssa afraid of dreaming, too? When a parent depended on you for their happiness, it was difficult to allow yourself to dream. Had Alyssa finally gotten the courage to cut the toxic strings? If she had, then Jack was wrong and Alyssa was strong. Leaving the familiar took courage. Yes, dreams were fragile things. Brooke couldn't remember the last time she'd entertained one. The pain of watching it float away unfulfilled was too great.

"Who's Gary?" Brooke asked, trying to keep herself focused on the present.

"I'm not sure. Maybe Gary Dunning, a guy we went to school with. But he left Comfort a long time ago."

"What does this Gary do?"

"He runs a trouble-shooting company out of Manchester. I've used him on a couple of cases where computers were involved."

"You mentioned Trish was having business problems—"

"A couple of complaints, not problems."

Brooke shrugged, the movement causing the unexpected

rub of shoulder against shoulder. "Maybe Alyssa wanted to help straighten those complaints out. Friend to friend. Just what were her clients upset with?"

"Timing. Trish was taking too long to make promised updates on their home pages. This was right after her brother died last year. She's mostly caught up now."

"Except for Cullen." The tan line on Jack's legs stopped at his ankle. His feet were white, the arch high and strong, the toes sinewy, powerful. She forced her gaze away before she developed a serious foot fetish. "Still, it's worth checking this Gary out. Got a pencil on you?"

He pretended to pat a shirt pocket. "No, sorry, I didn't think an attic rat would want to make a list."

Needing to create space between her and Jack and her too-eager response to him, Brooke scrounged around and found a pen next to the milk crates. "Doesn't sound like Alyssa got along with Cullen at all."

"They had a love-hate relationship. She teased him, but would never go out with him. She flaunted her many engagements in his face. He didn't like it."

"But—" Brooke started, confused again about Jack's relationship with Alyssa. "Didn't it bother you?"

"What?"

"Alyssa's flirtations?"

He shrugged. "They didn't mean anything."

Brooke knew she wouldn't be so forgiving if her lover flirted with anyone but her. And how could Alyssa have led someone else on while she had Jack? "Did Alyssa really get engaged six times?"

"Depends on who you talk to."

"I'm asking you."

He slanted her a shuttered look, then shrugged again. "Five or six. She wanted to escape, but she wanted her father's approval more."

"And he wouldn't give her his blessing?"

He shook his head. "So she broke her engagements. You have to understand. He was her only remaining parent. She needed to feel wanted by him."

Brooke did understand. She'd felt responsible for her mother's happiness. She'd felt the need to be the perfect daughter. And she'd failed miserably on both counts. She sighed. "The things we do for love."

She couldn't help herself and glanced at Jack.

Long lashes were wasted on a man, she thought. Maybe not. They did soften his eyes, making him look approachable. She sat down again and placed the journal back in her lap, making sure to leave plenty of space between her and Jack. "What kind of negatives do you suppose she wanted to destroy?"

Jack chuckled. "Our friend Tim is a little vain. She probably took a shot of him that was unflattering and used it as leverage to get something she wanted."

"You think it's an ice cream dripping down his chin or nose-picking type picture?"

"That would be enough to get Tim more than mad."

"Mad enough to kill?"

"I'll handle it, Brooke."

"I'm trying to help you."

"I know." He blew out a long breath, heavy with resignation. "I'll add asking Tim about the negatives to the list."

He snagged the pen from her hand and found a piece of scrap paper on one of Alyssa's piles. "Number one, talk to Gary. Number two, talk to Tim."

Jack was being much too indulgent, stirring confusion. After watching him jot down the note, she returned her attention to the book. A loose page floated out. The drawing was dated early June. Alyssa must have sketched it right before her accident.

"Oh." Brooke reached for the illustration depicting little Lauren and her beagle asleep on a quilt beneath a tree. Alyssa had captured every tiny detail from the smudge of chocolate on Lauren's lip to the bubble of slobber on Daisy's whisker, reflecting both the innocence of her subjects and their zest for life. "I didn't know Alyssa could draw."

Jack leaned closer to peer at the page. His bare shoulder brushed her bare arm. The warmth seared her skin, yet caused a shiver to slink up and down her body. "She's always been good at it."

"So is my mother. I can barely draw a straight line." Once again Brooke wondered if her mother hadn't chosen the wrong child.

"I'm sure you have other talents."

She smiled. "I play a mean game of Trivial Pursuit."

He chuckled. "You never know when trivia will come in handy."

Interspersed among the pages of sketches of flora, fauna and scenes from the resort were Alyssa's thoughts in bold, colorful strokes.

"Listen to this," Brooke said. "'I found the perfect gift for Jack's birthday yesterday. I'm going to have to put off buying it or I won't be able to resist giving it to him early.' When's your birthday?"

"Not till April."

"This is dated February. What did she give you?"

"A book I'd been looking for for ages."

Something a lover would be close enough to know, Brooke thought, suddenly, inexplicably jealous of her sister. Then she remembered Alyssa's condition and a spot of shame stained her conscience. She couldn't let herself be bewitched by a man who didn't belong to her.

Brooke read a few more entries, gaining insight on the resort's daily rhythm and Alyssa's wry view of life. "Sounds like your party was a blast."

"Let me see that." He took the journal from her, read the entry, then frowned. "I never knew she had a flat tire on her way home."

He thumbed through the pages. Brooke read along with him and had to keep reminding herself to focus on the words her sister had written rather than the wild honey scent of Jack and the ridiculous aching of her skin to rub itself against his.

Alyssa had documented a series of near-accidents, a feeling of being watched and a growing paranoia. Though she tried to hide her growing fear, it came through in her words. The writing stopped abruptly midentry two days before her accident.

"Look here," Jack said, pointing at the last entry. "She mentions someone erased files on her computer. I don't like this at all. She says her brakes were tampered with, too. If George at the garage hadn't noticed the fluid loss while he was pumping gas for her, she could have gotten in a serious accident."

"She didn't tell you about these incidents?"

"No." His frown deepened. "That's not like her."

"We'll add George to our list then." Brooke had another thought. "The deposit money that disappeared, did you find it?"

"No. According to the man who sent us the check, it hasn't yet been deposited."

"So money isn't the motive."

"Still could be, depending on whether you wanted the business to expand or shut down."

"Okay, so Cullen wanted to expand, right?" Brooke took the pen and paper from Jack's hands, turned the page over, wrote Cullen's name and drew a box around it.

"He wanted to offer more challenging experiences, but cost got in the way. With challenge comes a safety risk and more expense."

"But with Alyssa hurt, the business is on hold."

"Or prime for a split. Cullen has mentioned he wants to buy our shares and continue the business."

"Couldn't he do that on his own?"

"He could," Jack agreed. "But the Adventure Club has a good reputation. He'd have to start from ground zero. He's not a patient man."

Brooke scribbled a note. "What about Stephanie? You said she was safety conscious. Couldn't she turn Cullen around?"

"She enjoys climbing, but never really cared for the business. I think she's hoping Cullen will settle down if the business dissolves."

Brooke drew a box around Stephanie's name, connecting it with a line to the box with Cullen's name. "With Alyssa hurt, then the business is on hold and she gets her wish."

"More or less."

"And Tim?" Brooke added Tim's name to her chart.

"He's always worried about being sued. He wants things to stay as they are. He's confident of his skills at this level."

"With Alyssa hurt, he also gets his wish."

"Yes."

"And Trish?" A fourth box appeared on the paper.

"For Trish, the business is more of a chance for socializing than anything else. She likes to climb, but would be just as glad to meet somewhere for pizza." Jack kneaded the back of his neck. "On the other hand, with the business on hold, so is our promotional effort, which gives her extra time to spend on her own business."

"She was in charge of marketing?"

He nodded. "And having a hard time keeping up with her own work, let alone Adventure Club business."

All the boxes connected back to Alyssa, bringing her no

closer to understanding what could have gone wrong in their association.

Jack seemed to share her frustration. He leaned his head against the bookcase and closed his eyes. The dark fans made by his eyelashes softened his features, giving him a touch of vulnerability. His hands hung from his knees. She wanted to trace the bones with her fingers, feel the strength of his fingers touching her, caressing her.... She swallowed hard and hugged her knees close to her chest. These feelings were ridiculous. She didn't know the man. How could she possibly desire him? No, not desire, she corrected, lust. Because she was pretending to be Alyssa, and Alyssa was in love with Jack? These feelings were Alyssa's, not hers.

"The night before we climbed Devil's Grin, she got a bit tipsy and told me someone was trying to kill her. I didn't believe her."

"Why not?"

"This is Comfort, New Hampshire." He gave a short, dry laugh. "We're in the middle of nowhere. People come here to vacation, have fun. She can be a little brash, but almost everybody likes Alyssa. I thought she just wanted attention."

"Had she done that before?"

He raked a hand through his hair. Soft hair, she remembered. "It's kind of hard to explain. Alyssa couldn't ask for anything. Not directly. If she wanted company, she invited you over for dinner. If she needed help, she asked for it in a roundabout way. If she was scared, she made jokes about it."

"She didn't joke that night?"

"She was strangely morose." He frowned. "Looking back, I guess she was going the roundabout route. I just didn't see it. I thought she was a little stressed and needed a break. Your father had been riding her kind of hard. He tends to do that at the beginning of every season.''

Jack flipped through the rest of the pages, but they were all blank.

Until the last page.

Stuck against the back cover of the sketchbook was a folded piece of computer paper. Carefully Jack laid the journal flat on the wooden planks. Handling the note by the edges, he opened it.

Brooke gasped at the horrid sight. Seemingly in blood, someone had printed a grim poem.

''Reap what you sow.
Pay what you owe.
Sticks and stones
Will break your bones.
And when you die,
I won't cry.
Remember me, 'friend.'
I'll smile at your end.''

Chapter Nine

Jack swore, shut the journal cover over the bloody poem and shot to his feet, cracking the top of his head on one of the roof's supporting beams. Stooping, he rubbed his head and, paced the small area. This was what Alyssa had meant that day on the mountain.

Sticks and stones will break my bones.

But you'll be all right. You always are.

Not this time.

Why hadn't she trusted him? Had she thought he could be the one who wanted to harm her? Then why had she been so insistent on his presence on the climb?

Set Jack free.

She'd been in one of her independent phases. Had she been serious about leaving this time? Part of him wanted to cheer her goal, part of him wondered what had happened to all her good intentions. *Alyssa, Alyssa, what were you up to? Who did you rub the wrong way? Why didn't you let me help?*

"Is there any way to find out who wrote this?" Brooke asked from her position on the floor.

She looked small, like a little girl, soft and vulnerable, just as Alyssa had been all those years ago under that tough tomboy exterior. Just the peek of toes showed from beneath the length of the aqua oversize T-shirt Brooke wore.

Tented over her knees, the material hid all the delectable curves that had tempted him when he'd first climbed into the attic. The enticing shape of breasts, the enchanting dip between waist and hip. His hands had wanted to roam. His lips had yearned to taste.

She had him on edge, nervous and tight like a prowling mountain lion. Exercise, that was what he needed. He'd been confined for too long. His muscles were twitching from lack of action, not because Brooke Snowden's body was a temptation he found hard to resist.

"I'll send it to the state police lab in Concord, but I can guarantee it won't be a priority, and chances are they won't be able to tell much from it. The paper is your average copy store stock. The ink, even with the bloodlike Halloween font, looks like a common color printer type. If this person has more than an ounce of brains, he'd know to wear gloves while handling the paper. And you can buy latex gloves at any hardware store—even the one in Comfort."

"Trish deals with computers all day."

"So do Tim and Cullen and Stephanie. They all use them in their everyday jobs."

"Of course." Brooke frowned, studying the same page over and over again. "Someone really wanted Alyssa to die."

He saw her shudder from across the room, wanted to hold her, kiss away her frown. Instead he turned his back to her, and opened the journal to look at the note once more.

"Yeah." Not knowing who could do this was getting to him, slowly eating at him. Those he suspected had shared so much with Alyssa and him over the years. How could he not know which one of them harbored such evil? "Someone still wants her dead. The truck and the snake are proof of that."

Jack crouched beside Brooke. He reached forward to touch her, caught himself, and balanced on the balls of his feet. "It's dangerous for you to stay."

"I know."

How could he make her see the depth of his fear for her well-being? "I'm not sure you understand what you could lose."

Her brows lifted slightly. Her eyes shone with swirling passion. "I'm not sure you understand what I could gain."

"I'm talking about your life." His fingers clenched tightly.

"So am I. But I'm not alone. You're here."

Her eyes were deep and darkened with determination. And confidence. In him. The blow of recognition rocked him back onto his heels.

As protest galloped through him, he shook his head. "I couldn't protect your sister. What makes you think I can protect you?"

"Your love for her."

"Is that what you think?"

He should encourage her misconception. Allowing her to believe he and Alyssa were lovers would keep badly needed distance between them. Brooke was more than a distraction. She was a liability. He knew enough about her to believe she would not encroach on territory she perceived as belonging to her sister.

If he denied it, telling the truth, there was no way to judge what would happen. Would she yield to all that passion bubbling so close to the surface? If she did, could he handle it? He'd have to deal with his own troublesome feelings and he didn't want to do that. He didn't want to drown in all those messy emotions. There was no room in his life for that.

"Didn't you...love her, that is?" Brooke asked. Her gaze was direct, asking for truth, but there was tension there, too—as if she wasn't sure she wanted her question answered.

He sat beside her. Without thinking, he reached a hand across her shoulder to draw her into him. Mistake. Big mistake. A hum of contentment vibrated through him. A gnaw of primal hunger. His pulse tripped and raced. He took in a long breath, closed his eyes.

"We met in first grade on the first day of school," he said, seeing the image clearly in his mind. "She was a pixie with an attitude. It rubbed the class bully the wrong way when she ignored his taunting. He picked a fight with her and knocked her flat on her butt. When he went in for the kill, I told him he had to go through me first."

"What happened?"

"He declined." And Alyssa had not thanked Jack for his selfless actions. She'd told him exactly where he could go—until the bell rang and she had no idea where her classroom was. She'd stood there, petrified, afraid to ask for help, afraid to make a mistake. He'd pretended to be talking to himself, giving her directions as he went. She'd followed him like a lost puppy.

"She didn't have a mother," he continued, realizing how easy it had been for them both to fall into a pattern of mutual dependence. "Her father was always too busy. My father was gone. And my mother, well, let's just say, I wasn't her priority. Alyssa and I kind of formed a family by default. She came to my baseball games. I went to her soccer games. We cheered for each other."

"Oh." In the silence, he could almost hear her thoughts trying to classify what he'd told her. And he wasn't sure what he wanted her to glean from the dismal picture he'd painted for her. "You've been a team for a long time."

"Brooke—"

"We'll find who did this." She looked at him, confidence brimming once again. She'd gotten it wrong. He didn't mean to stir her into renewed action.

Eyes scrunched, face determined, she ticked off steps against a mental checklist. "One at a time, we need to let each of them think that we've figured out their secret, see if someone takes the bait. If someone does, we set up a trap and catch him."

"And you learned all those fine police procedures while getting your education degree?" He couldn't decide if he was angry or amused.

"Hey, those little tykes can be a handful at times."

She chuckled and the sound reverberated against his heart, heightening that damnable hunger, stirring fear and longing and a cascade of sensations with no convenient, practical label.

"Brooke?"

He silently cursed. He was getting too involved, forgetting too easily he was supposed to observe and protect. How could he explain the tumbling feelings inside him? How could he tell her he wanted to take her to bed, to ravish her as he'd never ravished a woman without sounding like some sort of sex-crazed maniac? But that was exactly what he wanted to do—lose himself in the wild green of her eyes, feel the softness of her body against his, around his. What would she think of him if she knew his thoughts?

"What?"

But he couldn't share them, because sharing them would be too dangerous. He needed to keep her penned in that little box marked Alyssa's Sister, Do Not Touch. Safer for both of them if he stayed removed and distant. Then why was it so damned hard to achieve? With a force of will, he pushed himself to his feet. "It's been a long day. You should go to bed."

There went those eyes again, green, swirling with warmth and promises he didn't dare linger on too long.

Come with me, sunshine. Share my bed so I don't have to be tortured by your restless movements on the other side of the wall. Impossible, of course. She was Alyssa's sister. He had to protect her—even from himself.

She shook her head with short, troubled strokes. "You go ahead. I'll be down in a few minutes."

"Your day starts at six with a kayak ride," he reminded her as he moved away from her warmth and headed for the cold ladder. The steps creaked under his weight. This was business as much for her as for him. They were both on Alyssa's side, both trying to find out what had happened to her and why. No emotions. No entanglements. A job, just a job.

She grimaced. "Are you sure that's necessary?"

"You're the one who was just insisting we needed to put you front and center to draw out our 'friend.'" Distance. This was better. Easier to handle. "Alyssa-would go."

"Don't remind me."

Was she asking for an out? "No one would fault you for leaving."

"No one but me. I've got to stay. I've just started to learn about Alyssa. There's so much more I don't know. I think…" She shrugged, fingering the edges of the journal now in her lap.

"What?"

She looked at him with such a sad expression his fingers bit into the ladder's wood to keep him from reaching for her. "My mother took the wrong child."

"There's nothing you can do about it now."

"Except find who put Alyssa in a coma."

"You don't have to—"

"I do. I feel I owe her for having so much while she had so little."

"You're telling me your life was a bed of roses?"

"Not exactly, but... You're going to have to help me out with this kayak thing. I've never been in one and I have no idea how they work."

She was withdrawing from him. Just like her sister. Into the dark? He didn't care. He didn't want to know the workings of her mind, her heart, her soul. Nothing good ever came out of the dark—only sadness, and he'd never quite gotten the hang of taming other people's demons.

"I'll be there, sunshine. Every step of the way." She looked so fragile with her satin skin and hair, yet he was beginning to think there definitely was steel beneath the softness.

"Jack?"

He looked up.

"Do you love Alyssa?"

"Yes," he said, then found he couldn't let the lie stand. With just a few words, he would destroy the wall he'd so carefully tried to erect. "I love her like a sister."

Closing his mind to the rush of feelings, knowing he was escaping, he forced himself to continue his descent and go to bed—alone.

THE NEXT MORNING, BOBBING gently at the water's edge, the kayak's opening hardly looked large enough to fit into. Brooke gulped her trepidation and held the paddle behind her with both hands as per Jack's instructions.

Pink still brushed the sky. A lone walker ambled the shoreline. A black lab tagged along, sniffing here and there, then trotted to catch up to its master. Most of the cottages lay in an early-morning mist, the picture of sleepy pastoral serenity.

The gray water lapped cold against her feet. Goose

bumps pebbled her arms and legs despite the wind suit she wore over Alyssa's black-and-red bathing suit. Her breath came in shallow spurts as she fought back the panic of her remembered near-drowning when she was sixteen. She wanted to be anywhere but right here, right now.

"You're sure I can't go for a run instead?" Was the opening getting smaller, the waves larger, or was her imagination playing tricks on her?

"Appearances, remember?" Jack had the audacity to smile, transforming the harsh landscape of his face into a pleasing panorama. "Someone may be watching."

"Yeah, appearances. You're having way too much fun with this."

His chuckle rumbled through her, setting off a chain reaction of absurd longing.

"Kayaking relaxes her, makes her start the day with a positive attitude."

"Don't think it's going to have the same effect on me."

Though Brooke could understand Alyssa's need. She used running on the beach for the same purpose. The communion with brisk air, saltwater, sandy earth and the fire of the sun got her day off on the right foot—even when it rained. There was something about letting the mind wander where it wanted in the openness of nature that did the body good. Maybe she could go for a run later—if she survived this ordeal by kayak. At least he didn't expect her to tackle the lake on her own. His own kayak waited on the shore.

"Can you promise me I won't get wet?" Brooke asked, doubt pooling acid in the pit of her stomach.

Jack tried not to smile, but wasn't very successful at it. "Chances are you won't."

"That's real helpful."

He tweaked her nose playfully. "Don't think I'll let you try an Eskimo roll your first time out, though."

"How comforting! What next?"

"Squat down facing the bow."

Holding the boat steady, he waited for her to comply. "Reach across the cockpit and hook the thumb of your left hand—no, keep gripping the paddle shaft, too."

Her cast reached only to her elbow, but still made maneuvering awkward. "What do you take me for, an acrobat?"

He was too near. He was too far. She'd never been a great athlete, but neither had she been a total klutz. Now there seemed to be a short circuit somewhere between her mind and her muscles.

"You've got it. Hook your thumb under the coaming behind the seat."

"What's a coaming?"

"The lip around the cockpit. Keep your right paddle blade so it rests on the shore. Okay now that you're balanced by the paddle, step sideways into the boat."

The boat bobbed harder under her inexpert movements and her brain fast-forwarded to an image of her splashing headfirst into the water, of the water rolling over her, swallowing her, dragging her down and down and down. She shuddered, dismissing the memory with a sharp shake of her head.

Jack steadied the kayak with one hand, her with the other. Her knees wobbled in response, setting the boat in motion again.

"You're doing fine. Lower yourself on the seat. Extend your legs forward until your feet touch the foot braces. Feel them?"

She nodded, more aware of his hand on her lower back than the pegs beneath her rubber sports sandals.

"Rest your knees against the knee braces. Swing your paddle around in front of you. There you go. You're all set."

"It's moving."

"It's supposed to."

She gripped the paddle with all her might, not budging a muscle, praying with fervency that the kayak wouldn't overturn. "Oh, God. I'm going to fall in."

"No, you're not. It's a very stable boat. You're an expert at this, remember?"

He waded into the water to his knees and stood next to her. He looked like a Renaissance sculpture in his gray neoprene shortie—chiseled straight out of granite and not leaving much to the imagination. A suit like that on a body like his ought to be outlawed.

Rubbing the back of her neck, he bent down as if to whisper a secret. A playful glint flickered in his eyes. This was part of the game, part of the show. Should anyone be watching, they would look like the lovers they were pretending to be. He'd warned her before they set off they'd have to perform as expected.

Taking her cue from him, she smiled up, fabricating a cheer she didn't feel, swallowing the acid rising up from her stomach. "Alyssa's an expert. I'm, well, not."

"It's not that hard. You'll get the hang of it in no time. Keep smiling, sunshine. You're supposed to be having fun."

"The time of my life."

Jack got into his own boat with swift ease. His movements were graceful and effortless as he paddled next to her. The muscles of his arms gleamed in the soft morning light. She was struck once more with the lean efficiency of his body.

"Hold your paddle like so. Now all you have to do is a cycling movement of your arms and shoulders so you alternate dipping your paddle in and bringing it forward."

"Easy for you to say. You don't have a cast on one arm." Her personal flotation device made her feel like a giant marshmallow, and along with her water-protected cast, hampered the ease of her movements.

He oared away and she almost reached out for the side of his kayak to keep it locked to hers.

"Lean forward a bit," he called softly. His gaze narrowed past her and skimmed the resort's horizon. Did he see anything out of place? "That's good. Don't slouch. Keep your head up."

"What do you see?"

"Nothing. Don't look at the paddles, look ahead."

That was a mistake. Looking forward made it seem as if the horizon jounced, giving her a slight case of motion sickness.

Don't look at the shore, look at the water. That didn't help, either.

The water was wet, dark, slippery. The shallow, undulating waves appeared to form a sleek, pewter creature who slithered as it surrounded her, ready and waiting to devour her should she make a mistake and roll this rickety craft over. The ripples from her paddle played on her imagination and gave the watery monster life.

Enough! For today, you're Alyssa. She loves the water. She's confident on the water. She's good at kayaking. Someone is out there watching. Someone who needs to believe you're Alyssa. Give it your best effort.

Brooke ignored her body's tension, the sweat slicking her palms, the dryness in her throat needing constant lubrication, and concentrated on smiling and stroking the water with the paddle. Her casted arm made the right dip more difficult, making the kayak go in a less than perfect line.

"Don't stroke so hard with your left arm and it'll even out the path."

Right! Nothing was going to even out the rolling in her stomach. This was not fun. But if Alyssa could do it, she would, too. Jack expected her to make this work. He was giving up his vacation time to protect her. The least she could do was try to flush out Alyssa's stalker.

Jack showed her various maneuvers—how to turn, how to slow down, how to reverse. Before she knew it, the shore was no longer within wading distance. Her movements grew easier. Part of her relaxed, giving in to the steady rhythm of paddling, the slurp of water around the oar, the sibilant slip of fiberglass through water. Even the shore didn't seem to bounce as much.

"I can see why Alyssa enjoys this," Brooke said, resting her paddle on the boat's bow.

"Kind of grows on you." Jack took a break, too.

The current bobbed them slowly backward. The sun had burned away most of the morning mist and the resort was coming to life. "Stephanie mentioned all of you paddled up to Devil's Grin."

"Devil's Run is joined to the lake by an artery called Devil's Arm." He pointed up ahead with his paddle. "I don't think you're ready for that."

He sounded distracted and his gaze remained on the boat ramp where Devil's Arm emptied into the lake. Two trucks and a sport utility vehicle were parked in the lot. A man fished from a canoe. Two teenagers were unloading kayaks from the back of one truck.

"What's wrong?" Brooke asked, observing the scene, but seeing nothing out of place.

"That's Cullen's SUV."

The bright red paint gleamed in the sunlight. "Fancy."

"Got to impress the clients."

"Is it unusual for him to be here?"

"This early, yeah."

"Want to check it out? See and be seen."

"Might as well."

They paddled closer to the shore. Cullen sat on a boulder, dipping a fishing line into the lake. As he spotted them, he waved a greeting.

"Up early?" Jack said as they neared. His demeanor was friendly, but his gaze was all business.

"Never went to bed."

"Rough night?"

"Hot date." Cullen smirked suggestively. "Got to get some relaxation in before heading to the office. How's the water?"

"Great!" Brooke said, surprised she meant it. "How are the fish biting?"

"They're avoiding me." Cullen laughed and shrugged. "Where are you off to?"

"Devil's Grin." Brooke studied Cullen's face, noted the slight rise of eyebrow.

Cullen shaded his eyes against the sun with a hand, hiding his expression. "Revisiting the scene of the crime?"

Scene of the crime? An unfortunate turn of phrase or a deeper knowing? Everyone had been told Alyssa's fall had been ruled an accident. Brooke shrugged as if nothing mattered. "Seeing if it'll spark some memory."

"Maybe that's not such a good idea." Cullen frowned, bobbed his line up and down in the water.

Jack's kayak bumped against hers. "That's what I've been trying to tell her."

"He thinks I'm too fragile." Brooke scrunched her nose in mock disgust.

"He's always read you wrong." Cullen's face grew serious. The brown of his eyes burned with a feverish zeal that made her want to recoil. "You're the toughest person I know."

"Thanks. I think."

The somber expression disappeared and was replaced by a gleaming smile, showing off a neat row of white, even teeth. "It's a compliment. But you were never good at taking them. At least not from me." Cullen glanced at his watch. "Guess I'd better get going if I want to get a shower in before the Bells and their two terrors show up at my office door."

"Lauren's parents are looking to buy?" Jack asked, clueing her to a fact she should know.

Cullen reeled in his line. "They figured they've spent the last eight summers here, they might as well buy."

"You'll only have one terror," Brooke said. "Lauren's coming over this morning for some craft brainstorming."

"That's a relief." He shouldered his fishing pole and waved. "See you later."

As they paddled away, Brooke asked, "What do you think?"

"About what?"

"Cullen. Was he watching us, or was he really fishing?"

"Hard to say."

"Then we need to find out."

"Paddling up to Devil's Grin isn't going to accomplish anything."

"If he's guilty, he'll follow us. He'll want to know if I remember anything."

This was her chance to prove to herself she could stand on her own two feet—or paddle with her own two arms, as the case may be. Tempting fate up Devil's Arm and Devil's Run was not her ideal way to spend a morning, but Alyssa would; therefore, she needed to. Determined, she headed for the mouth of the river.

"Okay, that's far enough." Jack reached across and snagged the grab loop on her bow. "You don't have to prove anything to anybody."

Except to myself. "Alyssa would go back to the scene of the accident."

He pointed at her cast. "You're injured."

"Alyssa would go injured or not. You said so yourself."

"You'll be paddling upstream."

His face was intent, focused; his will piercing—as agonizing to bear as the fear sitting heavy and uncomfortable on her shoulders. She'd always given in—to her mother, to the bullies of this world, to her fears—because it was easier, simpler to give in. There were no battles in surrender, no shots, no blood. Barely a ripple on the sea of life. But something in her was crying now, wanted to come out, wanted to be heard. If she turned away, if she yielded, if she gave up another slice of herself, what would be left?

Defiance lifted her chin. "Weren't you the one telling me I'm an expert?"

"Look—"

"If Cullen is watching us, then he'll expect us to go. He knows Alyssa. He knows what she'd do."

"Another day. This is your first time out."

"It's our chance to draw Cullen out. Make him make a mistake. Make him think I'm remembering things he might not want me to."

"The current—"

"Today it's the current. Tomorrow it'll be something else. You want to protect me. That's your choice. My job is to draw out this person with murder on his mind. It's my choice. You can't keep me under glass or you won't ever catch your criminal. Give me room, Jack. Let me go."

Without waiting for an answer, she flipped his grip from the grab loop with her paddle, dragged her oar through the water, and pushed past him. A surge of adrenaline rushed hotly through her. Her heart thumped hard in her chest. Her pulse drummed madly.

Alyssa would do this.

And for now, she reminded herself yet again, she was Alyssa.

Chapter Ten

Cursing, Jack followed Brooke up Devil's Arm. She was proving to be as much a magnet for trouble as her sister. He should send her home before she got herself in a situation she couldn't handle.

But he couldn't. Not if her presence gave him a chance to catch a criminal. For the umpteenth time he reminded himself that he'd made a promise to Alyssa, and intended to keep it.

Still, he was becoming too involved, finding it harder and harder to maintain the necessary distance needed to get through this unbearable situation. He tightened his grip around his paddle. What he needed was a break—one clue, one mistake that would crack this case wide-open. So far nothing had turned up on the truck—not on the computer, not at any body shop in the area. He was still waiting for the state lab report on the rope. And there would be more waiting while the poem page was analyzed.

In the meantime, someone had to protect Brooke from her reckless self.

As they paddled on to Devil's Run, in his peripheral vision, Jack spied Cullen's SUV backing away from the boat ramp. Instead of going left toward town, Cullen turned right and was hugging the highway. Slowly, way too slowly for a man with a collection of speeding tickets.

Was Brooke right? Had Cullen's jealousy where Alyssa was concerned finally driven him to attempt murder? But this type of crime required planning, patience, and Cullen wasn't long on either. He was more apt to lash out in the heat of the moment. What could Alyssa have done to him to bring out this methodical side of his personality?

"Slow down," Jack shouted to Brooke, letting his frustration seep through.

Putting her all into each stroke, she glanced at him over her shoulder. "Will you grab my boat again?"

"No." He caught up with her and let his kayak glide next to hers—as if keeping himself between her and Cullen on the highway would save her from a fate similar to Alyssa's. "Are you always this stubborn?"

The vibrancy of her sunshine smile snuck through his resistance once more, catching him unaware, soaking him with warmth.

"As a matter of fact, I'm just learning."

"Great." Why couldn't she have picked someone else to practice her new found independence on? The last time one of the Snowden sisters had tried to strike out on her own, she'd ended up in a coma. He didn't need this right now.

Giving a wide berth to the eddy created by mountain runoff cascading into river, he guided her past Devil's Falls. Cullen hung back, using scattered bushes as ineffective camouflage. Who did he think he was kidding?

As they rounded the curve into the relative calm of the bay, Devil's Grin stood before them in all its savage splendor. The curved ridge midway up gave the one hundred fifty foot sloping rock face its name. Worn smooth by wind and weather, the lip formed more of a smirk than a smile, almost as if the granite dared them to climb it. The cracks, scars and horns slashing the dark facade added to the pockmarked look of evil.

But for all its apparent menace, Devil's Grin was an easy ascent—especially for the six of them. The group had been hiking and rock climbing together through the New Hampshire wilderness since high school.

The only difference between that day and the thousands of other outings they'd gone on before was that one of their friends had had malice on their mind. Malice that had nearly turned into murder.

"Is this it?" Brooke asked, staring up at the rock facade, awe etched into her face. "Devil's Grin?"

"This is it." A chill went through him as his gaze scaled the rock.

"Where?" she asked tentatively.

He didn't have to ask what she meant. The spot was etched in his memory. "Just before the lip."

He pointed to the edge of the crooked rock smile. "It was a practice run for a group of businessmen we were taking out on a team-building exercise the next weekend. She was supposed to climb to the lip, then let herself fall, showing the clients the proper positions of arms and legs."

"She didn't make it that high?"

He shook his head. "The rope stuck. She lost her balance trying to free it." Having traversed away from protection, the unexpected fall had swung her like a pendulum. Her weight coming down on to the rope had spun her like a top. Her right side had smacked against the rock. "She hit her head." And she'd dangled from her rope like a broken doll.

"You went up to get her."

"Yes." He'd seen the mark on the rope. The sheath was torn. With unnerving pings, the nylon filaments below were unraveling one by one. A few seconds longer and Alyssa would have plummeted to the ground to her death.

"That's when she told you about someone wanting to kill her."

"Yes."

The rope. They got me.

I'll take care of it.

I was warned, Alyssa gulped. *Sticks and stones will break my bones.*

She'd tried to laugh, but only a rough rasp came out and it couldn't erase the sheer terror in her eyes, the blood pouring from the gash on her temple. There had been no time to ask why, to pry for details. His first priority had been getting her down safely. But before they reached the ground, Alyssa slipped into a coma.

At the river's edge, he and Brooke bobbed on the water. She studied the rock so intently, Jack wondered what she was seeing.

"The planned fall, everybody knew about it?" she asked.

"It was part of the exercise."

He couldn't remember exactly who had thought up the stunt. Cullen wasn't big on preventive precautions. Tim lived with the constant fear of being sued. Trish wanted things neatly tied, signed and sealed. But it was Stephanie who was most concerned with the human element of their part-time adventure business. She wanted everyone to feel comfortable and safe.

"They knew Alyssa would lead," Brooke said.

"It was her turn."

Brooke nodded pensively. "What happened when you got here?"

Each of her questions excavated a new layer of guilt. "To this spot?"

She turned to him, fixed her gaze on him and nodded. The determination imprinted on her face belied the fragility of spirit he'd come to associate with her, creating confusion within his own mind. He had the sudden impression that if she truly put her mind to something, she would succeed and nothing and no one could get in her way. Not even him.

His gaze returned to the rocky beach. The whole event came back to him like watching a video. The regular banter between Cullen and Stephanie had irritated him that day because his mind was heavy with worry for Alyssa's unusually thick cloud of sadness. She'd looked like his mother on the day she died, so helpless, so troubled, and so uncharacteristically closed-off.

"We'd taken a picnic lunch because that's what we'd planned to do with the businessmen. Thrill with a view, Tim called this exercise. The appearance of risk with all the comforts of home was Stephanie's take on the day. She'd made sandwiches. Trish brought fruit, some carrot sticks. Tim was in charge of napkins, garbage bags and water. Cullen brought along some wine, even though he was supposed to bring sodas. I had the climbing gear. And Alyssa provided the kayaks."

"Did she drink any wine?"

"No, she's not stupid. She's usually safe and focused when climbing."

I don't think you should lead this climb. Jack held on to the sling racked with the gear Alyssa would need to scale the face.

Why not? It's my turn to lead.

Our conversation last night.

Alyssa waved his comment away, and reached for the gear rack. He didn't let go, and she sighed with exasperation. That was the beer talking.

The beer then.

I'm not hungover. I'm fine. Everything's fine.

Jack looked up at the top of the stance. From up there, the view was magnificent. A blanket of green forest spread out, broken only by dark amoeba-shaped lakes and squiggles of rivers. To the north, the White Mountains poked at the sky. To the south, the world stretched on forever. "She loved the view from mountaintops. She said it made her feel as if she could fly."

Sit this one out. He checked her rope, her knots. In your frame of mind, you'll get impatient.

You'll be there.

Alyssa—

Please, Jack, let me go. I need this. I need to touch the sky.

And when she'd looked at him with those sad eyes, when he could feel her pain, when he knew that climbing calmed her down, focused her, how could he have done anything other than let her climb? So he'd relented and let her go.

And guided her to her near demise.

"So everyone had access to the rope," Brooke said, cutting into his self-indulgent thoughts.

"Everyone." He'd seen nothing wrong with the rope. How could he possibly have missed such a blatant clue?

"Where's the rope now?"

"The Fish and Game officers took it as part of their investigation. I'm still waiting on a report."

"Oh."

Jack had come back to Devil's Grin several times after the accident. To collect his gear. To look for clues. To examine every inch of ground and rock. Nothing had shown up. And being here again was a sharp reminder of how little progress he'd made. He was missing something—something that should be obvious.

And this closeness to the subject now blinded him to what might otherwise be obvious. His only hope, his greatest fear, was that the taste of revenge was so great, the would-be murderer would strike again—at Brooke.

Looking at her, he felt more of his precious distance melting. Her hair rippled with light under the breeze's soft whisper. Her cheeks were pinkening under the sun's golden kiss. The green of her eyes was alive with spring-like fervor. And he was falling deeper under the spell of her vital energy.

He wanted her. Had never wanted a woman with such keen hunger. Could no longer deny the plain and simple fact. But he also knew he could not have her. Not while she was under his care. Not while her life was in danger.

And after, while one of his own friends rotted in jail for the crime of Alyssa's attempted murder, Brooke would fly home, to her mother, to her sister.

The thought sobered him, saddened him, simmered a slow boil of unwanted anger.

"Let's go," he said. "There's nothing to be done here."

With a quick maneuver, he did an about-face and headed midriver. Distracted by Cullen's creeping SUV, his stroke hitched. Pushed by the current, Jack was pulled into an eddy, crashed against a jutting boulder.

Just a bump. Nothing much. He dipped his oar in the water. He pushed away from the rock. The crunching sound wasn't right. He leaned forward to take a closer look.

A patch on the front of his kayak popped off, shoving the boat sideways.

He saw the keeper hole, but before he could put his paddle into the water, the kayak was sucked in.

BROOKE WATCHED HELPLESSLY as Jack disappeared in the froth of water battering a ring of boulders with deadly intent. Had he hurt his head? Was he drowning? Fear, rampant and nauseating, surged through her.

"Jack!"

Paddling madly, awkwardly, she headed toward where she'd last seen him.

"Jack!"

Afraid to take her gaze away from the spot where he'd vanished, she didn't notice the water moving faster beneath her, the roil of foam from the waterfalls, the multiplying number of rocks.

"Jack!" she called, until her throat was raw from the effort.

A good-size boulder rushed toward her. She strained to avoid it. Her movements were jerky. Her paddle stroked air, unbalancing her. She lurched, overcorrecting. And the kayak rolled over, dumping her out of the boat, plunging her underwater.

The blue of the sky turned to black. Water roared all around her, dark and heavy. It sucked at her, pulled at her. Her arms and legs fought madly for purchase in the heavy water.

She was at the mercy of the river. In spite of her floatation device, she was going down.

She screamed her terror. Cold water choked her. Her lungs burned. Her mind spun wildly.

She was drowning. She was drowning!

No! Not again. Not this time. Fight! Live! Arms flaying, she reached out for anything that would stop her downward rush. The harder she struggled, the faster she fell.

Relax. Relax. Relax!

But instinct fought logic and the pulling of water increased. The water monster. It was eating her alive. *I want to live!*

One flaying hand bumped against the face of the rock as she passed it. Fighting despair, Brooke forced her limbs to calm. Her rear touched bottom. Water pushed her away from the rock. She rolled over and tried to swim up, but was sucked back down. She tried again. And again. With each passing second she grew more desperate for air.

I don't want to die, her mind sobbed with anguish.

Relax, Brooke. Relax. The voice came to her softly, a

flutter on her mind, and suddenly she grew calm, stopped fighting.

This time when she touched bottom, she pushed off the rock with her feet, and stroked downstream with the current.

Sun gleamed on the water's silver surface and she headed toward the light. Lungs bursting, she exploded out of the water, sputtered and gulped in air by greedy mouthfuls. Treading water, she oriented herself and swam toward the nearest shore.

She fought the current, but unbalanced by her cast, she was pushed closer and closer to the whirlpool of rocks and water spewing from the waterfalls. Her arms were tiring, but she defied her fatigue, and finally felt the river bottom beneath her feet.

Standing on shaky legs, she stumbled through the churning water and stepped on the rough shore. But she couldn't rest. Heart thudding, she used a hand to shade her eyes, and scoured the river, looking for Jack.

Then through the sparkling mist of water from the falls, she saw him, a frantic silhouette diving and surfacing. She gave a cry of relief. Never had a sight seemed more magnificent.

"Jack!" she yelled, jumping up and down to attract his attention. "Jack!"

He stopped, stared, then swam toward her in bold, powerful strokes. And when he reached shore, she launched herself at him, wet body against wet body, flung her arms around his neck, nearly clobbering him with her cast, and hung on to him as if she were hanging on to life itself.

"I thought you were gone," she croaked. "I thought you drowned."

His arms wrapped around her waist. His head snuggled against hers. His breathing was harsh and ragged against her skin.

"I thought you were gone," she whispered harshly, still feeling the raw, primal fear stampeding through her.

Then, as she hung on to Jack, she did what she hated most. She cried. A torrent of tears poured from her freely, unstoppable.

"I thought you were drowning," she bawled, holding him tighter, not really understanding why this near loss was ripping her apart.

"Shh."

Great sobs racked her chest. Shivers rattled through her. And the pain of almost losing Jack cracked whatever reserve of restraint was left in her.

She kissed him. Kissed his neck, his ear, his cheek. Her fingers tangled roughly in his wet hair. She found his mouth, found warmth, found heaven.

Her own breathing loud in her ears, she relished the taste of him, the roughness of his day-old beard against her cheeks, her wrists. A soft moaning sound of need escaped her throat.

"I thought I'd lost you," she mumbled against the hunger of his mouth. And knew she'd gone and done the most reckless thing in her life—she'd fallen in love with a man who was all wrong for her.

AGAINST THE BACKGROUND of the river and waterfall, old as eternity, beating against the rocks, wearing down, Jack was swept into a riptide of emotion.

In Brooke's arms, he was drowning in tides of passion and couldn't seem to rescue himself. Didn't want to be rescued. Not even when the waves of emotions were stealing his breath, making his heart pound, mushing his brain from lack of oxygen. Kissing Brooke like this was wrong. He couldn't afford the emotional toll. Yet he couldn't stop.

He'd almost lost her.

When her empty kayak had smacked against him after

his own less than graceful capsize, he'd frozen, then his stomach had knotted with nauseating tightness. Horrible, vivid images of her drowning, of her being battered against the rocks, of her lifeless body washing up on the beach had paralyzed him. Then he'd grown frantic searching for her, diving again and again into the cold, black water. He'd been crazy with the thought that he'd lost her to the river, to his own carelessness.

When he saw her on the shore, he'd nearly buckled with relief. His only thought was to reach her, hold her, and yell at her for taking ten years off his life.

The last thing he should be doing was kissing her. But, God help him, he couldn't keep his hands off her. They stroked, they learned, they memorized every delectable curve of her warm and wet body, reassuring him with every sizzling stroke that she was alive.

Afraid of water as she was, she'd fought for survival and instead of falling apart once she got back on shore, she'd worried. About him.

"I'm sorry." Her voice was gentle against his skin, reverberating against his neck as intimately as the pulse of his own blood. "So sorry. I should have listened to you. I wasn't ready. I shouldn't have… I was…I was trying…"

"It doesn't matter." He kissed her again, deeply, possessively. He felt her soften against him, felt his heavy, male satisfaction at her response, and knew he shouldn't have answered the primal call of base instincts. If he allowed this to continue, his own survival would be at risk.

"It matters. It matters a lot."

Heart still thundering in his chest, he skimmed his hands against her face and held her still. "No, it doesn't. What matters is that you're okay."

She nodded. Her grip on his shoulder loosened. She turned her glittering gaze to the shore along the highway. "Cullen…he followed us."

"He did." And the why would have to be addressed, but not here, not now. Need was still swimming strong between them, but his savage pulse was slowing and logic was returning. He had to get her home, keep her safe.

"He's the one then." She pushed away. Her eyes were fiery with warrior passion. Not for him, he realized with a sinking sensation, but for the fight. She'd picked her quarry and was ready to do battle. "He has to be. Why else would he have followed us?"

"You're jumping to conclusions."

Driven by her certainty, she shook her head. "We have to set a trap, corner him, force him to act."

"We need to analyze this. We can't go making accusations."

She nodded, distracted. "We'll wait until he's out with clients and search his house."

"Breaking and entering is against the law."

"So is attempted murder."

"We have no proof."

"He followed us."

Swearing, he raked a hand through his wet hair. "Brooke—"

She looked at him with her eyes wide, her feelings raw, open, and he was on that edge again, ready to lose himself in her sheer vitality all over again. "You could have died, Jack. You could have drowned."

I did. In your kiss.

And I didn't mind one bit.

"I'm an experienced kayaker. I was never in danger." He wanted to kiss her again, to feel her melt against him. But growing up in his father's criminal shadow, in his mother's tearful house, in this busybody town, he'd learned to do one thing well—hide his emotions.

For all of their sakes, he would have to suppress the depth of his feelings for Brooke now. Because she might be right and their list of suspects might just have been narrowed down to one.

A bully who always picked on the weak.

And *his* weakness right now was his fierce feelings for Brooke. He'd also become too predictable. He always used the same kayak. A kayak he'd bought for himself and stored at the Comfort Pines boathouse for convenience. Cullen would have known that, could have loosened the patch during his sleepless night.

Whoever had tampered with his boat had done a master job—just like the rope.

In first grade he'd told Cullen that to get to Alyssa he would have to go through him. Was Cullen sending the message that he was prepared to do so?

Chapter Eleven

Ordinarily Brooke wouldn't have gone back in the water, would have refused to go near the source of her close call with death. But after Jack had rescued both kayaks, recovered one set of paddles, then hidden his broken boat to be retrieved later, he'd set her on top of the remaining kayak and paddled them both home. With Jack's strong arms around her, holding her balanced, a feeling of self-confidence quickened in her in a way she could not explain. She was actually a little sad when they arrived back at the resort.

When they reached the cottage, Lauren was waiting for them on the freshly repaired step.

"What took you so long?" Lauren asked, her forehead creased in an odd mixture of anger and delight. That was what Brooke liked about children—they hadn't learned yet the strict adult codes of proper conduct and their emotions shone through their little faces like lights.

Daisy whimpered and tugged at her leash, determined to soak someone with her eager tongue.

"We had a little adventure we didn't expect. Come on inside. Have your parents left yet?"

"Hey, how did you know they were going somewhere?"

Brooke tweaked Lauren's nose. "Magic."

Lauren rose and whipped her arm from behind her back, presenting Brooke with a squashed muffin in a napkin.

"For me?" Brooke said, smiling.

Lauren nodded. "I saved it."

Brooke took the offering. "Blueberry. My favorite. How did you know?"

Lauren grinned widely. "Magic."

Jack unlocked the door and checked the house as if he expected someone to be hiding in a closet ready to pounce. Brooke settled Lauren at the kitchen table with a glass of juice and an arts and crafts book, Daisy with a rawhide bone from a stash she'd found in a cupboard, and headed toward Alyssa's room to change. Jack appeared next to her, but kept his distance. His muscles were tight and drawn, and she couldn't keep the small smile of satisfaction from reaching her lips.

"Don't leave the house without telling me," he said.

His expression was stark, unreadable. But Brooke had the private satisfaction of knowing his secret, the validation that her instincts weren't completely awry. With his steely control, Jack was denying the hot magma that flowed through his veins and had coursed unchecked at the falls.

In his kiss, his feelings had surfaced from great depths and poured through every touch, every possessive claim of hand and tongue, every powerful beat of his big heart. His own emotions frightened him. And that fear, that vulnerability had made her ache with tenderness for him, made her want to prove to him he had nothing to fear by loving her, by showing his feelings.

But she understood he needed to slip back into his cool detachment, to protect himself from what he didn't quite yet understand. She would give him time. He could not have kissed her that way if he didn't care for her. He could change. He could learn to show the enormous well of sensations residing in his heart. She knew he could. But she also realized that the change had to come from him to be permanent. Dealing with her mother had taught her that much. And Alyssa still stood between them, would stand between them until the mystery of her accident was resolved.

For now it was enough to know that she'd touched him as deeply as he'd touched her.

"I wasn't planning on going anywhere."

He nodded once. "I've got calls to make."

"I'll be here." She smiled.

He frowned, spun on his heels and disappeared into his room.

IN ALYSSA'S MAKESHIFT HOME office, trying his best to forget the gut-warming glow of Brooke's smile, Jack searched for paper.

How could Alyssa live like this? There were piles everywhere—on the desk, on the chair, on the floor, on the file cabinet, under the bed, in the closet—and none of them seemed to be constructed out of logic. Negatives were mixed with prints, receipts with order forms, books with random pieces of paper. He'd even found something that looked strangely like a high school essay. Even given her two-week absence, her wall calendar was three months behind. How did she find anything?

He'd spent hours trying to help her get organized after her father's stroke, setting up color-coded files to ease her tasks, rearranging her desk and supplies in bins and organizers for maximum efficiency. His effort seemed to have been for nothing.

After he and Brooke had found Alyssa's threatening note, he'd searched through her file cabinet for clues, could not make heads nor tails of her system and eventually gave up trying to find anything useful there.

He finally located a pad of paper amid a stack of empty file folders under the daybed. After clearing a space on the desk, he started two lists: one with the facts of the case so far, the other of things to do.

Interviewing friends who'd become suspects had gotten him nowhere. Inspecting the crime scene, every inch of Alyssa's climb, time and again had yielded no new clues. The rope had been his. He'd been there, seen the accident happen. He knew the time, the place, the weapon of choice. The usual analysis of forensic evidence wasn't going to get him anywhere. He already knew any prints would belong to one of them. He knew there had been an intent to commit murder behind the assault, had proof of it in Alyssa's words and in the bloody note.

What he didn't have was concrete motive.

Which led him back to his suspects. None of whom had attempted to flee. None of whom had made a mistake—so far.

What had Alyssa done? What had she seen? What had she heard?

There were no clues beyond the note, and a wish list. And a rope. His rope.

The sound of giggling came through the closed door. Jack turned to it, taking in the joyful noise. He rose, opened the door. To keep an eye on them, he told himself as he sat back down. Keeping them safe was, after all, his job.

He glanced at his lists once more and picked up the phone. His first call was to Rafe Bates at the Comfort Marina.

"What do you mean the patch popped? I fixed that sucker myself. It should have held through Armageddon."

"That was my thought, too. I want you to have a look at it and give me your take on it."

"When can you get here?"

"After lunch."

"I'll be waiting."

Jack heard Rafe swear as he hung up. Rafe was proud of his work, treated the boats that came to his shop with more care and sensitivity than their owners. If someone could figure out what had caused the patch to pop, Rafe was the man.

Jack overheard Lauren and Brooke talking. He couldn't make out the words, but sensed the warmth of the conversation. He glanced in their direction and found them sitting, Brooke cross-legged, Lauren on her heels, on the living room floor busily cutting up pictures from catalogs. Daisy was sprawled on her side between them, sleeping contentedly. As he listened to them, tension dissolved from between his shoulders.

His next call was to George Stern of George's Garage, the only service station in town, to talk about Alyssa's cut brake line.

"Was a clean cut, it was. It's the only reason I brought it up to her. You know how careless Alyssa can be. Never seen anyone get into as many close calls as she docs. That Jeep of hers looks like it's been through hell and back and it's only a couple of years old." He clucked. "I always say that some people shouldn't be allowed to have a license."

"Back to the brake line, George. Why didn't you tell me about it if you suspected foul play?"

"Not foul play. Not really. I mean, I woulda told you if I thought it was truly foul play. She's a good kid, she is, and I don't want no harm coming to her."

"George—"

"She said she was drivin' on some rough terrain. And between you and me and the fly on the wall, she could make even a paved road seem like an outback trail. Now, don't you sigh at me, young man. I'm just callin' it as I see it. She made me promise I wouldn't tell you. Said you'd give her a lecture and she didn't need another one when she already got one from me. So I fixed it.''

"Did you keep the tampered line?"

"Yep. Got it right here."

"I'll be by this afternoon to look at it."

As he hung up, Jack realized he'd maneuvered his chair to give him a view of Brooke and Lauren in the living room. At that moment, Brooke looked up, caught him in the act of staring at her. She shot him a bright, breezy smile. His heart thudded hard once in his chest. He swiveled away and forced his attention back to his lists.

After a few tries, Jack located Lieutenant Ed O'Hara of the Fish and Game Department.

"How's Eddie?" Jack asked, referring to Ed's son who'd gone and lost himself up on Devil's Back last fall. Jack had tracked the boy to a deep and narrow crevasse. Thinking he could jump over the opening with a full pack on, Eddie had landed short and ended up with a compound fracture of the leg. When Jack found him, Eddie was suffering from blood loss and hypothermia. His condition had been touch-and-go for a few days after he was rescued.

"The leg's almost back to normal." There was a pause. "You're gonna ask for a favor."

"Just checking on the tests you were going to run on the rope and carabiners from the accident at Devil's Grin."

"Still at the lab."

"When do you expect a report?"

"End of July, maybe later. Depends how busy they get with priority cases."

Jack turned the answer over in his mind. An accident like Alyssa's wasn't considered a number one priority. Waiting for the lab results was going to take too long. "What kind of tool might have caused the rope to fray with a good yank?"

Ed cleared his throat. "The fraying was ragged, Jack. All preliminary indications are that the break was due to natural causes."

"You're right, Ed." Jack drummed the eraser of his pencil against the pad of paper listing the logic of his thoughts, of the facts. "I'm going to ask a favor."

"Has new evidence cropped up that you haven't told me about?" Ed asked tentatively.

Asking would complicate his task, make more work for him. Paperwork was a bitch no matter what the profession. But more than speed and a lightened workload, Ed valued truth. Jack was counting on Ed's high moral principles.

"Alyssa Snowden received a note threatening to break her bones a few days before the accident. I'm sending it down to Concord for testing, but I'm not holding my breath for prints."

Through the silence, Jack heard the muted sounds of Ed's office. Though he wanted to rush Ed's answer, experience had shown him the best way to get a yes out of Ed was to let him come to it in his own time.

"All right," Ed said on a long exhale. "I'll see what I can do."

"Thanks, Ed. I really appreciate it."

"Can't make any promises, but one of the techs owes me a favor."

After he hung up, Jack checked Ed off his list and reached for the Manchester phone book to look up Gary Dunning, the computer nerd Alyssa had wanted to consult about Trish.

Lauren and Brooke's voices floated to him once more. Again he turned to them. He found he liked the homey sounds of woman and child. Part of him wanted to join them on the floor and do something crazy like cut up pictures in a magazine, get his fingers messy with glue, drink grape juice from a plastic cup.

A vague memory floated up from the recesses of his mind. His mother. A sandbox. A yellow Tonka dump truck. A matching bulldozer. She was making engine noises as she guided the bulldozer to the truck and dumped a load of sand in the cargo area. Her feet were bare. Her jeans were rolled up. He made a roaring sound as he drove the dump truck to the corner of the sandbox and released the load. They both laughed. When exactly had the laughter stopped?

Jack shook his head and returned to his self-appointed task.

His talk with Gary led him in a circle. Yes, Alyssa had called him. She'd asked him a few questions about his business and the cost of hiring him for a consultation.

"How long ago?" Jack asked.

"A couple of months. She said she'd get back to me and never did. I assumed she decided I was too expensive."

No cutting old friends from back home a deal with this guy. But then back home was someplace Gary had worked hard to leave behind. "Do you know if she wanted to hire you for the resort or for some other project? Did she mention anyone else involved?"

"It sounded as if it was personal."

Jack thanked Gary and hung up, feeling no more enlightened than when he'd started his inquiries.

He drummed his pencil, made more notes, thought back to the kayak incident that morning, to Cullen's interest, to Brooke and how unprepared she was to deal with someone like Cullen. She might have some steel in her spine, but she was too trusting, too open, too easily trapped in emotional storms. And that made her an easy target for someone hard and driven like Cullen, for someone with revenge on his mind.

Reluctantly Jack picked up the phone one more time and

placed a call to Matt Bender, an ex-cop turned private detective. Once Matt finished watching Brooke for him while he went out, Cullen would now have a tail. If he made any move toward Brooke, he would be stopped.

JACK EMERGED FROM HIS ROOM just as Brooke and Lauren were cleaning up after making a treasure keeper from some empty chocolate sampler boxes Brooke had discovered in the pantry. Lauren was pleased with her effort. She'd glued animals and flowers all over hers, and as her first treasure, she'd placed the leftover inch of Daisy's chew stick inside.

Daisy stirred from her nap, and tail wagging wildly, headed for Jack. She got several licks in before he turned her over and scratched at her belly, sending her to doggy heaven, judging by her contented grunts.

"I've got to go out for a couple of hours." Jack wore his business face once more. She thought she'd seen him relax while he was on the phone. The set of his shoulders hadn't been as tight, the lines on his face not quite so tautly drawn. "I don't want you to go anywhere until I get back."

Brooke placed the last of the catalog cuttings into a garbage bag and handed the scissors and modge podge pot to Lauren. "I'm going to walk Lauren home in a few minutes."

"I'll do it."

Scooping up her own treasure keeper decorated with daisies, sunflowers and Anne Geddes babies, she got up. "It's only a couple of cottages down."

"I said I'd do it."

Her brows rose in question. Had something happened while he was on the phone? "What's up?"

"Nothing. I just want to know you're safe."

She studied his face, found no enlightenment in his features. Watching over her was starting to take its toll, and she didn't know what to do to lighten his burden. "Okay. Let me find Daisy's leash and they'll be ready to go."

"Is Jack the boss of you now?" Lauren asked as she followed her into the kitchen.

Brooke laughed. "No, I just let him think he is."

"I'm serious, Brooke," Jack said. "I want you to stay here."

She looked at him over her shoulder. "I know. I've got some reading to finish. Don't worry about me."

Five minutes later, the craft idea was boldly inserted on the weekly schedule for next week, the neon-yellow leash was secured to Daisy's collar, Lauren's treasure box was safely tucked under her arm. Lauren reached up for Jack's hand. As if he'd done the task a hundred times before, his hand folded gently over hers.

"I'm taking Al—your Jeep. I'll be back by three," he said. "If I get tied up, I'll call."

"I'll be here."

She watched them walk down the path toward the beach, man, child and dog. He was a good man. A little overprotective, but a good man. Someday he would make a terrific father.

She sighed and moved away from the sight. Or maybe it was all an illusion. Maybe she'd seen the heat, the desire, the vulnerability in his eyes because she'd wanted to see them. Maybe she saw not the man he could be, but the man she wanted him to be.

Brooke, Brooke, Brooke. She could see her mother tutting and shaking her head, her disapproval vivid in every perfect line of her face. *How do you get yourself in these situations?*

"I don't know, Mom," she answered the ghost of her mother as she headed toward the kitchen. "Maybe because I care."

And no matter how many times she got hurt, she just kept on trying again and again. When would she learn?

Brooke fixed herself a sandwich and retrieved a couple of Alyssa's journals from the attic nook. Feet tucked under her on the love seat, she read.

Through the illustrated journals, Brooke was getting to know her sister. Alyssa's fears, her relationships, her suspicions became part of her. The sadness and loneliness that seemed to dwell in her sister's soul echoed eerily through her. They might have grown up separated by three thousand miles, but they had each shared a cold and lonely upbringing at the hand of their parent.

The more she read, the more it seemed as if Alyssa feared happiness. Whenever it came too close, it appeared as if she felt she had to punish herself. Brooke recognized her own coping mechanism against hurt, pain and disappointment. But whereas Alyssa punished herself by hurting the people close to her, Brooke went out of her way to please. Alyssa sought conflict; Brooke avoided it.

Neither strategy had worked. Both had ended up feeling somehow deficient. Would this have happened if they'd had each other to turn to?

On the small pad she kept in her purse, Brooke took notes on each of their suspects. Alyssa wrote of Cullen's eely business ethic, of a sensitive secret Tim hid, of Trish's annoying need to best her, of Stephanie's stupid infatuation with Cullen, of Rick's—Trish's brother—inappropriate fixation on her before his death.

And she wrote of Jack, giving Brooke a whole new insight into the man who tried so hard not to feel.

He was a man of his word. If he made a promise, he kept it. That fact had come through in Alyssa's writings, and Brooke took a deep comfort in such basic principles. Brooke was also starting to understand why Alyssa hadn't shared her fears with Jack. Her emotional need for this man, for his support ran deeper than even Jack probably suspected. He was her anchor in this world that seemed so harsh and cruel to her. And if her plans to leave had indeed been real this time, maybe she'd been trying to shed her dependence on this strong man to see if she could stand on her own.

Just as Brooke herself was trying to do now.

Maybe they weren't as different as Brooke had thought they were.

A car stopping beside the cottage tore Brooke away from her reading. Trish climbed out of a silver Trooper, a plate of cookies in one hand.

"Made a batch of double chocolate, chocolate chunk cookies and thought I'd drop some by. I know they're your favorite," Trish said as Brooke opened the door.

"That's sweet of you."

Trish shrugged. "An excuse, really. I wanted to see how you were doing."

Brooke invited Trish in. "I'm doing great. I've got iced tea in the fridge. Do you want some?"

"Got coffee?"

Did she? With their adventure this morning, they'd skipped that awful morning coffee ritual, but surely if Alyssa drank the stuff, there would be some in the kitchen. The question was, where? "Sure. I'll make a pot."

Brooke filled the coffeemaker with water and searched the cupboards for coffee grounds. "What brings you out here in the middle of a workday?"

"That's the thing about owning your own company— you make your own hours. Besides, I had to get away. Tomorrow's the anniversary of Rick's death, and Mom's insane with grief. She's been over crying her eyes out. I finally put her to bed and decided to drown in chocolate."

"I'm so sorry to hear about your mother." Did Trish

resent her mother's tears? Or did the messy show of grief heighten Trish's own sense of loss?

"It's to be expected. He was her only son."

"You're her only daughter."

Trish shrugged, and Brooke wondered at the relationship Trish shared with her mother. Had this been another point of connection with Alyssa? Alyssa's mother had abandoned her; Trish's favored the eldest son.

"While I was mixing the batch of death by chocolate," Trish said, smiling sadly, "I thought about you, how you'd be sad, too, and decided to see how you were doing."

This was not good. She hadn't gotten that far in Alyssa's journals yet. She knew enough about Rick's death, what had caused it. She had no feelings for the man she'd never met, had no idea how Alyssa felt about him other than the few entries about his unwanted romantic attention. But Trish's compassion at such a sorrowful time touched her.

Trish appeared at the kitchen door just as Brooke located an unopened can of coffee in the pantry. "You forgot, didn't you? Is that why you're going through your old diaries?"

Brooke silently cursed the blush firing her cheeks. She turned her back to Trish, scooped coffee into the coffee-maker's basket and pushed the On button. "I'm still trying to sort everything out."

"He loved you, you know."

When Brooke turned back to face her guest, Trish was leaning against the doorjamb, arms crossed beneath her breasts, brows furrowed. A studious expression narrowed her blue-gray eyes. Was she not acting enough like Alyssa? Was that what was encouraging the suspicion in Trish's demeanor? But upon closer inspection, she thought maybe Trish was not as much suspicious as trying to hide her own strong feelings. Her eyes were rimmed with red, as if she, too, had cried her eyes out along with her mother.

She'd lost her brother just as Brooke had lost her sister so many years before. Empathy softened the edge of her mistrust.

"I know," Brooke said, stuffing her hands into her shorts pockets and leaning against the counter. "He was family. I loved him, too."

"He would never have tried to scale Devil's Back if it weren't for you."

The accusation went straight to Brooke's heart. The sting jerked her hands right out of her pockets.

"He would have done what he damn well pleased, and you know it." Brooke snapped the lid back on the can and shoved it against the counter wall. Where had that come from? Had she gleaned more about Rick from Alyssa's writings than she'd thought?

A small, knowing smile creased Trish's features. "So you do remember that."

Thank you, Alyssa, and bless you for keeping a journal!
"What else do you remember?"

Brooke squared her shoulders and stared Trish straight in the eye. "That I don't like to be badgered, or made to feel guilty, especially about things I can't help."

Trish laughed, running a hand through her loose dark-blond hair. "You know I was worried about you when Jack told us about the amnesia, but I should have known better. Nothing's going to keep you down, is it?"

"No, nothing." Brooke filled a mug with coffee and handed it to Trish.

Still smiling, Trish accepted the offering. "Good. I couldn't bear to lose my favorite rival so soon after losing my brother."

After that confession, the atmosphere seemed to lighten. They talked like real friends about Rick, about business, about life in general. They ate cookies, and drank coffee, reminding Brooke how much she missed her friend, Crystal, and their weekly girls' night out.

It wasn't until Trish left and Brooke reached for one of the diaries that she noticed her notebook was missing.

Chapter Twelve

The next day, when Brooke questioned Jack about setting a trap for Cullen, he infuriated her by saying he had everything under control. She resented having to pull information out of him, resented his cool detachment tempered by the hot look in his eyes when he thought she wasn't looking. *Show me. Tell me.* But forcing him to talk only seemed to make him retreat more deeply, so she reluctantly accepted his distance.

Which didn't mean she was planning on sitting by idly. Being Alyssa was teaching her that she had a strength inside her she never knew about. Even as playing Alyssa was forcing her to keep more and more of her emotions under constant guard, it was also freeing her to become more physically daring.

She was also getting antsy.

Jack soundly rejected her notion of going to Trish's home to retrieve the missing notebook, but Brooke didn't give up on the idea. She still had the cookie plate to return, and if Jack could leave her alone for more than a minute, she'd head for Trish's house off Maple Run.

The opportunity presented itself two days later, when Jack was called in to help out with a rescue off the North Bridge. She was just about to leave when Tim knocked at the door.

"Shouldn't you be covering the bridge accident?" she asked, trying very hard not to let her irritation show. She needed every minute to make it to town and back before Jack knew she'd left the house.

"I've got a reporter on the story." He seemed ill at ease. His gaze darted left, then right, which didn't raise her confidence level. Was he looking to see if there were any witnesses to his presence? Why did he need privacy?

She'd been so sure the suspect they wanted was Cullen that she hadn't stopped to consider anyone else. Then her notebook had disappeared after Trish's visit. And now here was Tim looking shifty. She was back to three suspects, which did nothing to calm her irritation.

Suddenly it occurred to her that Tim's timing was a little too perfect. He'd deliberately waited to get her alone, without Jack hovering and protecting. Had he done the same thing to Alyssa? Watched her, waiting patiently for an opportunity to strike? Was his unseen gaze the one Alyssa spoke of in her journals?

"Can I come in?" Tim's voice was harsh and tight.

"I was just going out." She reached for her purse to prove her point. "Can't this wait?"

"No, uh, it can't." His gaze avoided hers. He shifted his weight from one foot to the other, and cleared his throat. "I need them."

"Need what?"

"Don't play games with me, Alyssa. We both know the amnesia is just another one of your games." He shook his head and his gaze narrowed, turning his choirboy good looks into something hard and unyielding.

"I'm not. I have no idea what you're talking about."

He adjusted his perfectly set glasses. "I want the negatives."

"What negatives?"

He glanced around once more. "Can I come in? I don't want to get into this outside."

Impatient with the interruption, Brooke sighed inwardly and opened the door to let him pass. "I really need to get going."

"This won't take long." He pivoted to face her. A certain desperation appeared in the set of his eyes, in the lengthening of his features. "I want the negatives of the photos you took from the town forest trails behind my house."

"You'll have to be a little more specific." She hung on to the doorknob in case she had to make a sudden exit. She didn't like the way Tim's face was getting red and mottled.

"You're having fun, aren't you? You're enjoying seeing me beg. Well, fine, you're getting your way. I'm begging. Give them to me."

There was something pitiful about a grown man groveling, even if the words were full of spit and fire. She took no pleasure in it and sought a way to ease the tension mushrooming between them. "Okay, why don't we go into my office and look through my files."

He blushed, shifted his weight and cleared his throat.

"I see. You've already been through them."

He looked up, pleading. "I had to. You were in the hospital. Nobody thought you'd make it. I couldn't take the chance anyone else would find them." His brow knitted. "You didn't leave me any choice."

"If the negatives you're looking for aren't with the others, then I have no idea where they are."

"Then let's look elsewhere. Where do you keep your other blackmail material? Surely, I'm not the only one you're holding by the throat."

"The amnesia is real, Tim. I don't remember."

His eyebrows pulled together, creating deep wrinkles on

his forehead. His eyes were mere slits, and his lips were pressed tight. No need to hire a psychologist to figure out that Tim's anger was running deep. A trickle of fear slid down her spine. What if he didn't believe her? Would he get violent? How to soothe him? How to make him go away? How to get herself out of this situation?

"I don't know where the negatives are, Tim. If I did, I'd give them to you."

"Just like that?" He snorted incredulously.

Brooke desperately tried to put herself in Alyssa's skin. How would her sister handle him? Alyssa respected his work and his climbing skills, but she'd also written a few scathing passages about her less than favorable opinion of him as a human being. And the person in front of Brooke was the human being, not the journalist, not the sportsman.

"Why not?" Brooke asked, throwing Alyssa's truth at him to protect her own lie. "I'm sick of this place. I want to get out. But I don't want to leave with bad feelings all around. I was planning to make things right."

"Yeah, that sounds like fiction to me."

"It's the truth."

"Truth is my business. I know it when I see it." His lips twisted in a sneer, he shook his head. "But fantasy is something else. You'll never leave here because you can't. You need Jack to function, and you want your father's approval so badly it's pitiful to watch you with him. You'll never be more than a backwoods girl. You haven't got the guts it takes to make use of your talent."

She swallowed back her own anger. Fanning these flames was going to get her nowhere but deeper into trouble. "Then what are you worried about? If I'm so gutless, what are the odds I'd use those damning negatives against you?"

"Revenge. You've been such a witch lately. You say you want to make things right. Well, it sure feels like you're out to destroy everything and everyone who's ever loved you.'' He raked both his hands through his hair. ''The awards, Alyssa. I can't let those pictures show up with the awards coming up soon. It would ruin everything. Not just for me, but for my staff. Can you understand that? They've worked hard and I don't want their reward clouded with small-town closed-mindedness.''

''What exactly are you doing in those pictures?''

''Nothing,'' he answered too fast as his gaze slid away.

''Then why are you so worried?''

When he looked at her again, sadness drooped his eyes. ''Because I like it here, and I don't want to have to leave.''

She considered his words, then nodded. ''What if I made you a promise not to use the negatives?''

His pale-blue eyes studied her for a long time. ''I'd have a hard time trusting you. But I guess I don't have much of a choice.'' He stalked forward and hurried past her through the still open door. At the bottom of the stairs, he turned around. ''Whatever you do, Alyssa, please don't show those photos until after the awards. Not for me, for my staff.''

''I promise.'' Hugging the door, Brooke felt like crying. Was Alyssa really manipulating her friend with those negatives? Why blackmail? What could she possibly have wanted in return? What could she have hoped to gain? It seemed like a cruel game and she wanted no part of it.

BROOKE FOUND TRISH'S HOUSE easily enough. The small Victorian was on a large lot. The fully leafed maples, birches and oaks surrounding the house on three sides effectively hid it from all but the front neighbor. When she called Trish's number before she left, there was no answer, but she was relieved to find Trish's silver Trooper wasn't in the driveway.

Brooke drove around the block twice and parked around

the corner on Cemetery Street. Cookie plate in hand—just in case—she rang the doorbell and got no answer, then tried the knob. It turned under her hand. Drawing a deep breath, she walked in as if she were expected.

All the drapes were drawn, giving the living room a shadowy feeling. The air smelled of apple and cinnamon potpourri, but with all the windows closed, the air also carried a certain staleness. The furniture had the clean, simple lines of Danish teak. The cushions on the sofa and two chairs were a neutral beige. The carpet was sand-colored. Even the few prints on the wall were black and white inks framed in plain, neutral tones. And everything in the room was immaculate—as if the room was just for show, as if no one really lived here.

The kitchen, the den, the two bedrooms looked just as stiff and formal and colorless. Even the office was perfectly neat. Two computers sat on two desks, each displaying a whirling geometric screen-saver design.

The only visible papers were newspaper clippings about Trish's brother's death. One of the pictures showed a man smiling as if he had a secret. His eyes reflected a mischievous sparkle. His features, Brooke decided, looked remarkably like Trish's. They could have passed for twins, she thought with a gasp.

Putting the clippings on the desktop, Brooke started a methodical search of the office, careful to replace everything exactly where she'd found it.

She was halfway through the drawers on the first desk, when something caught her eye—a piece of colored paper that seemed out of place. The letters RTC appeared in a bold circle like a logo. She was about to reach for the file and sensed she was no longer alone. With controlled calm, she closed the drawer and turned to find Trish staring coldly at her. Trish's gray T-shirt and black pants did nothing to light up the dullness of her dark-blond hair, put a spark in her gray-blue eyes, or liven up the ash color of her skin.

"What are you doing here?"

Brooke swallowed hard. There really was no explanation for her presence here. Truth was her only weapon. "I'm looking for the notebook you took from me the other day."

Trish's body tensed, her jaw locked tight, her expression froze into a deep scowl. "Why would I want anything from you?"

"I don't know. You tell me."

"It's you who takes from people, Alyssa. Not me. Unlike you, I mind my own business."

The barb was sharp and pointed and backed with a hefty dose of resentment. How far did this resentment go? Were the competitions Alyssa enjoyed so much more one-sided than not? Brooke shrugged as if nothing mattered, but her gut twisted. "It was there. You were there. You left. It was gone. What else am I supposed to conclude?"

"That maybe you forgot where you put it. It wouldn't be the first time you parked your brain in one room and your body in another."

"I looked. I couldn't find it anywhere."

"Did you find it here?"

Brooke lowered her gaze and shook her head. "No."

Trish's face crumpled with little girl hurt. With a stiff arm, she pointed down the hall toward the front door. "Get out. You're not welcome here."

Brooke left with the feeling she'd made a terrible mistake. Trish had gone out of her way to be compassionate on the anniversary of her brother's death, and Brooke was rewarding the previous day's kind gesture with suspicion and invasion of privacy.

She was doubly sure of her faux pas when she got home. Retracing her previous search, she looked through Alyssa's journals, beneath the lamp table, behind the curtains, under the cushions on the love seat. Finally she palpated the area beneath the love seat. Her hand struck something hard. She dragged the object forward.

Her stomach felt as if it had dropped all the way to her feet.

There was her notebook covered with dust bunnies.

SOMEONE WAS WATCHING THEM. As he walked toward the resort office, Jack unobtrusively scanned the area, every shadow, every corner. He saw no one, but the feeling persisted.

He wished Brooke would be content to stay at the cottage. Her need for movement was making his job harder. But claiming she was bored, she insisted on going to the resort office every morning with a stop at her father's first.

She was making things worse without even trying. Her presence was putting all of their suspects on guard instead of tempting them into making a mistake.

And then there was Walter. She talked to him as if he cared, and didn't let his nonresponsive attitude dim her effort. He'd seen the puzzled look in her father's eyes, seen the softening of his demeanor and wondered how long it would take for Walter to start asking questions.

Neither did she seem to understand that her un-Alyssalike behavior was starting to get noticed by the staff.

Brooke was acting too steadily and too dependably at the office. He'd seen her go out of her way to make people feel at home, especially the children running around the resort. Her paperwork was done much too efficiently. Worse, she was taking to life at the resort as easily as if she'd been born here, handling routine and problems with equal proficiency, with that sunshine smile always ready to shine.

Jack opened the office door and saw Brooke busily working at the computer. "Lunchtime."

"I'll be right with you."

As she typed, a wide, pleased smile graced her lips. While she tidied her desk area, she whistled. This was getting way out of hand. He much preferred those times when she did manage to be like Alyssa. It was safer that way. Emotions didn't get involved. And he could remember she was just a means to reach a greater goal.

After shouting a quick goodbye to Franny across the great hall, Brooke fell into step with him. He stuck his hands into his shorts pockets. Shrieks of kids having fun came from the water and from the tennis courts, which they were presently using as an in-line skating rink. People strolled lazily around them on their way to the beach or the small souvenir shop inside the office. All this slow summer comfort was starting to get to him in a way he couldn't understand no matter how long he spent analyzing the anomaly.

"Don't whistle while you work," he said, with more irritation than he planned.

Her head snapped in his direction and her smile faded. "What?"

"Don't whistle while you work." He frowned, wondering how to get her to smile again. "Alyssa doesn't whistle, she grumbles."

"Oh."

"Don't sway your hips." Every sensual roll of those bright red shorts heated a craving best left unsatisfied.

She glanced at her pelvis. "Sway?"

"Alyssa walks like she means business."

"And I don't?"

"No," he grumbled.

A half smile teased her lips. "Oh, I see."

He gritted his teeth. "And stop being so damned cheerful."

"The clients like it."

"But it's getting you too much attention from Franny and Walter."

Deep inside he wished he could bask in the sunshine of her smile more often, and that irritated him as much as his lack of progress on this case.

He'd learned that the kayak had been tampered with, but it was impossible for Rafe to narrow down the exact tool used. Anyone could have done it. Examining the brake line at George's had not proved enlightening, other than to cement his conclusion that the cut was deliberate. So far, Cullen was acting just like Cullen, and Matt, the P.I., had nothing to report. Cullen had done nothing suspicious or out of line. No word from Ed yet. He'd give him a few more days.

Jack still felt it all came down to the rope. His rope.

"And didn't I tell you to stay away from Trish?" When he'd heard from Matt about Brooke's breaking and entering escapade while he was busy working the North Bridge accident, he'd wanted to strangle her.

"Who says I've seen her?"

She tried for nonchalant, but her eyes, her cheeks, her mouth betrayed her. He found a certain satisfaction in the fact she couldn't lie to him.

"I've got spies everywhere." Small-town gossip had its advantages in his line of work. Even if Matt hadn't followed Brooke, Mrs. Hastings, who lived across the street from Trish, had put in her neighborly report. "What happened?"

"Didn't your spy tell you?"

"Mrs. Hastings can't see through walls."

She nodded and hooked her arm through his elbow. The sense of rightness had him faltering for half a step. "Ah, the front neighbor. Trish caught me and sent me home. End of story."

"It could very well have been," he reminded her.

"I found the notebook. Cullen—"

"Is only one of four suspects."

"But—"

"But nothing. I'm trying to keep you safe. I can't do that when I don't know where you are or what you're up to. You've got to keep up appearances." He frowned. "You've got to be Alyssa."

"Oh." She flashed him that mysterious half smile again and wreaked havoc on him.

"And don't look at me that way."

Where Alyssa's eyes bore sadness and ice, Brooke's warm and vulnerable gaze fired heat and longing in his veins. A longing that was starting to feel like torture. It was pure hell to hear Brooke's bed sheets rustle on the other side of the wall every night, to imagine her long limbs tangled in those sheets, to want to ease her restlessness with slow lovemaking that would leave them both feeling languorous and sated.

He groaned silently at his body's instantaneous response to his thoughts, and was taken aback when the cottage door sprung open under his less than gentle twist.

"You've got to remember to lock the door when you leave," he barked.

"You were the last one here, hotshot." Laughing, she brushed a soft kiss on his cheek as she glided by. Every atom of his body responded with deepening hunger. Without even trying, she was making him feel things he didn't want to feel.

"What do you want for lunch?" she asked, as she set her purse on the kitchen counter. "Keep it simple. My kitchen repertoire is rather limited."

I want you—any way you'll let me take you. On the kitchen table. Against the counter. On the floor. He cleared his throat. "A sandwich will be fine."

No matter how well she fit here, she'd be going back to California in less than a week. His life was here in Comfort. He didn't want to be anything else but a small-town cop. And he'd never made the mistake of confusing fantasy with reality before. Not with Lily and Malcolm Chessman's examples to follow. He wasn't about to start now.

As he closed the front door, he felt that unseen gaze bore through him. The scent of danger was getting stronger.

STEPHANIE TOOK TO COMING around the cottage every day after work. Jack usually excused himself during those visits, closeting himself in Alyssa's office. Brooke wished she knew what lead he was following, wished he'd be more open with his suspicions and the results of his investigation. Though they'd spent the past few evenings alone together, playing Trivial Pursuit, Monopoly or pun-filled games of Scrabble, their conversation, by some mutual agreement she couldn't remember making, stayed on "safe" subjects like the weather, or sports, or resort business.

Brooke enjoyed Stephanie's company. Stephanie had an irreverent view of life, not to mention that her daily dose of gossip gave Brooke a good overview of life in Comfort. They never spoke of the accident nor the amnesia, but something about the way Stephanie looked at her put Brooke on alert and kept her from relaxing completely in the woman's presence. Could she be trusted? What blackmail article did Alyssa hold against her best friend?

After Jack closed the office door, Stephanie leaned forward. Her long brown ponytail cascaded forward. Her hazel eyes twinkled with mischief.

"Jack is so romantically challenged. How did you get him to change his mind about marriage?"

It was not a subject Brooke particularly wanted to discuss. She tried to disguise her creeping blush by opening the window behind her wider. Her mind raced for an answer and she sought to slow it down by taking in the sounds of the resort. Children's laughter drifted in on the warm afternoon breeze. A blue jay's reedy gurgle echoed from a nearby pine branch. The scent of lake and forest made Brooke inhale deeply. She relaxed and turned back to Stephanie.

"The accident jolted a dose of reality in both of us." Brooke shrugged.

Stephanie frowned as she picked up her glass of iced tea and set the rocker in motion with one foot. "There's something different about you."

Brooke tried to brush off her sudden unease with a laugh. "Is that good or bad?"

Stephanie stopped the rocker and drank a slow sip of tea. "I don't know. It's just different."

"Maybe I'm mellowing with age." Brooke gave a short, mirthless laugh. "Or maybe the knock on my head is making me see everything a whole new way."

"Yes," Stephanie said as a thoughtful expression masked her features. "Maybe you are."

"What about you?" Brooke asked, diverting attention from herself. "Why are you pursuing Cullen when you know there's no future in it?"

"I'm not stupid." Stephanie tossed her ponytail over her shoulder. "I know he'll never give me what I want. But right now he's being attentive, and right now I need attention."

"There's got to be someone better."

"Around here?" Stephanie snorted. "You've got to be kidding?"

Brooke tapped her thumbnail against her teeth. "You know, I met someone at the office the other day I know you'd like."

Stephanie shook her head and waved her hands as a look of horror spread over her face. "You know I don't date vacationers. It's not what I want."

"Would it be so bad?"

"I know you want to leave, Alyssa, but I like it here. As much as I bitch and moan about my family, I couldn't bear to be away from them."

"I can't blame you." Alyssa had written about the closeness of Stephanie's family and her own envy at their loving bonds. They'd often included her in their celebrations. What was one more when there were already a half dozen of them around the table?

Brooke recalled the early laughter of her childhood and couldn't help wondering what would have happened to her family if they'd stayed together. Would it have fallen apart anyway? Brooke had longed for closeness many times while growing up. "It limits your options."

Stephanie sighed and swirled the spoon around the glass. "A sad fact of life that can't be helped. *Ticktock, ticktock.* I'm not getting younger. Cullen may be my last chance."

"What about Tim?"

"Tim?" She wrinkled her nose. "He's about as romantic as a stone. Cullen for all his faults has a lot of passion."

"But maybe steady and dependable is better in the long run than hot and heavy and over in a flash."

"Maybe not." Stephanie shrugged, jumped up, set her glass aside and reached for the bag she'd placed by the lamp table when she came in. "Oh, by the way, I brought you a new wreath for your door. The one you've got is starting to look faded." She pulled out a wreath of orange tansy and blue and white gypsophila added to a base of goldenrod. "It's the last of my goldenrod from last summer."

After removing the rose and herb wreath from the front door, Stephanie carefully anchored the new one.

"It's beautiful! When do you have time to do this with your job?"

Tossing back her ponytail, Stephanie stepped back, then made an adjustment to center her masterpiece. "Keeps evenings from getting too long and me from falling into a deep pool of self-pity."

"Do you sell these?"

She shrugged and gave Brooke a queer look. "You know I only make them for friends and for Mom's church."

"I guess I'd forgotten that. My brain still feels like Swiss cheese sometimes. You'd do really well at craft fairs with the wreaths."

Stephanie waved away the suggestion, then shyly cocked her head. "You think?"

"I know."

"You have changed." Stephanie drained the last of her tea, then smiled. "But I like it."

"I'm glad," Brooke said. And she was.

ALYSSA HADN'T CHANGED. *Never would. This was just a new game. She didn't care about others' feelings, went about her business as if they had none. Or maybe she did, and that was her pleasure, twisting, torturing, seeing how much twitching she could get before her quarry cracked.*

The time had come for the grand finale. They were on the lake again, enjoying the early-morning quiet before the rest of the resort awoke. A loon cried out a warning. They didn't even seem to notice. They were having too much fun when they should be worried about what was going to happen next.

One more adjustment and the surprise was in place. Then open the valve, turn the ignition switch and set the timer for midnight. The witching hour. The hour of truth. The hour of redemption.

"Good night, princess. Sleep tight."

Comfort would not soon forget these fireworks.

Chapter Thirteen

The nightmare was coming back. The dark images crept into his sleep until he saw himself balanced on the edge of a black precipice. The rock beneath his bare feet cut into his flesh. He tried to pull himself out of the fog, to turn and claw for the rope that connected him with safety, but it dissolved between his fingers and he teetered helplessly with nowhere to go but down into whirling, uncontrolled chaos.

Hanging on by sheer will, he watched them fall again and again, first his mother, then Alyssa, then Brooke, spiraling into the abyss below, swallowed by the darkness. He couldn't reach them, couldn't save them. He gripped tighter, holding on to the rock with the smallest of finger- and toeholds as rain and wind beat savagely against him.

A loud crack reverberated through the rock. He looked up. A figure, dark in silhouette, stood at the top of the stance, dangling a rope just out of reach. Laughter, cold and heinous, whipped with the wind, loosening his hold.

Then the falling started all over again as the silhouette pushed the people he loved one by one over the edge. *No!* Vertigo nauseated him. *Stop!*

He reached out, trying to grab a hand, a sleeve—anything—that would stop the madness of this senseless dying. Something caught, jerked at his arm and pulled. Then he was falling, too. Down into the dark, endless chasm.

Jack awoke with a start to the sound of retreating thunder. Rain splattered through the screen of his open window onto the foot of his bed. A quick glance at the clock radio showed that it was barely eleven—not even an hour since he'd gone to bed. He got up to close the window. A blast of cold air pebbled his bare skin. In the next flash of lightning, he caught a reflection of his face on the glass.

Crazed.

Haunted.

Every time he failed to save them.

They'd both counted on him. He'd let both of them down.

And now there was Brooke.

She was the next victim, and his nightmare was warning him of a dire outcome.

He scraped a hand over his face, trying to erase the images. But they would always be there until he got answers to his lingering questions, until he was sure of Brooke's safety.

Three more days and he would be sending her home.

Needing a change of scenery, he pulled on a pair of jeans and headed to the living room to check the windows.

A teakettle purred in the kitchen, black against the red-hot burner. Dressed in one of Alyssa's oversize T-shirts and a white fleece cardigan, Brooke stood in the kitchen. Between the stove's light and the open refrigerator, radiance surrounded her like a halo, making her glow.

She was an angel. Offering hope.

He shook his head and dismissed the notion. She'd given him nothing but trouble since her arrival. Three more days before he shipped her home. Three more days before his responsibility toward her ended. He swallowed, tasted regret.

A strike of lightning flashed blue through the house. Thunder cracked right on top of it. Brooke jumped, gasped. The light in the fridge surged, then died.

"Hang on. I'll find you a flashlight." He knew she didn't like the dark, didn't draw comfort from black shadows the way Alyssa did.

"Jack?"

"Were you expecting someone else?" He probed for the drawer, bumped his hand against her hip, felt a surge of heat flood through him.

"I thought you were asleep." A little tremor rippled through her voice, making him want to gather her in his arms and kiss the fearfulness away.

"The thunder took care of that." He wouldn't sleep again tonight, not with the nightmare so raw and fresh on his mind. Lifting the lantern out of the drawer, he flicked on the switch, then set it on the counter. "Why are you up?"

Like a moth, Brooke sought out the light. Her skin took on the soft patina of gold in the dim light. His fingers itched to touch her, trace the smooth exposed curves of cheek and hand, to skim beneath the shirt and explore the more tantalizing mounds of breast. The need for the reassurance of life after his morbid nightmare, he rationalized.

"Why are you up?" he asked.

There was a nervousness to her movement as she snagged a short strand of hair behind her ear. "I was cold and decided to make myself a cup of tea to warm up." She whirled to the pantry and rummaged for tea. "Did someone forget to tell New Hampshire it was June?"

He answered her smile with one of his own. "You know the state motto, don't you?"

"Live free or die."

She breezed by him and it took all he had to keep from

snagging her midflight and pressing her body to his. Chemistry, that was all. Emotions, feelings could be controlled with logic.

"We believe in following the beat of our own drum."

She laughed as she plucked two mugs from the cupboard. "Snow in June and T-shirt weather in December?"

"That about sums it up. Let me light a fire and see if we can chase that chill away."

Her smile faded and a flash of something warm and needy lit her eyes. Carefully she turned away. Her busy fingers ripped cellophane wrapping from the box of tea, turning the easy task into a marathon affair.

Walking away was difficult, but he did it. Giving in to lustful impulses would do neither of them any good. He knelt in front of the fireplace and concentrated on the task of starting a fire. "What are you making?"

"Making?" Her voice sounded a bit rusty.

"You were standing with the fridge open before the lights went out."

"Oh, yes. Well, there isn't much left. There's the strawberries Lauren and I picked this morning. Orange juice. Lettuce. Half a cucumber. A small chunk of cheese." She chuckled. "And dark chocolate from Alyssa's secret stash."

"Secret stash?" Trying to ignore the warm tripping of his blood at the sound of Brooke's voice, he built a pyramid of balled newspaper and kindling, then reached for the long matches in the holder on the wall.

"In a coffee can behind the flour."

He smiled. That was typical Alyssa. "Any crackers to go with that cheese?"

"I'll look." She was sounding more relaxed now.

The fire took and spread, eating greedily at the kindling. The sounds of Brooke bustling in the kitchen chased away part of the remnants of his dream and replaced them with frustration. Want, it was there, powerful and restless, stalking inside him like a starving beast.

She took the quilt from the rocker's back and spread it on the floor in front of the fireplace. She laid out a plate of cheese and crackers, and one with strawberries and squares of chocolate. She went back to the kitchen, returned with two mugs of what smelled like peppermint tea, and handed one of them to him. The domestic tranquillity of the scene should have lulled him into relaxation, but it didn't.

He added a log to the kindling, noticed the slight shake of his hand. Orange flames soon surrounded the wood, shooting warmth and light into the living room. He gave the fire all of his attention, sensing that shifting it to Brooke would get him in a world of trouble.

"Does the power go out often?" she asked as she settled on the quilt. Her voice hitched as if she, too, was trying to find the right string of conversation that would keep them on safe ground.

He cleared his throat. "Now and again. Lightning must have hit the transformer. It's a pretty wicked storm out there, but the power should be on again in no time."

She handed him a cracker topped with a slice of cheese. Their fingers accidentally touched. She recoiled to her side of the blanket.

He toyed with the cracker, rearranging the square of cheese this way and that, and pretended he hadn't felt the spark between them.

"What made you decide to become a cop?" She sipped her tea, watching him over the rim of her cup with those deep green eyes.

Staring at the cracker in his hand, he shrugged. "It just felt right."

"Does your father work in law enforcement?"

"You could say that." The fact that his father had spent

most of his life on the other side of prison bars certainly had inspired him.

"You never talk about your parents. Where's your father now?"

Just the train of thought he needed to forget his inappropriate lust for Brooke. Jack stuffed the cracker and cheese into his mouth, tasted neither. "Serving a life sentence in the state prison."

"Oh."

His father had stolen his mother's heart, then he'd wiped her bank account clean and taken off with all his mother's heirloom jewelry, except for the ring that had been on her finger. Unfortunately for Malcolm Chessman, his next victim hadn't been so easy to manipulate. The killing had been accidental, but murder was murder, and Malcolm was now paying his debt to society.

"What about your mother?" Brooke persisted.

He made the mistake of looking at her then. A storm might be raging all around them, but in the dim light of the fire, all he saw was her and the sunshine she brought to a room by her mere presence. Her skin glowed in the firelight. Her hair shone. Her eyes were impossibly dark. From the low light, he tried to convince himself, not from desire.

"My mother is dead."

"I'm sorry to hear that." She wrapped the cardigan tighter around her middle. "What happened?"

"You're a curious woman, aren't you?" He turned back to the fire, poked at the log. Sparks reeled in tight swirls. "Part of my charm."

Lily Haywood Chessman had been a sad creature. Her long, dark hair, white skin and large eyes had lent her a fey appearance that made people want to take care of her, and she was more than happy to let them. Malcolm's betrayal had stolen more from her than her earthly fortune.

He'd also pirated her spirit. The townsfolk who had made sure Jack had meals when Lily succumbed to one of her frequent bouts of depression also made an effort to paint another picture of the girl who had become his mother. But the image never quite fit the reality of the person with whom he lived.

"She killed herself."

"Oh, Jack, I'm so sorry."

His grip tightened around the poker as he stared into the flames and saw the past. He'd rushed home from school like he always did and found his mother passed out on the living room couch. Her hair was spread around her head on the cream-and-periwinkle pillow like coiled snakes. Her skin had been ice-blue. Cold. Dead. "An overdose of sleeping pills and antidepressants. She suffered from insomnia and constant anxiety."

"Oh, no." Brooke's hand touched his shoulder. "What a horrible accident."

He wanted to shrug away the compassion in the gentle contact, but couldn't seem to contract the muscle needed to accomplish the task. "One that could have been prevented."

"How old were you?" Brooke laid her head against his, wrapped her other arm around his shoulder. A sigh of contentment whispered through him as her warmth wrapped around him in downy comfort.

"Seventeen."

"A boy."

"A man," he countered and jabbed at a log. "Old enough to see the signs and get help."

"You were just a kid. You weren't her guardian."

"Who else was there?"

She hugged him tighter. Something hard and painful lodged in his chest. "Is that why you look after Alyssa? To redeem yourself for your failure?"

He shook his head, felt the stubble of his beard rasp against her too-soft skin. He leaned forward trying to squeeze much needed space between them. "When I met her, Alyssa acted tough, but I could see the sadness in her eyes."

"She'd just lost her mother and her sister. And you were just a kid, too."

"She still needs protection."

"Why?" Her breath pulsed against his cheek. He leaned into the softness until her lips grazed at his cheek as she spoke. "She's a grown woman. She can take care of herself."

"Alyssa isn't able to form close relationships. There's always a contradictory need to please and yet reject."

"Push/pull."

He wanted to pull Brooke into his lap, knew he should push her away, yet did nothing while the fire in his veins grew hotter. "Alyssa charms, then she strikes. She takes risks to prove to herself that she's good enough, but I don't think even she realizes it's her father's approval she wants. It's never going to come. Walter's too far gone in his own world of hurt. I tried to explain that to her, but she can't seem to stop her destructive pattern. She mostly acts without thinking. Then she's remorseful, but it's too late. Someone has to help her pick up the pieces."

"So you appointed yourself."

Jack didn't answer. He swirled the poker in his hands, watched the charcoaled log fall apart and grow dark, watched the flames grow taller around the fresher log, watched the hot, blue section of flame crisp and crackle at the dry bark. "She has nobody else."

"Still, it's pretty arrogant of you to think you're completely responsible for your mother or Alyssa's actions." With a hand on his chin, she turned his face until their gazes met. He swallowed hard. "Who worries about you?"

He turned away, back to the fire, wishing the answer to all his uncharacteristic confusion would appear in the flames. A rough laugh escaped him. "All the old biddies in town are always dropping off casseroles and baked goods, along with the gossip."

"Who worries about you?" she asked again. The green of her eyes darkened, deepened, drawing him in.

Ignoring her question, he reached around her for cheese and crackers. They tasted like the magnesium carbonate powder he used for climbing, and didn't do a thing to sate his hunger.

The log in the fire popped. Lightning flashed blue on the walls. Thunder burst in hammered blows.

"I should go back to bed," Brooke said and started to get to her feet.

Before he could think, his hand reached for her ankle and tugged. "Stay."

She shook her head. "I, uh, I don't think that's a good idea."

"The fire's just getting warm."

"Yes, well." She looked like a deer poised to take flight. He should let her go, but he couldn't.

A fresh downpour pounded against the roof. "Stay."

She sat back down, tucking her feet beneath her, and drew the plate of chocolate and strawberries between them. "What do you need to make sure your case gets prosecuted properly?"

Safe enough territory, he thought, until she popped a square of chocolate and a berry into her mouth. He imagined the chocolate melting on her tongue, the strawberry exploding with juice. He gulped down the tea, which thankfully had grown cold, but couldn't get rid of the spark instigating jealousy in his own mouth. "I have to establish that the suspect had motive and opportunity to do the act. That he or she did it with the specific intent to commit murder.''

''Doesn't the threatening note support the intention?'' She held a strawberry by its green cap, twirled the stem between her fingers. The berry hovered right by her lips as she spoke.

''Not unless there's a way to prove who wrote the note.''

She popped the fruit into her mouth. He silently groaned. ''And you said that the lab wasn't likely to turn up any prints.''

''No. It all comes down to the rope.''

She broke off another square of chocolate. He snagged her wrist and drew it to him. He opened his mouth, tasted the tips of her fingers as he took the chocolate from her hand, and wanted more.

Her hand was shaking when she withdrew it. Her voice sounded edgy when she spoke. ''What about a profile? Do you guys do that? Wouldn't it help you to narrow down the suspects?''

Tension was stringing him tight as she fidgeted, her T-shirt rucking up higher on her thigh. ''We're too small for that. The Comfort P.D. has only five full-time officers and three part-timers.''

''But you and I could create a profile to eliminate one or two of them.'' Her T-shirt rode ever higher as she reached for a strawberry. His pulse thundered through his veins, igniting heat and flaring desire that was getting harder and harder to control.

''I've been thinking a lot about Alyssa's would-be killer. My theory is that revenge is involved, and it sure looks like any of them could be nursing a grudge against Alyssa, if her journals reflect the truth. And if he or she is letting that need for vengeance simmer, then the planned attempt is no surprise. The need to witness the perceived justice also fits.''

Tugging her T-shirt down to her knees, she sighed and frowned. She picked through the berries as if they required all of her attention. "It still could be any of them."

"Unfortunately."

He was still staring at the delightful play of light dancing on her cheeks when she looked up from the berry bowl. She offered him a strawberry and something in him snapped. His heart stopped and started again as hot flesh met hot flesh once more, causing a chain reaction of primal hunger.

Swearing softly, he shoved the plate of chocolate and fruit out of the way and reached for her, pressed himself against her, and kissed her, deeply, thoroughly. The taste of strawberries and chocolate melded against his tongue, transforming itself into a potent elixir.

His hand glided over her thigh, up her hip, down to her waist and climbed up her rib cage until the softness of her breast beckoned him to stop, savor and explore. He liked the feel of her skin, the scent of summer-heated flowers sprinkled across it—subtle, fragrant, mind-muddling. He loved the way she responded to him, melted for him, moaned for him. He was lost, he knew, but he didn't care. He wanted more, much more.

Breathing hard, he pulled himself from her mouth, framed her head between his hands. "I want you."

"I know." She licked her lips. The rapid up and down movement of her chest caressed his own bare skin, fraying his control. "It's not wise."

"No. Not wise." But he couldn't seem to kick the logic back on track. His fingers freed the cardigan's buttons from their holes, and he shoved the material off her shoulders.

"You're not what I need in a man."

His hand paused on the flatness of her stomach, felt the shiver of delight that rippled through her. "What do you need?"

"I need someone who'll love me as I am, who won't be afraid to tell me, to show me how he feels. I need a man who's not afraid of his own deep passion."

"I'm nothing like that." His hand drifted south to the damp strip of silk between her legs, hot and ready for him. "But you want me."

"Oh, yes."

He pushed aside the silk, reveled in the satiny moistness waiting for him. "We're all wrong for each other."

Her breath hitched. Her eyes grew unfocused. Her hands were pulling at his shoulders, trying to draw him closer. "Logic doesn't seem to make a lick of difference in this case."

"No, it doesn't." He yanked the T-shirt over her head. It snagged on her cast, reminding him of why she was here. "You're leaving in three days."

"I'm staying until this is settled."

"No, you can't." His breath caught at the sight of her breasts. The crooked angel pendant rested between them. He tasted one luscious peak, then the other. She sighed her pleasure, so he did it again. "I have to go back to work and I can't afford to worry about you."

"I can take care of myself." Her voice had a dreamy, faraway quality. He teased her nipple with the tip of a finger and gloried in the hardening bud, in the arch of her back stretching to meet his caress. "I've been taking care of myself for a long time."

"Alyssa thought she could handle the situation on her own, too. Now she's in a coma."

"But I'm not Alyssa."

"No, you're not."

"Then shut up and make love to me."

His pulse throbbed hot and wild in every drop of his blood. "Are you sure?"

She guided his hand to her liquid center. "Um, yes."

Her flaring passion growing fast out of control seemed to temper the urgency of his own need. He smiled. With slow, consummate care he went about discovering just how far he could tease her before she exploded beneath him in the most grandiose of fireworks shows.

SHE'D GUESSED RIGHT. Jack's strong, sensitive fingers knew just where to find her most responsive spots. Every inch of her was alive in a way she never thought possible. She was in heaven. She was in hell. And it was glorious.

His hands stroked the fires of Hades on her skin. His body, hard and lean against hers, felt like sin itself. She was heading for damnation and couldn't remember why she should care. She'd never before felt such a sense of abandon. It was heady, freeing.

"I've gone and done something terrible," she whispered between kisses.

"What?" he asked, his voice distracted as he found another weak spot of flesh to torture with intense pleasure.

"I've gone and fallen for the wrong man."

He kissed her again. Hesitated. His breaths sounded like a runaway train in her ears. He rolled away from her, leaving what felt like a gulf between them. Her body, down to the bone, ached, actually ached for his touch. His eyes were so dark, so deep, the sight took her breath away. He traced her lips with a fingertip, sending shivers of pleasure coursing madly through her body.

"Point of no return," he said huskily.

He replaced his finger with his mouth and kissed her senseless. She reached for the zipper of his jeans, heard him gasp as she cupped the fullness of him in her hand.

He shed his jeans, her panties and rolled until she straddled him.

She leaned forward, grazing her nipples, the cold gold of her medal, against his chest. Spearing him with her gaze, she laced her fingers with his, swiveled her hips until she found the pulsing tip of him and tortured him as slowly and as deliberately as he'd tortured her, until he could take no more.

In a swift move, he pinned her beneath him, slid into her, and possessed her. There was no other word for the sensation of claiming that buzzed through her. Breath catching as if she'd just run the whole length of the West Coast at top speed, a tremor built deep inside her until she thought she would die from the sheer intensity of the sensation. Then she exploded, saw a million stars, a whirlwind of color, tasted eternity and wanted it to go on forever and ever.

"I love you," she said against the still convulsing body of the man she loved. He owned her body, soul and heart. And she had no idea what to do about it.

I LOVE YOU. Her passion-filled voice echoed in his mind, seemed to reach deep inside him, touch something he'd thought long dead. She was a force as elemental as the storm outside. She was pure sunshine, and she was his, all his.

He was alive, thoroughly, utterly alive. Every cell, every atom sang with the sensation. In his arms, he held the lost half of himself, and he never wanted to let her go.

I love you, he wanted to say, but could not bring himself to say the words. For the first time, he understood the soul-dimming pain his mother might have experienced at his father's departure. "Stay," he said instead, hugging her closer. *For now. Forever.*

"I'm not going anywhere."

In the afterglow of their spent passion, he could believe the nightmare would end. She would go. She had to. That was reality. But for just one night, he wanted to believe in the fantasy, so he let himself relax.

And just as he let the last of his nightmare slip away, something made him sit bolt upright. He tensed. Pulling on his jeans, he scanned the room for the origin of his discomfort.

Before he could analyze the situation, the cottage was rocked with a wall-shaking blast.

Chapter Fourteen

Jack rolled her into the quilt, threw her over his shoulder and sprinted out the door. After putting her back on her feet, he jammed the nightshirt over her head. Numbly she pushed her arms through the sleeves. He rewrapped the quilt around her shoulders, held it for a moment.

"Stay here," he said. "You'll be safe." With a quick kiss to her forehead, he spun and disappeared, leaving her stranded on the beach.

"Jack!" she shouted, but he seemed not to hear her over the roar of fire and thunder. Dread snaked through her. She started after him, but her legs felt like wooden blocks. Fear as she'd never known paralyzed her. She could not lose him. Not now. Not when she knew she loved him.

Her throat convulsed. She swallowed the nausea surging to her throat. He'd be back. He had to.

Wild-eyed, all she could do was stare at the flames as they had all but engulfed the small cottage. *No!* The scream ripped silently through her, tearing at her chest, shredding her throat. *No!*

Fingers clamped tight around the quilt's edge, Brooke couldn't move. Her heart pounded. Then the shaking started and rolled through her in cold waves.

I'm sorry, Alyssa. I'm so sorry. Pressing her fists against her mouth, she tried to hold back the tears wrenching at her to be free, tried to will the frenzied shaking to stop.

It was happening all over again. Losing her sister twenty-four years ago had caused a wound that refused to be cauterized. Watching the cottage burn now was like losing another part of herself. The memory of little-girl laughter and tears went up with the smoke. Pain sliced at her breastbone and tears gushed down her cheeks.

The last thing she'd wanted was to destroy her sister's life. She thought she'd be taking care of her twin by being Alyssa again. Instead she'd failed her, taken away all she had left.

She wanted to run from the scene, hide from the pain shredding her raw, but her limbs refused to obey. *Jack, come back. Please come back.* Caught between the past and the future, she stared at the fire consuming the cottage, numb with shock. The scene imprinted itself with vivid detail as the past was erased with every greedy lick of flame. All of Alyssa's memories were in that house. All her possessions. Her equipment, her cameras, her art.

And Jack was somewhere in there, too, fighting the fiery monster.

Jack, where are you? Another knife of pain stabbed through her. *Please, please come back.* Her mind went on overload.

A small crowd gathered and buzzed with questions. The fire engine's siren pierced the night over the lingering rumble of thunder and shrieked closer.

Firemen shouted once they arrived. Hoses sprayed water. But the cottage was crumbling. And so was she. Her legs wouldn't hold her any longer. She sank to the rough, cold sand while rain plastered her hair, the quilt and the nightshirt to her skin.

"Alyssa, oh, there you are." A frantic Franny, dressed in an oversize purple sweat suit and bright yellow slicker, squeezed her into a tight embrace. "I was so worried when I couldn't find you. Where's Jack?"

"With the fire." And every second he was out of her sight was killing her slowly. If he got hurt, if he died.... But he wouldn't. He couldn't. She just couldn't bear it.

"What happened?"

Brooke's gaze wouldn't stray from the house. Angry red flames poured out windows and doors. Black, acrid smoke swirled skyward, tainting the air with its stink. Wood splintered. Windows burst. And the fire roared like a beast possessed.

"I don't know," she said shakily. Drugged with love and contentment, she hadn't noticed anything wrong until Jack had scooped her from the floor and raced out the front door. "An explosion. We barely had time to get out before the fire."

"But you got out and you're safe. That's all that matters." Franny squeezed harder, then pulled her up. "Come on. Let's go to the great hall. You can stay with us."

Brooke shook her head. "No, not now. I want to stay here, wait for Jack."

"Okay, then." Franny wiped the run of tears from Brooke's cheek with a swipe of her palm. "I'll stay with you. You shouldn't be alone."

Hugging each other, they sat on the sand and waited silently while chaos ruled around them.

From the eerie smog of rain and fire emerged a hunched figure. As it drew closer, Brooke made out the lump of her father in his wheelchair.

The effort it took to push the wheels on his chair was written in every strained muscle of his face and neck. When he finally noticed her, he stopped. His eyes widened, his cheeks quivered; he fell to pieces. Tears poured from his eyes. Hiding his face in his hands, he wept with huge body-shaking sobs.

Brooke rose and went to him. "Daddy?"

"I thought…you were gone."

She crouched beside him and wrapped an arm around him. "I'm here, Daddy. I'm here."

Franny joined them, and together, they watched the house burn to the ground. Sometime during their silent vigil, Walter reached for his daughter's hand and he didn't let go.

THE FIRE HAD BURNED HOT and fast. There was nothing left of the cottage, except the foundation and the granite chimney. The rest was a charred pile of debris. The fire department would have to sift through the remains for their final report, but the preliminary findings were not reassuring.

Over Franny and Walter's objections, Jack insisted on taking Brooke to his home. There was no way he was letting her out of his sight until he saw her safely on an airplane to San Diego.

Never had he felt so frightened as when the explosion had nearly devoured them. If she'd been hurt… He tamped down the emotions tightening his throat. Emotions would only get in the way now when he needed to depend on logic. Tomorrow morning, after they got her some traveling clothes, he would drive her to Boston and send her home. She couldn't stay. It was too dangerous. He couldn't risk losing her.

Looking like a stray cat caught in a storm, Brooke sat on the edge of the bed in his spare room while he stacked the climbing equipment into piles on the floor. He'd tossed the gear there carelessly after Alyssa's accident and hadn't had a chance to take care of it since then.

"Do they know what started the fire?" Brooke asked, eyes still wide with shock. She tightened a dry blanket around her shoulders and shivered anyway.

Carabiners clinked as he dropped them beside the maple straight chair. "They found part of a timer and some propane tanks. They were set in Alyssa's darkroom right under your bedroom."

The meaning of his words made her gasp and reach for her heart. "I was meant to die."

"Yes." The thought had his heart knocking hard, anger pouring into his veins faster than magma from an exploding volcano. Someone was going to pay for this.

Jumping to her feet, Brooke became agitated, prowling the room like a caged tigress. "Tim, he came by the other day. He wanted some negatives back and was upset when I couldn't produce them for him. He was worried about the awards." She stopped, turned to him. "Do you think...?"

Anything was possible. "The tanks had Cash Propane printed on them."

"Stephanie?"

He wrapped one of the ropes on the bed into a mountaineer's coil and tossed it on the ground. "I doubt she'd use her own family's product to off you, but at this point, nothing can be ruled out. Except for Cullen."

"Your P.I. was with him."

"Cullen's been out of town for a couple of days, taking a course. Behaving himself, for a change."

Jack caught a rope bag with his elbow as he looped a second rope into a coil. The bag fell to the floor with a clunk. Curious about the out of place noise, he looked inside and found a small automatic camera.

"Yours?" Brooke asked.

"Alyssa's." He turned the camera over in his hands. "She took pictures during the picnic at Devil's Grin."

Launching herself in his direction, Brooke grabbed the camera from his hands and looked at the counter. Tapping the small window, she looked up at him, excitement vibrating on her face. "She took twenty pictures. We need to get it developed. Right now. Maybe there's something on there. Come on. Let's go!"

He grabbed her wrist and pulled her back to him. Because he couldn't help himself, he wrapped his arms around her waist and kissed her. "It's going to have to wait until the pharmacy opens at nine."

She linked her arms around his neck and kissed him back. "Do they have one-hour processing?"

"We're not completely deprived."

"That's what we'll do then," she said as she laid her head on his shoulder. He rubbed the side of her neck with a thumb and buried his face in her hair. She smelled of smoke and rain and summer. And he could not let her melt away his resolve. For her own good, she had to go home.

With one hand, Jack turned down the comforter, exposing light blue sheets. "In the meantime, you're going to take a nice hot shower and go to bed."

Clinging to him, Brooke shook her head.

"You're exhausted. There's nothing we can do right now. Tomorrow, the fire chief should have more information, I'll have our suspects rounded up, and we'll get Alyssa's film developed."

"The only way I could even consider sleep tonight would be in your bed with you."

When she looked at him with those big, green eyes, his heart skipped a beat, then thundered. Even though she'd said he wasn't what she needed, she loved him, he reminded himself. And she was what he needed. In her arms, he'd felt complete.

Tomorrow—today—she'd be gone. But for now, she was here, and she wanted to spend what was left of the night with him, in his bed. What harm could it do?

I'm fine, Jack. Go to school. I'll be all right.

Please, Jack, let me go. I need this. I need to touch the sky.

The difference this time was that he was in control. He was allowing Brooke to walk all over him for purely self-ish reasons—one last taste of her before he sent her home.

Gently he scooped her into his arms. As she snuggled against him, he pressed a kiss against her temple. "Shower, then sleep. Just like the lady ordered."

HOW COULD THIS POSSIBLY have happened? Everything had been perfectly planned. Everything had been perfectly ex-ecuted. How could they have gotten out of the cottage alive? How could she? Alyssa was like a damned cat. But she had to run out of lives sooner or later.

In the shadows of the boathouse, the sound of the gently lapping water, of the rain pitter-pattering on the tin roof, of the wind sighing through the trees brought calm, clarity, focus.

"I should have thought of this before."

Was there a man more predictable than Jack? The town hall clock could be set by the sureness of his habits. Yes, he'd been acting out of sorts since Alyssa's accident, but at his core he was the same. And even Alyssa's flighty behavior had pockets of dependability. It was all so clear now. The missed element had been one of humanity.

What couldn't Jack resist? A soul in need of rescue.

What would send Alyssa headlong into trouble without a second thought? A little girl looking for her lost dog.

WAITING FOR THE FILM TO BE developed was straining Jack's patience to its limit. Because of the fire, he now had a reason—and an urgency—to have their suspects rounded up for questioning. The captain himself was han-dling the paperwork. In a few hours, those assembled would all be cooling their heels in the holding cells at the station. Jack was itching to be there to witness their interrogations.

He glanced at his watch for the hundredth time since they'd arrived at the pharmacy. They'd used up ten whole minutes buying Brooke a pair of jeans, a T-shirt and some running shoes at the general store. She'd used five more getting out of his sweatshirt and shorts held on with a belt, and into her new clothes. They'd stretched drinking a cup of coffee to half an hour at the River's Edge Café. Now they were prowling the pharmacy's aisles, picking out necessities for Brooke, both of them keeping an eye on the machine in the corner as it spat out prints.

"There's a flight to San Diego this afternoon." Loss clawed at his heart, but he had years of practice at closing off the pain. He handed her a travel-size tube of toothpaste. "You're going to be on it."

"I'm staying." She swapped the travel tube for a full-size one.

"You don't have a choice."

She considered the merits of two hairbrushes, put one in the basket and the other back on the display. "You can't make me."

"I'll blow your cover."

"I'm still staying."

He cursed her stubbornness. She simply smiled at him, making him want to kiss some sense into her. But if he touched her, if he kissed her, he would be the one whose mind was scrambled.

She was going to be on that plane if he had to drag her kicking and screaming. He couldn't take a chance with her safety.

Irritation twanged through his every nerve. At Brooke, because her smile cracked his detachment every time. At himself, for letting her get to him. Couldn't she see she had to leave?

Jack was standing by the counter before the last print dropped and grabbed them from Stella before she could pack them neatly into their bright blue envelope.

"Anything?" Brooke asked, standing on tiptoes to look over his shoulder. This morning she smelled of his soap and that sweetness that was uniquely hers. The intimacy of the scent made his detachment slip another notch.

Jack whipped through the prints, once, twice, three times, then let out a sigh of disappointment. While he paid Stella, Brooke took over the stack.

"That's a nice one of you," she said, examining a print of his face as they walked out of the pharmacy. "What did Alyssa say to make you smile that way?"

"Probably one of her silly jokes."

Brooke stopped abruptly, making him turn to face her with a hand on his forearm. "Look!" Her voice became animated as she pointed to something in the background. "Over there. Who's that?"

Jack took the print and squinted at it, trying to make out the details. Someone was crouching beside the neatly aligned coils of rope. The head was bent forward, making the person appear to be headless. "I don't know. We all wore red climbing pants and white T-shirts for the practice climb—it's the Adventure Club uniform."

"We've got to blow this up!"

"The pharmacy'll have to send it out to get that type of work done."

"Then drive me to the resort. I'll use the office computer. There's a photo shop type program on there."

Hand in hand, they raced to the car, and Jack stretched several traffic laws getting them to the resort.

While Brooke scanned the photo into the computer, Jack took out his phone and tried to track Ed O'Hara from the Fish and Game Department.

"Just got the results." A heavy squeak came from Ed's

office, then the crinkling of paper being shuffled. "There weren't any tool marks, but when they ran the chemical processing for sizing, lubricants, preservatives, etc., they found the midmark had been soaked with DEET."

"DEET?" Jack jerked in his chair as if he'd been slapped. At a mountain-rescue team meeting a few years back in North Conway, they'd done an experiment. A rope had been soaked with DEET, then they'd used it in a tug-of-war. The rope had snapped. Who else had been there? Tim? Trish? Not Stephanie. Cullen?

"That's right, DEET."

"Just at the midmark?" The site of the break.

"Looks like it was injected into the core."

And they'd all been wearing bug repellent because of the black flies, so the smell wouldn't have appeared out of place. But he couldn't recall any greasy feel to the rope. The midmark. Of course, the tape would have hidden the stain.

"Premeditation," Jack said.

"Looks like it."

"Thanks, Ed. I owe you one."

"I'm counting on it."

Jack stood behind Brooke, one hand resting on the back of the office chair, the other on the desk's edge. "How's it coming?"

"Almost there."

Slowly the pixels rearranged themselves as the new enlarged version of the background loaded onto the screen.

The body was female. The patch of hair barely peeking above the shoulders was dark blond.

"Trish."

And she was switching one coil of rope for another.

Jack reached for his phone and was about punch in the station number when a woman ran into the office. Her hair was a chaos of dark curls around her head. She hung on to the knob as if it were a lifeline.

"Alyssa, have you seen Lauren?" Her voice was tight and high.

"Not since yesterday," Brooke answered as she ordered the computer to print a copy of the screen. "Is anything wrong?"

"I told her to stay close to home." Mrs. Bell's words tumbled one on top of the other. "Now I can't find her anywhere. I thought she was with Robby, but he hasn't seen her since breakfast."

Brooke rounded the desk and went to the distraught woman. "We'll find her."

"Something's wrong." The woman held up a neon-yellow leash and gulped in air, trying to hold back tears. "It's Daisy's. I found it by the path that goes into the woods. Lauren loves that stupid dog. She would have gone after her. What if she's lost?"

Brooke looked up at Jack. "We have to go look for her."

Jack swore silently. If he searched for the child, he risked Trish getting away and losing justice for Alyssa. But if he went after Trish and Lauren was hurt, he'd never forgive himself. And that left him no choice at all.

He called the station, told the captain about the print, asked how the suspect roundup was going. Stephanie and Tim were in custody, but Trish and Cullen were missing. He gave the captain Matt Bender's number and asked to be kept up-to-date.

Snapping the phone shut, he joined Brooke. "You stay here, Mrs. Bell, I'll find Lauren."

"Thank you," she whispered, tears bright in her dark eyes. "I'm going back to the cottage...in case she comes back."

"That's a good idea." He handed her a card. "Here's my phone number. If she comes home, call me."

She nodded and hugged the card to her chest. With quick, jerky strides, she left. The office door slapped shut behind her.

Jack strode to the store side of the office and plucked several water bottles from the upright cooler.

"I want you to stay here," he ordered Brooke.

"I'm coming with you."

"If anything happens to you..." he started, shaking his head at her. He couldn't afford to let his thoughts stray in that direction.

"I can't just stay here and do nothing." She leaned toward him and whispered harshly, "Alyssa would go, and I'm still Alyssa for now."

He jabbed the office door open and headed for his car. Trish should be in custody soon. There was nothing to fear. But everything in his life had been turned upside down in the past few weeks. The lead feeling in his stomach had nothing to do with indigestion and everything to do with Brooke and her safety.

Yet he knew that part of him would worry about Brooke even as he searched for the lost child. With Brooke within sight, he could concentrate on the task at hand. "All right. Stay close and do what I say."

He grabbed a pack from the trunk of his car, stuffed water bottles into the side pockets and exchanged his running shoes for hiking boots. Together, they trekked to the trail head. The sooner he found Lauren, the sooner he could take care of Trish.

And maybe, just maybe, when all this mess was over, when Trish was safely in prison, he could convince Brooke to stay.

LAST NIGHT'S RAIN HAD GIVEN way to heavy fog in the morning. Even with noon just a few ticks of the clock away, a heavy mist remained, clinging to skin and hair and clothes in a sticky film, exaggerating the peaty smell of the earth, distorting sounds. The thick gray on the dark of the forest reduced visibility to mere yards.

The track was narrow—invisible to her. But Jack seemed to know his way around it, so Brooke followed confidently. He stepped in long, sure strides, stopping now and then to read an imperceptible mark on the ground or against a tree trunk.

After an hour, Brooke had no idea where they were. The forest seemed to be closing around them, holding them prisoner. They were going up, but seemed no closer to a summit than when they'd started. *Poor Lauren,* she thought, *the kid must be petrified.* Jack had ordered her to be quiet in order to listen for Lauren, to hear the smallest sounds of the forest around him, so she didn't dare call out Lauren's name, but every instinct in her urged her to do so.

Jack stopped, frowned, dropped his pack and walked a circle. "Stay."

Brooke took the opportunity to rest. With the tail of her T-shirt, she wiped her sweaty face. Jack's absence soon made her nervous. Then it hit her that the woods were much too quiet. Where were the birds? The chatty chipmunks? The heavy-footed squirrels, cracking twigs and leaves with every hop? The air was heavy, barely breathable, as if the fog seemed bent on suffocation.

"Jack?" she ventured, rising to her feet.

"Right here." Silently he stepped from the mist and she breathed relief.

"Anything wrong?" she asked. His face was stark, his expression unreadable, and she knew that something had to be wrong to put him on such stiff guard.

"I'm not sure. The signs don't make sense."

"What do you mean?"

He frowned. "The tracks, Daisy's and Lauren's, they just stop as if they were both abducted by aliens."

"How can that be?"

Shaking his head, he sat beside her and took a long draft from a water bottle. "I don't know."

"So, what next?"

"Let me think."

Brooke sat, but soon started feeling fidgety. She wanted, needed, to talk but kept silent and watched Jack's expressions as he sorted out his options.

Finally, she could stand the silence no longer. "We don't seem to be going anywhere."

"The tracks are leading up there." He pointed toward a barely visible rise above the tree tops. Swaddled in wisps of fog, the granite outcrop looked sleek, dark and menancing—almost like a reptillian monster's spine. "Devil's Back."

The name jogged something in her memory, but she couldn't seem to hang on to the fleeting thought. "How could Lauren have walked this far? She's just a little girl."

"She's not walking. She's being carried."

"Trish has her?" Brooke sprang up. The surge of adrenaline coursing through her body demanded action, but she didn't know which direction to go in. Swallowing hard, she concentrated on Jack. "How long have you known?"

"Just now. The bit of fur on the tree trunk is too high for Daisy." He got up and pointed out the sign. "This one is too deliberately placed." He gestured at the ground. "See how those tracks stop there, then there's nothing, as if the tracks were scrubbed?"

She couldn't really see anything. The floor of decomposing leaves and pine needles looked like a blank slate to her. But something about the color nudged at her consciousness. "Jack? What's the name of the company whose deposit went missing?"

"RIM TEK Corporation. Why?"

"RTC. Their company colors wouldn't happen to be gold and black?"

"Gold and dark brown."

She seized both his upper arms in her fists. "I know where the check is. In Trish's file. I saw something with RTC that day when I was looking for my notebook. She hid the check so you'd have to climb." She squeezed his arms tighter. "Devil's Back. Isn't that where Rick died?"

"Yes."

The newspaper clippings came back to her. "Jack, it's the anniversary of Rick's death. The newspaper articles said it was an accident. What really happened that day?"

Jack turned away from her, dislodging her grip on his arms. Shading his eyes with a hand, he gazed at the tip of mountain visible above the tree tops.

"Rick and Alyssa had an argument right before the climb," Jack said. "Rick stalked off, saying he was heading back home. He started rappelling without doing his safety checks. He lost his grip and fell. The rope wasn't tied on properly. It slipped out of the carabiner. There was nothing left to catch him."

Brooke rubbed her arms, but could feel no warmth through her cast. "Trish brought me cookies the other day. She said it was because she knew I—Alyssa—would be sad. She'd been crying. She'd tried to hide it, but her eyes were swollen and red. The motive *is* revenge, Jack."

"She wanted to see remorse."

"And didn't." Would Alyssa have acted differently if she'd been in Brooke's place? Would she have understood Trish's torment, how to soothe her?

"Trish hadn't talked about the accident in a long time,"

Jack said. "We all thought she'd finally accepted it was a senseless tragedy, no one's fault."

"What were Rick and Alyssa arguing about that day?"

Jack shot her a glance over his shoulder. "Commitment. Rick was ready to make one and Alyssa felt she had a bad track record where engagements were concerned. She wanted time and space to think about his proposal."

"Alyssa wrote that in Trish's eyes, Alyssa always got what she wanted. To Trish, it must have looked like Alyssa wanted Rick out of her life."

"And the accident couldn't have happened at a worse time." Jack shouldered his pack. "Rick owned a black pickup. I thought his mother sold it after the accident."

As he walked, Jack spoke into his phone. In rapid, clipped tones, he ordered a unit to search the old barn on the Witchell family farm and look for Rick's truck. He gave the rescue team their position, their destination, and a synopsis of their situation.

Brooke dogged his footsteps. "Would Trish hurt Lauren just to get back at Alyssa?"

As he holstered the phone, his jaw flinched. "I don't know."

"Here," he said after a while. In his hand he held a tuft of Daisy's brown hairs that he'd found caught on the rough bark of a pine. Even Brooke could tell it was too high off the ground to have lodged there naturally."

"She wants us to follow her."

Jack nodded. "To Devil's Back."

AN HOUR LATER, BROOKE THOUGHT she heard a whimper. "Did you hear that?"

Jack rushed forward up a steep incline. Brooke scrambled after him, slipping on the boulders' moss-slicked surface.

"Lauren!" Her voice echoed in the mist.

"Quiet! Listen."

The noise came again, a whimper, a yip, a frightened bark.

"It's Daisy."

They topped the incline and found themselves surrounded by trees on one side, a cliff on another, a pile of boulders on a third and a narrow path split by a crevice on the fourth.

"Lauren!" Jack called. He cupped his ear, listening for an answer.

When it came, they both looked down. The pitiful cry had come from deep inside the crack.

JACK MADE A CALL TO ALERT the rest of the rescue team that Lauren had been found, then methodically set about to save the child. The crevasse was too narrow for his body. Brooke insisted on climbing down. Jack finally relented when he saw no way around it. The rescue team would take at least an hour to reach them, and Lauren was petrified.

He studied his surroundings in order to decide the best way to execute Lauren's rescue. A shudder ran through him as another piece of the puzzle clicked into place. Trish had been part of the rescue team who had found Eddie O'Hara last fall not far from here. She'd known about the deep, narrow cracks.

Lauren's presence here was no accident.

Brooke was lying on her stomach reassuring Lauren while he set up for a rappel. He checked and rechecked every inch of rope, every carabiner, every bight until he was certain the system would hold. Rappelling was the most dangerous maneuver in rock climbing. Lowering Brooke would require all of his concentration.

"Come here," he called to Brooke. She made him stand near the edge so she could continue talking to Lauren while he adjusted a sit harness around her body. When he'd done all he could to ensure her safety, he reached for her, hugged her, kissed her.

Holding the rope taut, he prepared to let her go. "You'll be fine."

She smiled at him. "As long as the spiders don't get me."

"Spiders. For Pete's sake, Brooke, you wrapped a snake around your shoulders."

"It was a pet."

"You didn't know that."

"How else would a boa constrictor end up in a cupboard in New Hampshire?"

She was scared. He saw the signs in the roundness of her eyes, in the sweaty swipe of her hands against her jeans, in her attempt to make light of a situation that must have her heart beating faster than hummingbird wings. He looked deep into her beautiful green eyes. "You'll be all right."

"I know."

Lauren sobbed.

"It's okay, Lauren," Brooke reassured. "I'm on my way down. Just hang on for a little bit longer."

With a nod and a deep breath, Brooke stepped off the edge into the crack. Using his voice to keep her calm, he guided her every step. He breathed a sigh of relief when she reached Lauren, but didn't let his attention wander for even a second. He wanted this rescue over, but knew he couldn't rush things.

"I've got her," Brooke called up, triumph in her voice.

Joy speared through him, but he quickly snuffed it. He couldn't let his concentration wander until they were all safe. "Tie her to your harness like I showed you."

"The ledge is really tiny, Jack, and the crack goes down deeper."

"Don't look, just tie. I'll pull you up as soon as you're ready."

"I can't take them both." He heard the hesitation in her voice. "Daisy's too squirmy. I'm…Jack…"

He guessed her dilemma then. If she carried the puppy, she risked the child's life, but if she left the dog behind, it would panic and fall deeper. "Can you tie her to anything?"

"There's a stub of branch, but I'm not sure it'll hold."

"It'll have to do." The rescue team could go down and get the dog. The important thing was getting Lauren and Brooke out safely.

Brooke carefully explained to Lauren her every move, promised the child to bring her dog back to her, then signaled her ascent.

"I've got you."

Just then he heard a swish behind him. Something cracked. Sharp pain filled his head. Blackness swamped his consciousness.

"Brooke!"

Chapter Fifteen

Brooke heard Jack's cry and looked up to see the rope snaking down toward her. She rounded forward over Lauren's body as the rope whipped past them, striking her on the back, nearly throwing her off balance and off the small ledge.

"Oops. Forgot. Rope!"

Brooke snapped her head up. A chill raced up her spine as a silhouette appeared over the lip, dark against the gray of the sky. "Jack!" Something was terribly wrong. "Jack!"

"He's taking a bit of a nap right now."

Trish! Dread curdled in Brooke's stomach. Trish was here, not in police custody and she'd hurt Jack. *Please, no, let him be all right.* Brooke wanted to cry, to race to him, but had to keep her head clear until Lauren was safe. She forced herself to think past the fear churning her insides into a knot.

"You've got to help me get this little girl up to safety."

"Wish I could, but the rope slipped from my hand. Sound familiar?"

"Wanting to kill me is one thing, Trish, but Lauren has nothing to do with this." Her voice was sharp and cutting, but Brooke didn't care.

"You're right, of course. And I'm not completely heartless. I'll tell you what. You get the rope back up to me and I'll see what I can do.''

At the harshness in Trish's voice, Lauren started crying, hanging on to Brooke with all of her might. Her little body shook with fear. Brooke did her best to calm the trembling of her own body.

"I'm going to put you down for a second so I can get the rope to the lady, okay?''

"Noooooo! Don't let me *gooooo!*"

The crevasse was dark and tight, making it hard to see and maneuver. Brooke flattened against the rock. She shifted Lauren to her right side, cradling her with her casted arm, freeing her left arm. Daisy whimpered and tugged at her restraint, bumping against Brooke's legs.

Painstakingly, Brooke inched the rope up her leg and into a coil. "I'm going to throw the rope up, Trish."

"Okay." The voice was coy, playful.

"One. Two. Three.'' With all her might, Brooke heaved the coil, watched it rise, then fall back toward her. Whipping her arm forward, she bent over Lauren to avoid getting lashed in the face with the whistling rope.

"Oops!''

"Trish, this is no game. Lauren is petrified.''

"Okay, okay. Try again.''

Brooke wanted to swear and pound into Trish, but could do neither, so she once again methodically coiled the rope. Her fingers ached from the effort. Her shoulder protested. Sweat slicked her face, her arms, her back. The quivering Lauren was becoming a heavy burden.

"One. Two. Three,'' Brooke called up.

"I've got it." The rope went taut. "Ready?''

Sick foreboding shivered through her. *No, I don't trust you for one second.* But what other choice did she have? Yet, she couldn't bring herself to give Trish total control of their ascent. "Hang on a minute.''

Brooke bent down and untied Daisy. There was no way she was going to trust Trish twice. Once she got to the top and released Lauren, she would have only one chance to rescue herself. She sandwiched the squirming puppy between herself and Lauren and felt the two trembling bodies of dog and child. "Hang on tight."

Swallowing hard, she closed her eyes and prayed for courage. Alyssa was the risk-taker, not her.

Alyssa! Help me with this. Show me how you climb.

Taking a long, deep breath, Brooke forced the panic down, forced herself to concentrate on her task. She looked up, studied the rock. A thought, soft like a whisper, touched her mind. *One step at a time.*

As she signaled her readiness to start up the sheer rock facade, a sudden calmness washed over her. *One step at a time.* "Climbing."

"Climb," came Trish's response.

"Hang on tight, Lauren."

Brooke lifted her foot to a jutting piece of rock, reached for a crease with her hand. Her tense muscles relaxed. Her mind cleared. Hand- and toeholds seemed to pop out from the rock. The route over the straight face appeared as if drawn on a map.

As she neared the crest, she stopped and reluctantly loosened the knot securing Lauren to her. "When I say go," she whispered in Lauren's ear, "you start running as fast as you can. Can you do that?"

Lauren shook her head.

"Look at me." Slowly Lauren lifted her head. "You're a very brave girl and I really need you to help me. When I say run, you run as fast as you can. There's a rescue team coming up the mountain and they're looking for you. Your Mom's really worried about you. Run. Okay?"

Lauren nodded. "Hang on."

"What are you doing?" Trish asked.

"Looking for a hold."

Two more steps and Lauren's body cleared the top. Heart pounding, Brooke quickly released the rest of the restraint, shoved Lauren away from the crevasse and shouted, "Run!"

Puppy and girl shot down the path.

At the sight of Jack prone on the ground, Brooke gave a cry of despair. Blood poured from the side of his head. "No, no!"

Trish's laughter cracked the air. "That's right, princess. Cry for your lover. You deserve to suffer like you made me suffer."

Just then, Jack lifted his head. Determination was etched into his face as he crawled toward Trish. With a glance, he signaled the object of his determination. A loop of rope was coiled around Trish's foot.

Trish took a step forward, tightening the rope against the heel of her hiking boot. "You were always a sucker for little kids. Too bad you didn't have as much consideration for your friends."

"Rick's death was an accident." Brooke edged away from Trish, looking for better support than the toehold crumbling beneath her foot. Every muscle in her body was screaming a protest as her toes reached for a fat knob.

"You took him away from me. You're always acting like some high and mighty princess, treating the rest of us like peasants sent to do your bidding. He wasn't a toy, you know. He loved you. He was my brother, my business partner." Her eyes glittered with anger. Her face was taut, her posture rigid. She was almost shaking from the intensity of her feelings. "That's over now. You're never going to take anything away from anyone again."

Trish planted her hiking boot against Brooke's chest. "Goodbye, princess."

Just as Trish shoved, Brooke brandished her casted arm

like a weapon. The hard cast connected with Trish's shin with a thunk, knocking the woman off balance. Jack pulled on the rope, jolting Trish completely off her feet.

Momentum continued to carry Brooke sideways. Unbalanced, she fell.

Her body bumped time and again against the tight sides of the crevasse. She tried to slow her descent, but only managed to bloody her hands and tear her jeans. Holding her arms up, she protected her head. Finally the rope caught, yanking her to a stop. Like a horror movie soundtrack, her scream echoed up and down the crevasse. She dangled for a moment before she heard the wonderful sound of Jack's voice.

"Brooke?"

"I'm all right." Her voice was choked with tears. Every muscle in her body shook with relief. "Get me out of here."

Ten minutes later, Jack's hands were reaching for her. He buried his face in her hair and held her so tight she could hardly breathe. She felt the hard pounding of his heartbeat against her chest, saw the shaking of his shoulders, heard the hitch in his voice. "I thought I'd lost you."

She knew he was thinking of Alyssa and *her* fate at Devil's Grin. Fisting her hands into the back of his shirt, she drew him closer and kissed him repeatedly.

"I'm all right," she croaked. She was safe in Jack's arms. As the rush of adrenaline receded, her legs felt like jelly, and her body started shaking uncontrollably. "As long as you hold me, I'll be all right."

Over the sound of their ragged breaths came the shouts of the rescue team hurrying up the path.

THREE HOURS LATER, Jack had reluctantly agreed to allow his head to be stitched and bandaged at the medical center. Brooke and Lauren had been examined. Their scratches had been doctored. Lauren and Daisy were safely back with their family. Trish was in custody, and Jack was just as glad to have someone else throw the book at her.

He'd fought to stay detached, but as he'd watched Brooke struggle with every fiber of her being only to fall back into that crevasse, he'd become fully involved—body, mind…and heart. God, yes, especially his heart. Every blooming bruise on her face and body reminded him how close he'd come to losing her. He was scared, petrified to lose her still.

He didn't want to let Brooke out of his sight, out of his reach for one second. He wanted to take her home, lock her inside and never let her go.

"Let's go home," he said, when the doctor agreed to sign her discharge.

"No." She climbed off the examining table and stuffed her feet into her running shoes. She looked pitiful in her bloody T-shirt and ripped jeans. She'd had the doctor cut off her fake cast, had ripped off the fake scar on her temple, and against his advice, had given her real name. "First I have to make a phone call, then you're going to take me to see my father."

Every instinct in him wanted to scream no, but he nodded.

She looked up at him, a layer of uncertainty dancing in her green eyes. "Alyssa, she's back."

"Back?"

"Out of her coma."

Frowning, he shook his head. "How do you know?"

"When I was climbing out of that crack with Lauren, I sensed her." Brooke's hands curled into his shirt. "Just like when we were kids."

Could this be true? Could Alyssa have defeated her coma? Joy shafted through him, but it was soon tempered with logic. How could Brooke possibly know this?

"I've got to call Mom."

He ushered her into a chair. "Here. Use my phone."

As he watched her dial, he sensed that if Brooke was right and Alyssa was back, Brooke would leave him and he would have to let her go.

The world seemed to dim right there and then, and he clasped the forgotten protective shield around his rapidly breaking heart.

ALL OF HER LIFE BROOKE HAD struggled to live up to expectations. She'd done everything she was supposed to do, and it had never been good enough. Alyssa's accident and her own adventure at Devil's Back had shown her it would never be good enough. Life could be snatched away at any second. She didn't want to die a failure of her own misguided presumptions.

Ordering Jack to leave, she slammed into her father's home and found him in his usual spot by the window—watching life pass him by. Pity rippled through her, but she shoved it aside.

Walter gasped at the sight of her battered condition, but Brooke wasn't in the mood for his belated concern. She was angry at him and she was going to let him know. She dragged a chair and planted it right in front of him.

"I'm Brooke," she announced. "The daughter that, for whatever reason, you agreed to pretend was dead twenty-four years ago."

His eyes widened and his skin paled, but Brooke continued. "Even with Mom's explanation I don't understand why you and Mom decided to do something so stupid, and frankly at this point I don't care. But Alyssa has just woken up from her coma, and I think after all the hard times you've given her in the past twenty-four years, the least you can do is fly out to California and tell her you're glad she's alive."

Without waiting for an answer, Brooke rose. "We're leaving tomorrow morning. I'll make the arrangements. Be ready."

With that, she walked out on him, leaving him stunned and silent. As soon as the door closed behind her, she sank onto the wooden ramp, put her head into her hands and cried.

"That was some speech," Franny said as she lowered herself beside Brooke.

The sounds of children playing amplified the chaos in Brooke's mind. She didn't know how she felt about anything anymore. Everything was all jumbled—love, anger, joy, despair. Leaning her head against the door, she dangled her hands between her upraised knees. "I don't understand how they could have done what they did. Don't they realize what it's cost all of us?"

"I think they do, that's why they're stuck where they are. Walter could have gotten out of that wheelchair years ago, but he was afraid that if he did, Alyssa would leave."

Brooke shook her head. "But he treated her horribly."

"All he had after your mother left was his dream. He found out too late it wasn't enough." Franny reached for one of Brooke's hands and squeezed it in hers. "Judging by what your father's told me over the years, Alyssa is very much like your mother. He took his anger out on Alyssa when what he really wanted to do was love her."

"Then why didn't Delia take Alyssa and leave me behind?"

"She knew exactly what she was doing. She couldn't let go, either—not any more than she could stay. She didn't want him to forget her, and she didn't want to forget him." Franny gave Brooke's hand another squeeze. "I'd hate to see you make the same mistake."

"What do you mean?"

"Jack cares for you very much."

"It's not enough." Brooke's gaze sought Franny's. "You should know that. Why do you stay here with Delia's ghost between you and Dad?"

Franny gave a small, helpless smile. "Because I love him."

"And you'll let him go back to her just like that?"

Franny rose and dusted her bottom. "He was never mine."

LEAVING JACK BEHIND in Comfort was the hardest thing Brooke had ever done, but she had to finish what she'd started before she could contemplate any kind of future. She had a big decision left to make, and given her parents' example, it wasn't one she was going to make lightly.

At the nursing home, she got the squealing reunion with Alyssa she'd once envisioned. She rushed into her twin's arms, felt the secret hug, though weak, squeeze her with warmth, and cried her eyes out as she and Alyssa tried to fill in the void of over two decades. After two days of near-constant conversation squashed into the narrow hospital bed together, they simply held each other.

"Think they'll work out their anger at each other?" Brooke asked, looking at their mother and father huddled on the patio off Alyssa's room. Their stiff body language conveyed the long road ahead.

"I don't know. I think Delia has a crush on one of my doctors."

Brooke's eyebrows rose. "The ice queen?"

"Not so icy when she's around Dr. Dan." Alyssa placed a hand coyly against her cheek and mimicked her mother's voice. "Oh, Dr. Dan, it's so nice of you to stop by. I just had a couple of questions."

They both dissolved into giggles.

"That should be interesting to watch," Brooke said, leaning her head against Alyssa's. "Dad apologized to

Franny before he left. I think he finally realized how good she's been to him."

"Too good, if you ask me."

They all still had a long way to go to repair the broken bonds of their family, but forgiveness and the willingness to try would start them on the road to healing.

"What about you?" Brooke asked. "What are you going to do when you get out of here?"

"Physical therapy for one thing. The doctors say it'll be a while before I regain full use of my arm." Alyssa shrugged. "I'm thinking of staying in California for a while. I've wanted to get away."

"I know."

"This is the perfect opportunity to try out my wings."

"Sorry about your house. Your photographs were pure art."

"There was nothing there but bad memories anyway. I'm just glad you weren't in bed." A wicked smile bloomed on Alyssa's face. "Which makes me wonder, where exactly were you?"

Heat fired her cheeks, but Brooke ignored the question. "I'm going back to Comfort."

It was a risk. A big one. If she was wrong about Jack's feelings, she could be asking for a world of hurt.

"I kinda figured you would." Alyssa hugged her sister. "Jack needs someone to love him."

If Brooke had learned anything in the past few weeks, it was that she could be only herself. She wasn't going to let her chance at happiness slip away just because her expectations didn't quite match reality. Jack might not be the man of her dreams, but he was the man of her heart. And she loved him.

Brooke leaned her head against Alyssa's. "What was the New Year's wish list in your journal all about?"

Alyssa sighed. "I'd made up my mind I was leaving—

with or without Dad's blessing. I also realized I'd trampled
a lot of toes over the past few years. I wanted to set things
right, wish those in my life well. Just like I wanted them
to wish me well, so I had all these plans...."

Brooke visualized the list. "What did you want to talk
to Gary about?"

"Without Rick, Trish was having a hard time keeping
up with the business she and Rick had started. I was going
to get Gary to help her get back on track."

"Only a good lawyer can save her now."

Alyssa plucked at the edge of the blanket. "She was
never good at losing."

Brooke gently jostled her sister's shoulder. "Neither
were you, as I recall."

"At least I can admit defeat now and then."

"True. Sometimes you used to let me win." Brooke
reached an arm across Alyssa's shoulders and hugged her
tighter. "What about making Cullen walk the straight and
narrow. What's that all about?"

A smile twitched at Alyssa's lips. "Cullen's really not
a bad guy, just a bit of a braggart. He hated losing real
estate deals over what he called 'silly stuff'. He bragged
about having a housing inspector in his pocket. I told him
he was smart enough to deal with his problems legally. He
scoffed. I videotaped him in the act and told him about
it."

"You didn't! How did he react?"

"Predictably." Alyssa ran a hand through her hair. "He
pitched a tantrum worthy of a two-year-old, then he
calmed down. I told him I was keeping the tape as insurance until he proved he could walk the straight and narrow."

"That must be why he followed Jack and me, to see if
I'd remembered the videotape and what my intentions
were."

"Well, he said Stephanie had already chewed him out and I couldn't dish out anything harder than she could."

"Good for her!"

Alyssa clucked and shook her head. "Threw me for a loop. I never thought of Cullen and Steph as a couple, but you know, she can cut his ego down to size. All he needs now is a little push to help him get over his fear of commitment." Alyssa giggled. "The video's in the office safe. Why don't you give it to Stephanie when you get home?"

"You're wicked!" Brooke said, loving the plan. "What about the negatives?"

"They're in the safe, too."

"What's that all about?"

Alyssa shrugged. "It's Tim's secret to tell, not mine."

"Not even to your long-lost sister?" Brooke teased.

"No." Alyssa turned to her sister. "Hey, with you staying, it looks like I've also found a new manager for the resort. One Dad would approve of."

"I can't wait." A mixture of anticipation and trepidation swirled though her. She loved the idea of running the resort, but worried about Jack's reaction to her relocating. "Remember how scared I was of the place when we were kids?"

Alyssa nodded.

"I love it now. Everything about it. The woods, the people, even the water."

"Especially Jack."

"Especially Jack," Brooke agreed, wondering what he was doing now, if he missed her as much as she missed him.

Alyssa touched the scar on her temple. "It took a coma to knock some sense into me. As soon as they let me out, I'm going to start rebuilding my collection of equipment and my stock of photographs."

"You'll have those back in no time. You're free to follow your dreams now."

"Yes." Alyssa's gaze searched the horizon outside the hospital window.

Brooke nudged her. "Scared?"

"Petrified."

"Me, too."

Arms linked, drawing comfort from each other, the twins leaned back against the pillow.

"We'll be okay," Alyssa said.

"More than okay. We've got each other again."

Epilogue

Standing in the airport lounge, waiting for Brooke's flight to land, Jack had never been so nervous. The daisies and forget-me-nots in his hands felt alien. The collar of his shirt was choking him. And he was sweating buckets by the time the jet rolled up to the arrival gate.

Brooke had proven she could take care of herself. She didn't need him. She'd even told him he wasn't what she needed. Yet she was coming back to Comfort, coming back to him.

In just a few short weeks, she'd become his sunshine, the center of his life. Through her, he'd learned to love, to dare to dream.

Examining his life since Brooke's departure had shown him that, in truth, Alyssa and his mother were both lost souls before he'd entered their lives. He'd done the best he could to protect them. His failure had been in not insisting they take part in solving their own problems.

While growing up and in his job, he'd experienced only the negative side of emotions. Love had come at the price of duty and responsibility. Brooke had shown him a whole new side to passion—one that would require a lifetime of exploring to appreciate completely.

What else could he do, but be here waiting for her?

Passengers started flowing out of the gangway. And

there in the middle, bright as a summer day with her green shirt and flowered skirt, was Brooke. When she saw him, she smiled.

He couldn't help himself, he smiled back, and at that moment all of his anxieties fled. He opened his arms and welcomed her with all of his heart.

"Hi," she said shyly and she snuggled up to him. "What are you doing here?"

The sound of her voice was a melody. As he hugged her closer, he inhaled her soft summer scent, absorbed her feminine warmth. He was in heaven. "I came to get you."

"Why?" She looked up at him, her eyes bright with hope.

A full sweep of emotions trampled through him as he held her. She was exactly where she was supposed to be. And he was alive. Fully. Completely. "Because I love you."

"Oh."

"I want you to spend the rest of your life with me."

"Oh."

He saw doubt and hesitation in her eyes. There was only one way she would believe him. With the heavy tramp of hurried travelers all around them, he got down on one knee.

"Jack?" Embarrassment coloring her cheeks, she plucked at the sleeves of his shirt. He took her hands in his, stilling them.

"Brooke Snowden," he said in a loud, clear, authoritative voice, then let it soften and carry all of the emotions pouring from his heart. "Will you marry me?"

Traffic slowed around them. Travelers no longer seemed in such a hurry to get where they needed to go.

"Well, come on, girl," someone said, "don't keep the poor sap waiting. What's it going to be?"

She reached down and pulled him up. Wrapping her

arms around his neck, she looked at him with those wonderful eyes full of life and sunshine and said, ''Yes, Jack, I'll marry you.''

A roar of cheers and clapping sounded around them, but lost in a kiss, neither of them heard.

The romantic suspense at

HARLEQUIN®
INTRIGUE

just got more intense!

On the precipice between imminent danger and
smoldering desire, they are

When your back is against the wall
and nothing makes sense, only one man
is strong enough to pull you from the brink—
and into his loving arms!
Look for all the books in this riveting new
promotion:

WOMAN MOST WANTED (#599)
by **Harper Allen**
On sale January 2001

PRIVATE VOWS (#603)
by **Sally Steward**
On sale February 2001

NIGHTTIME GUARDIAN (#607)
by **Amanda Stevens**
On sale March 2001

Available at your favorite retail outlet.

#1 *New York Times* bestselling author

NORA ROBERTS

brings you more of the loyal and loving,
tempestuous and tantalizing Stanislaski family.

Coming in February 2001

The Stanislaski Sisters

Natasha and Rachel

Though raised in the Old World traditions of their
family, fiery Natasha Stanislaski and cool, classy
Rachel Stanislaski are ready for a *new* world of love....

And also available in February 2001 from
Silhouette Special Edition, the newest book in the
heartwarming Stanislaski saga

CONSIDERING KATE

Natasha and Spencer Kimball's daughter Kate turns her
back on old dreams and returns to her hometown, where
she finds the *man* of her dreams.

Available at your favorite retail outlet.

Where love comes alive™

Harlequin invites you to walk down the aisle...

To honor our year long celebration of weddings, we are offering an exciting opportunity for you to own the Harlequin Bride Doll. Handcrafted in fine bisque porcelain, the wedding doll is dressed for her wedding day in a cream satin gown accented by lace trim. She carries an exquisite traditional bridal bouquet and wears a cathedral-length dotted Swiss veil. Embroidered flowers cascade down her lace overskirt to the scalloped hemline; underneath all is a multi-layered crinoline.

Join us in our celebration of weddings by sending away for your own Harlequin Bride Doll. This doll regularly retails for $74.95 U.S./approx. $108.68 CDN. One doll per household. Requests must be received no later than June 30, 2001. Offer good while quantities of gifts last. Please allow 6-8 weeks for delivery. Offer good in the U.S. and Canada only. Become part of this exciting offer!

Simply complete the order form and mail to:
"A Walk Down the Aisle"

<u>IN U.S.A</u>
P.O. Box 9057
3010 Walden Ave.
Buffalo, NY 14240-9057

<u>IN CANADA</u>
P.O. Box 622
Fort Erie, Ontario
L2A 5X3

Enclosed are eight (8) proofs of purchase found on the last page of every specially marked Harlequin series book and $3.75 check or money order (for postage and handling). Please send my Harlequin Bride Doll to:

Name (PLEASE PRINT)

Address   Apt. #

City   State/Prov.   Zip/Postal Code

Account # (if applicable)   **098 KIK DAEW**

HARLEQUIN®
Makes any time special ®

Visit us at www.eHarlequin.com

*A Walk Down the Aisle
Free Bride Doll Offer
One Proof-of-Purchase*

PHWDAPOP

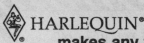

If you enjoyed what you just read,
then we've got an offer you can't resist!

Take 2 bestselling love stories FREE!

Plus get a FREE surprise gift!

HARLEQUIN®
INTRIGUE
opens the case files on:

TOP SECRET BABIES

Unwrap the mystery!

Follow the clues to your favorite retail outlet.

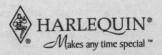

HARLEQUIN®
Makes any time special ™